THE WEDDING PLAN

JEAN ORAM

COMPLETE LIBRARY OF CONGRESS CATALOGING-IN-PUBLICATION DATA AVAILABLE ONLINE

Oram, Jean.

The Wedding Plan / Jean Oram.—1st. ed.

ISBN 978-1-928198-82-6, 978-1-928198-43-7 (paperback)

Ebook ISBN 978-1-928198-35-2

First Oram Productions Edition: May 2020

Cover design by Jean Oram

ACKNOWLEDGMENTS

Thank you to my fans who can't get enough of Blueberry Springs and my real-life feeling characters. You're the reason I write!

Thank you as well to Donna W., Mrs. X., and Tessa S. who are subjected to the convoluted, full-of-gaps mess called a first draft and try to see through the mud to pick out the gems. And thank you to Margaret C., Rachel B., Erin D. and Emily K. who see the almost-there versions and help me polish it into what my readers fall in love with today.

Thank you!

XO,

Jean Oram

Writing Luke and Emma was a fun challenge. I'm not wealthy, and I'm quite confident I will never find myself in a position where I have to manage a two-point-five emergency fund like Luke does. I've also never had to work with a debutante coach like Emma did.

And because Emma grew up privileged, I received advice from an editor to create her as an unfeeling snob. (Insert here: Jean's scrunched nose of distaste.) That wasn't what I wanted and I was fairly certain my readers didn't either. I wanted to spend time with a heroine who was so much more than her upbringing and, oddly enough, I think what helped me give Emma's character a nudge toward grace was coaching my son's soccer team.

On the last day of the season I had been poking about online to see what a debutante coach might teach her students and was struck by the list. I don't know about you, but I've always had an image of what debutante training might look like—thanks to TV and movies—and my guess is that you likely have a similar image of impossibly snobby girls walking around while balancing a book on their heads as an exercise to improve posture.

So what struck me when I found this training list was how unassuming it truly was. Many of the listed items were things my parents had tried to instil in me such as good table manners, rules of introduction, and being punctual. But most of all was this: Appreciation and thank you notes.

Bestill my heart. I read this piece the same day I walked off the soccer pitch after nine weeks of coaching 15 five and six-year-olds. It had been a fun and challenging season with lots of laughs and growth. However, I couldn't help but be disappointed when after the last session, not one parent thanked any of us moms for coaching their kids in the heat, the wind, the cold, the…everything, two times a week.

We didn't even get a single goodbye.

It's true I'm a strong believer in showing appreciation—I still send handwritten thank you cards after Christmas—but I'm even more of a believer after walking off that field laden with equipment and feeling taken for granted. I don't expect much as coaching is its own reward, but it still surprised me. (Especially since the kids didn't want soccer to end.)

So, I suppose what I'm getting at is that maybe debutantes are on to something, because after all, who would say no to a little more grace and appreciation?

And so, in the end, I tried to make Emma as down-to-earth as felt right, her attitude slowly becoming more relaxed as the story progressed, and as she and Luke coaxed the best from each other. (True love at its finest!)

I fell in love with Blueberry Springs in an all-new way writing *The Wedding Plan* and I had a lot of fun taking Luke and Emma out of the big city and their lives of privilege when I stuck them in a tiny cabin out in the mountainous woods. The two learned a lot about themselves as well as how to care for each other and their community.

I hope you enjoy the dynamic between these two lovers as their relationship unfolds and they learn to love with all of their heart.

Happy reading,
Jean Oram
Alberta, Canada 2017

P.S. Canadian singer/songwriter (and writer) Leonard Cohen passed away while I was writing this series and Luke's last name is a tribute to him and all those days I'd spent moaning to my mother as she listened to his "awful" songs that I soon learned to love as well.

The Wedding Plan

*E*mma Carrington stood in the room at the top of the lighthouse overlooking the Atlantic Ocean, her hands in Luke Cohen's, as a man they'd paid to perform their secret wedding ceremony trotted through the legalities of their union.

She glanced down at her ringless finger. Were they really going to do this? Was she really about to run off with the man who'd proposed to her sister only a few months ago? Who had been her own fiancé for less than twenty-four hours?

She swallowed her doubts as she watched the man she'd been attracted to for years. Luke would not become a true husband. Their marriage was merely a four-month contract to help him claim an inheritance from his late grandparents. She'd even dressed down, in capris and a casual top, to show him she could keep her head in the game. What had happened in their past would not impact their ability to work together. The past was finished business.

So why was he wearing a nicely cut suit that made him look the part of a genuine groom?

When she'd gone to him with a business proposal last week they'd both been perfectly clear that the only thing real about their partnership was the bottom line. Definitely not the attraction that still sizzled and snapped between them from time to time. Aspen had been a mistake. A moment of weakness due to extenuating circumstances.

But she *was* totally getting hitched to the catch of the country club. Oh, those old biddies would simply die if they found out she'd secretly swooped in and married him.

Emma found herself smiling despite the fact that she knew she'd never tell a soul about this part of their business deal. She'd sign her name on the marriage certificate and then, in four months, sign it again on their divorce papers, walking away with her agreed portion of the freed inheritance. A nice chunk she'd use to beef up the marketing budget for her new, all-natural cosmetic line, which would launch the month after that.

Luke caught her eye and his expression softened from intense seriousness to amused disbelief as he shook his head and chuckled.

She whispered, "I know, right?"

How totally crazy is this?

He flashed her a private smile that hit her in the chest, stealing the air from her lungs. Man, he was handsome. He was tall, athletic, and had that rich-man powerful thing going on. But that wasn't what consistently caught her eye, as practically every man in the country club had that commanding air. No, it was the lurking hint of humanity that would zip out and tag her every so often, catching her off guard and sending her heart beating with an irregularity that would alarm most cardiologists.

She sucked in a deep breath, focusing her thoughts.

Healthy, safe products. That was why she was marrying him. She needed his expertise to help place the finishing touches on her project, as well as launch it internationally. He was here because she'd offered him a sizable chunk of any potential profits —not because he still had the power to leave her breathless, and they both wanted to do something about it.

"You may kiss the bride."

Emma dropped her hands from Luke's and gaped in surprise at his security agent, Zach Forrester, who'd been licensed to perform the ceremony. They'd discussed this beforehand. No kissing. They'd added that little rule right after swearing the lighthouse museum staff to secrecy and making a nice donation to their preservation fund as a thank-you.

"You may kiss the bride," Zach repeated easily. He was tall and smart, but apparently had little in the way of a memory. "Or the groom. Whoever wants to go first can dive on in and make this official."

Nope. Emma was *not* kissing the groom. She'd rather poke herself in the eye with a mascara wand. Because if she kissed Luke she might discover that Aspen, which she'd excused as a one-off mistake that had left her off-kilter for months, had actually been about her and Luke and whatever it was that simmered just below the surface.

They had to work side by side for the next five months and their boundaries needed to be maintained with a steady hand. No exceptions. No messy, complicated or distracting kisses allowed. And just because they'd become spouses, and were standing in a beautiful old lighthouse with the sun reflecting off the ocean, it did not give her permission to break the rules.

Luke suddenly pulled her body against his, stealing her breath and stilling her mind in that way that was unique to him. He gave her a dreamy, knee-weakening kiss, full on the mouth. She didn't know whether to push away or to enjoy how his lips felt perfect against hers.

Before she could decide, he released her, his expression unreadable. It was then she realized that everything about their agreement was going to become not only distracting, but very, very complicated.

Luke Cohen was a married man.

Married to a woman he'd never once considered as wife material.

Emma Carrington, an old family friend, was cute, flirty and fun, but a bit of a princess who drifted toward things that were high maintenance. Which was fine. He could financially support weekly manicures, highlights, waxing and whatever else women put themselves through to look glamorous. But he didn't go for ex-models who laughed and flirted their way through life, worrying if their butts looked fat in their jeans. He preferred a strong, intelligent woman who didn't need him every minute of the day.

Not that he found Emma clingy or lacking in intelligence. She just wasn't someone he'd ever pictured as his wife. Other things, definitely.

His lips crooked into a smile as he thought of their mutual "mistakes," as she'd called their sporadic forays past the friendship line. Their satisfying—his word, not hers—unions had been intensely hot, and he had no doubt that the two of them would succumb to a few more over the next several months as they worked together.

She'd brought a sound business plan to him, proposing he share his knowledge and experience in exchange for a fifth of the profits. He didn't get offers like that every day. He'd leaped on it, not because he needed the cash, or the headache of launching her new line on top of running his family corporation, Cohen's Blissful Body Care, but because being associated with her all-natural, organic, safe products would shine a much-needed positive light on Cohen's.

Luke skimmed Emma's curvy form with his gaze. She was dressed as though she planned to go clamming, wearing minimal makeup, and he had no doubt that the former debutante meant to keep her word. Business only. He didn't need to worry about her stringing up tentative hopes for him to crash into with their fake marriage. She wasn't going to assume the union meant something beyond the piece of paper it was written on.

Unlike him. He'd gone in for the kiss.

He wanted to be furious with Zach, but he wasn't the only one who hadn't kept his head in the game. The man had acted like a wingman and Luke had jumped at the setup like a puppy being reunited with its owner.

He'd already started his and Emma's ill-matched partnership off on the wrong foot by sweeping her into his arms. But it was difficult to regret that when she'd felt so right there, and that was without even thinking about the way she had softened against him, making him greedy for more. More of her body, her laughter.

Trouble.

That's what kissing Emma was. She'd given him an apprehensive look when he'd released her, quickly shifting into her Placid Debutante Shut Down mode, as he'd mentally dubbed it. She'd straightened her spine, with her chin tucked in ever so slightly, as though she was about to saunter down a catwalk, her face washed of emotion. Polite and eerily mask-like. Distant. Proper.

Not good, in other words. But come on. She had to know that slipups and a few cases of it-is-what-it-is were bound to happen. He'd seen the way she gave him those secret, sly appraising looks that darkened her eyes with a telltale hint of attraction. And as for himself, he had a sixth sense for whenever she drew near. He'd feel that rush of heat flood his body before he even saw her. He'd spent a lot of years unsuccessfully trying to rid himself of the troublesome reaction, to no avail. And now they were moving to a small mountain town where they could explore their attraction in the privacy of their shared headquarters.

Although he'd be smart to stay within her parameters, as she'd very knowingly *not* offered an affair, but a lifeline. In other words, he needed to keep his libido on ice and his thoughts on business, not tug at the boundaries of their agreement to see how much it might flex.

However, where Emma was concerned, it seemed he was rarely able to keep his eye on the ball.

The limo that had been parked outside the red-and-white lighthouse pulled up.

"Emma?" Luke asked. She was on the sidewalk, looking up at the building they'd just gotten married in.

Married.

Wow. That still packed a punch. His mom would be disappointed in him, his dad angry for sneaking in the side door to claim the inheritance before the deadline, nullifying the will's contingency clause which would have immediately granted the money to Charlotte, Luke's mother. Franklin had designs upon the money, having fairly assumed that Luke wouldn't make his claim due to the existing marriage clause. If his father got the money it would be gone the next day, assuring that Charlotte would never have the wherewithal to leave him. Her parents had worked hard for that money and it was their legacy, one that should go to her, not their son-in-law. But now, with Emma's assistance, Luke could assure that the money would end up where it belonged—in his mother's hands—by making the claim himself and controlling its dispersal.

"Ready?" Luke asked, as the limo driver moved to open Emma's door, a salty ocean breeze ruffling her golden locks. "We have a long flight ahead of us." He didn't even want to think about how the Carringtons, the formidable Joan and Jack, would react to him sneaking off with their youngest daughter—even though she was nearing thirty and by all accounts independent. They'd always sheltered her more than their eldest, Olivia.

"Are you sure Zach won't tell anyone?" Emma asked once they were in the car, the privacy glass separating them from the man in question who'd climbed in next to the driver.

"Zach is solid." The man was an ex-spy, and even though he'd decided to act as a wingman today, Luke knew he could keep a secret.

"He didn't honor our wishes."

"Sorry," Luke said quickly.

He should regret the kiss, since every time they touched it seemed to draw him deeper. It was undeniable that there was something between them, although he guessed it was mostly a case of "I can't have her, so I want her" that would be quickly cured once they started working shoulder-to-shoulder and their innate differences came to light.

There were no galas for Emma to attend in Blueberry Springs, no doting gaggle of debutantes for her to gossip with, no big corporate events to stage. Just constant work in a tiny place that rolled up the sidewalks before suppertime.

Plus his ex-girlfriend, Olivia, would be around, bringing up reminders of the past and how he'd consistently chosen her over Emma and their pulsing attraction. Because, again, Emma wasn't wife material, and he was nothing more than a "mistake."

The car pulled away from the curb, taking them to the airport.

"This feels dirty," Emma declared.

"Dirty?" Luke's hands moved to the edge of the leather seat on either side of his knees. He gripped it hard, reminding himself to keep them there as his gaze drifted toward Emma's shapely legs. She had delicate ankles, tanned skin, and he was unable to resist the memory of how those legs had once felt wrapped around him, his hands lost in the cascade of her long, soft hair. Their frantic coupling had been surprisingly invigorating, addictive. Wild and free. Unlike anything he'd ever experienced.

Again, working together should cure the desire to repeat that night. He was a determined, hardworking man and she was a former model. Hardly a match that would find a professional partnership arousing.

Just keep lying to yourself, buddy, the devil on his shoulder chided.

"The secret husband part." Emma waggled her bare ring finger and he struggled to focus on her words. "Marrying so we can free up the money in your grandparents' will. I always took you as being on the straight-and-narrow." She was watching him, reassessing him, and he wasn't sure how it made him feel.

Since becoming CEO of Cohen's he'd been trying to fix past secrets, deceptions and lies, not create more of them to manage. It looked like he may have screwed up on that mark.

"Maybe not dirty, but definitely naughty," she added with a playful wink, her voice slightly breathless.

His mind kept repeating the way she'd said *naughty.* Two simple syllables that set his imagination on fire.

He cleared his throat. "It's just a way to slip through a loophole."

"But it's also like…" An impish smile lit up her face. "…a secret life away from the stuffy, elite, insincere snobs we call friends." She gave his knee a squeeze and his body jolted from the contact, a flash of heat twisting through him.

She didn't like the socialites they mingled with? That meant he didn't know Emma as well as he thought he did. And that could become a sizable problem. One he didn't know how to solve.

EMMA STARED at the tiny cabin that was to be her and Luke's home and business headquarters for the next five months—while married for four of them. It was nestled among towering pines on the side of a rolling hill. All around were craggy, snow-covered mountains, and below, the small town of Blueberry Springs.

Beside her, Emma's sister said, "It's small, but it's cute."

Bundled in a thick winter coat that barely zipped up over her large baby bump, Olivia handed Emma the keys.

"I need something bigger," Emma stated in near panic, as she turned her attention once again to her new abode. This was not what she'd asked the real estate agent to line up as the All You headquarters. She'd requested a four-bedroom home that could accommodate them, as well as provide individual office spaces. Not a one-bedroom cabin in the romantically snowy woods.

"There aren't a lot of leases in town, especially ones that run less than a year."

"I told the real estate agent I don't mind paying for a full year." Emma couldn't keep still. She felt like a lab rat knowing a lethal injection was coming. She was suddenly too warm in her parka, but at the same time knew she would freeze if she unzipped it. January in the mountains, unlike South Carolina, wasn't a friendly place temperature-wise, and in the airport she'd swapped her light sweater and capris for a turtleneck and jeans.

She worried that Luke, who was currently busying himself with their previously shipped belongings, now piled in the back of the pickup truck he'd leased, was going to turn right back around and leave as soon as Olivia was gone. This wasn't what Emma had offered as part of the deal when she'd lured him out in the pursuit of profits—profits he likely didn't even need. "I'm calling the realty office."

"Em, this is all there is," Olivia insisted patiently.

"There has to be somewhere with enough bedrooms for both of us. I can't believe you signed the lease on our behalf."

Emma, unlike her sister, didn't have a degree from Harvard Business School to fall back on. She had a fluff degree and little experience, having spent most of her career smiling for a camera as she modeled Carrington Cosmetics. She needed Luke to help get her all-natural, organic makeup out into the world and into the hands of women. They needed it. *She* needed it.

Both Emma and her late grandmother had been affected by

the toxins found in cosmetics, but only Emma had survived her toxin-induced bout with cancer. She knew how much the world needed safer products, and she'd sold almost everything she owned in order to make it this far, since the board at Carrington Cosmetics didn't believe in the products, or her, apparently. And now Olivia had just about guaranteed that Luke—her only hope —would walk.

"Emma," Olivia said, "you'd have to commute if you stayed in another town."

"Fine. We'll commute."

"The closest place is probably over an hour's drive away. Derbyshire has nothing, Rockwell Falls, the same."

Emma closed her eyes with a sigh. The little log home wasn't going to serve their needs. Especially when Luke's wedding kiss had just about knocked her off her feet that morning.

Married. Wedding. Kiss. Spouses.

She needed some space to sort herself out again, to refocus.

She knew what it was like to face the fear of finding a lump in her breast. What it was like checking each month after the "all clear," fear thick in her throat until her thorough self-exam came up clean.

She knew what it was like to undergo radiation and chemotherapy, watching her beautiful complexion become hidden by rashes and her precious locks, part of her very identity, fall out. She knew what it was like to wear a wig in stifling heat and humidity. The fear that someone would point out that she was no longer the pretty face of Carrington, and ask who she was now.

Women deserved to be able to put on Carrington makeup every morning without worrying that it might one day take their life. But what if Emma couldn't pull it off? What if the bad press from last summer that had surrounded the news of her Carrington Cosmetics-related illness torpedoed the new, safe product line? What if she lost every penny she owned and had to bamboozle some old guy from the country club into becoming her sugar daddy just so she didn't end up homeless?

She had to do whatever it took to keep Luke on the project.

"I should go say hi," Olivia said uncertainly, glancing in Luke's direction.

"No!"

"I don't want to be rude."

Emma softened her tone. "He'll understand that you're busy and want to give him time to settle in." She began herding her confused sister toward her new vehicle, an SUV that was better equipped for the winter roads than her old Porsche had been.

Olivia gave Luke an awkward wave as she passed the truck, propelled by her sister. The last time Olivia and Luke had seen each other she was refusing his marriage proposal. A proposal Luke had accepted on Emma's behalf and neither had plans to reveal seeing as they'd be divorcing within months. To say there was unfinished business between Luke and Olivia was an understatement, and Emma didn't need a fight between them added to her day's laundry list of problems.

Just one more reason to stay focused on work instead of Luke. She didn't need to upset her pregnant sister, who had miscarried once years before.

When Olivia's vehicle disappeared down the steep, curving driveway, Emma joined Luke at the truck's tailgate and hefted a box into her arms. She couldn't help but notice that his attention kept straying in the direction Olivia had gone.

"Can you believe she rented us a place with no bellhop?" Emma said lightly.

Luke barely smiled, now eyeing the log cabin with a skepticism she understood.

She smiled. "Here we go! New life. New adventure." She carried her box through the fresh snow and up the creaking steps, hoping the place was larger inside than it appeared.

She juggled the box as she unlocked the door, surprised at

how bright and sunny the open-concept cabin was despite being sheltered by so many trees. It could be the effect of the pale yellow log walls or the varnished pine floors reflecting light and happiness throughout the place, but whatever it was, it worked. The cabin was chilly, though. Emma noted a fire was dying in the massive river stone fireplace dominating the sitting area opposite the front door.

To her immediate left was a simple galley kitchen, and she set her box down, intent on exploring what was through the two doorways to her right. Could there possibly be two bedrooms? She stomped the snow off her boots and walked farther into the cabin. Opening the first door revealed a queen-size bed covered by a patchwork quilt where the pieces had been stitched into the shape of a moose head. The second door led to a bathroom with floral wallpaper, a pink tub and matching toilet.

She swallowed hard. One bed.

Optimal conditions for most newlyweds.

Emma went back to the front door, bouncing off Luke's chest as he wrangled two suitcases. He backed out onto the porch again as shyness overcame her.

"You sure you didn't tell her we got married?" she asked, her voice sounding strained to her own ears.

Luke's jaw tightened.

"There's only one bedroom," she explained quietly, figuring it was best he heard it from her rather than discover it for himself and leap to conclusions about her intentions.

"Then we can't live here," he said simply, putting the suitcases down on the porch and crossing his arms.

"I know." She straightened her shoulders, struggling not to feel overwhelmed. She needed to appear in control. She channeled the words of her former debutante coach, the duchess Francesca Marie.

Put it behind you, dear. Spine straight, shoulders back, chin up but not out. Show no fear, only strength. Pleasant smile. You can have a cry about it later if you need to, but right now you're the strongest person in the room, because nothing touches Emma Carrington.

Luke was watching her and she felt her chin wobble from the struggle of holding it all in. She really needed to have that cry the duchess always promised she could have later.

"I asked for two offices and two bedrooms," she whispered, barely trusting her voice.

Luke had her in his arms, squeezing her tight, before the first tear fell.

It was supposed to be easy now that he was on board. She didn't need help from a real estate agent or her sister when it came to appearing as though she was swimming in waters she had no business being in. Luke was going to see just how much knowledge she lacked, and find an exit clause in their contract so he could escape this big, unsolvable mess.

"I don't know how to cook," she admitted, clinging to him. Nowhere in town would deliver meals halfway up the mountain. She couldn't even feed the poor man.

He laughed. "You're going to make a few million before next Christmas. You're supposed to show the world you can't say 'Carrington' without saying 'caring,' remember? Real products for real women. Real beauty, pure makeup and all that."

So he *had* been listening during the flight as she'd nervously talked his ear off about what she wanted for All You. Other than the fact that she hadn't been able to shut up, she'd thought she'd sounded very knowledgeable and like a true business partner.

However, the fact that he was using her words to try and build her up again made it even harder to hold back her need to release her sense of desperation and failure in a flood of tears. It was that genuine side of his. She didn't know how to brush that off like the Duchess had trained her to.

"We're lying to everyone to get to your inheritance," she blurted out against his cold parka, realizing that their fake marriage was bugging her more than she'd like to admit. She was already omitting enough truths to her family, and she felt like a big cheater for sidestepping Luke's grandparents' requirements for claiming his inheritance. He needed to work alongside his wife for a business quarter plus a month in order to claim the money. They were going to do that, but not in the spirit intended by the loving couple who had worked side by side for over forty years.

Emma felt Luke let out a long sigh as he pressed her against him, his head lowering to hers as though he could no longer hold it up due to the weight of their combined personal failings.

"We'll get through this and it'll all be worth it," he promised, his voice steady, strong.

How? How was she going to survive this?

"One day at a time," he added, as if hearing her internal question. "If we wake up, it means we made it through yesterday and are one step closer to what we want out of life."

The tension in her chest eased off at the honesty of his words.

"You're right." She had survived worse. She'd survived cancer, after all.

But her illness had felt out of her hands, unlike this. The success of the product line was all on her.

That meant if she wanted to keep women safe from common cosmetic toxins, she had to pull it together.

She stepped back from Luke. "Thank you for the pep talk."

"Hey, what are husbands for?" he joked.

He shouldn't say things like that. It made it feel as if she could trust him, count on him.

She swallowed a lump in her throat and dragged her suitcase over the cabin's threshold, not daring to speak. She came back onto the porch to grab the other one.

"This place reminds me of Aspen," Luke said, surveying the surrounding woods from his spot on the porch.

"Aspen is done business," she replied quickly.

"Is it?" he asked, his tone curious.

"Yes." She could feel the weight of his gaze, the phantom feel of his body pressed against hers, the tightening celebration of hers in response.

It had been at a business retreat for both family companies in Aspen that Olivia had turned down Luke's marriage proposal, choosing to marry Devon, her long-ago love instead. It was in Aspen that Emma and Luke had turned to each other in a night of blistering passion as their dreams and what they believed to be true of their worlds had come crashing down around them.

The press had discovered Emma's toxin-loaded bone marrow was a result of prolonged use of Carrington Cosmetics and, later, that a malignant lump had been found in her breast. They'd exploited the news to the fullest extent, and when Luke had tried to speak up for Carrington products, whose chemical components were well within legal limits, the public's eye had turned to Cohen's and their own ingredient lists, giving them a black mark, as well.

It hadn't taken long for the board at Carrington to ask Emma to step down as their model, spokesperson and face of the company, leaving her with nothing more than the lowly job of organizing company picnics and such.

Add in the fact that Olivia had kept a very large personal secret from both Emma and Luke—Luke being the man she'd dated on and off again for over a decade—and both had been feeling hurt and betrayed, their attraction seeming like the only thing real, the only thing they could rely on. Their night together in Aspen was one Emma had best forget, especially since he had turned around several days later and proposed to Olivia, who'd just returned from Blueberry Springs single once again.

Maybe Emma had used Luke. Maybe he'd used her. But it was done, and she refused to believe that anything had been forged between them other than trust in each other. And she would use that to launch an international product line from a one-bedroom cabin in the woods if she had to. She just had to figure out how to keep Luke happy enough to stay.

He was staring out into the wilderness that surrounded them, his forehead crinkled in thought, his lips turning down. Then he walked down the steps with purpose, muttering something about earning his keep. At his truck he gave her a distracted "back in a bit" and climbed into his truck, leaving her there on the side of the mountain.

Luke let himself into the tiny Blueberry Springs real estate office, which seemed to double as a stationery store and accounting firm. It had been difficult to find, the storefront being only about ten feet wide, sandwiched between a florist and a mechanic, just down from a burned-out place on Main Street. He hadn't minded driving around the quiet town, though. Seeing Olivia Carrington had brought up some unpleasant emotions.

He'd known he'd see his ex-girlfriend eventually, but hadn't thought it would be first thing. However, the strangest part about seeing his ex after several months was the absence of heartbreak. They'd dated sporadically, mostly at their parents' urging, and he'd expected to feel more than just anger on Emma's behalf for how Olivia's issues had led the press to her sister last summer, slamming her publicly. But that's all there'd been in the way of emotion. That and a bit of self-berating for proposing to her after she'd broken up with Devon, her first choice. Luke and Olivia… he wasn't sure if they'd ever truly been in love. At least the way everyone talked about. Mostly, being a couple had been easy, as well as socially beneficial.

It was possible his feelings of anger had been written across his face because, despite her upbringing, Olivia hadn't come over to the truck to say hello. He wasn't sure what he would have said if she had.

"Hi, can I help you?"

There was a woman sitting in the small office. She was mostly hidden behind a large monitor that looked about the same age as the youngest bottle of whiskey back in his Charleston, South Carolina penthouse. Old for a monitor, young for a good whiskey. Luke quickly sent off a text to his cousin, Cash Campbell, reminding him that the wine room and everything in it—including the whiskey—was off-limits while he house-sat and took over some of Luke's CEO duties at Cohen's.

He almost put his phone away before thinking twice. *And dating Alexa is still off-limits.*

Can we flirt? came an instant reply. *She's totally hot.*

Luke sighed. Cash had a way of going through women and Luke depended on his assistant being happy as well as focused on her work. The last thing he needed was Cash creating a distraction or a mess.

I hear unemployment's a blast these days, Luke replied.

Touché.

The real estate agent—or accountant or whatever she was—cleared her throat. "Just coming in from the cold so you can text?"

"I need a place to live, as well as office space." If Emma couldn't secure a decent location, he would. She'd hired him to take care of issues, after all.

"Then you've come to the right woman." She smiled and stood up, leading him to a bulletin board on the wall. She perched a pair of reading glasses on her nose. "Here are our current offerings."

"Minimum four bedrooms. Or two bedrooms, two offices or dens. I'm not fussy about its architectural influence." He scanned the board. It was fairly bare, with listings for only eight homes and businesses. He glanced around for a second board. "This it?"

"Yes." The woman smiled with pride.

"What about your competition?" Surely there had to be more than this.

"We're it." She was still smiling.

Maybe everyone posted online to cut out the middleman.

She moved to a coffeepot set near her desk. "Would you like a coffee while you look?"

"Sure. Dark roast. Two skim, two raw sugar."

He really wanted to come back to Emma with a success story to hand her, to prove he was worth keeping around and wouldn't try and sneak kisses all the time.

Well, he might still try to do that, but he'd make it worth her while with a bit of on-the-fly problem solving.

The woman began dumping powdered creamer into a disposable cup and Luke resisted the urge to shudder. The coffee she poured looked weak and nothing at all like his preferred Starbucks venti dark roast.

He gave a polite smile and thanked her as she handed him the cup.

"Anything coming up soon?" he asked.

"I haven't heard of anything."

Surely that couldn't be true. Luke had a feeling she was simply not sharing the most primo places, having pegged him as an outsider. He knew how small towns worked. You took care of your own, like one big happy family.

He handed her his business card. "My name's Luke Cohen."

Her smile didn't change to one of recognition as she introduced herself as Greta.

"I donated the roof on the continuing care wing last summer."

"Oh, that's nice, dear. That was needed, wasn't it?"

He'd done it as a thanks to the town for allowing himself and Jack Carrington to land a helicopter on the local soccer pitch when they'd been worried about Olivia. Turned out she was just fine, with her new fiancé, Devon Mattson, and wasn't in need of rescue by anyone. As well, there had been no feathers in need of smoothing over due to the unauthorized landing. Still, it had felt nice to literally put a roof over the heads of some senior citizens and create some positive PR for Cohen's at a time when they were taking a hit right alongside Carrington Cosmetics for having harmful—but permitted—toxins in their products.

"CEO of Cohen's Blissful Body Care. I'm working with Emma Carrington on Carrington Cosmetics' All You products." The very products that had saved the town's pretty meadows and river from a proposed electric dam project.

"Oh, you must know Jill Armstrong," Greta replied.

"I don't." The name sounded familiar, though, and he was fairly certain Emma had mentioned her in passing.

"She creates her own soaps and lotions, many with medicinal effects thanks to knowledge of plants and flowers passed down to her from the Ute people. She sells them at the farmers' market."

Right. Jill had sent Emma a care package of her creams to help her deal with radiation rashes.

His phone buzzed with a message.

Did you go back to Charleston?

It was Emma. Heat infused his cells just like it did when she was around. Great, she affected him through text, too. He was in for a long five months.

I'm sorry about the cabin. I promise I'll find us something suitable.

He probably should have given her a proper goodbye, or at least given her a hint as to where he was going despite wanting to surprise her with a solution to their accommodation issue.

"I need a place to live and work out of," he said firmly. "Immediately. Preferably two places. Money isn't an issue." He tried not to look at his watch as a hint to hurry her up. He wanted to close on a place tonight.

Greta made a thoughtful humming sound and turned to the board, looking at it as though expecting something perfect to materialize from her meager offerings. There was a listing of the cabin they were staying in and she tapped it affectionately. "This one is taken, but it's lovely. You would have liked it." She carefully removed the listing, as though afraid to tear the paper.

"It's dated, drafty, minuscule, heated by a fireplace, and remote. There's no internet and the cell service is horrible. It's less than sufficient. "

"My father built that cabin."

"It's quaint."

Luke? Are you there?

He sighed and texted back. *I'm at the real estate office.*

Finding anything? I like hot tubs.

He liked her in hot tubs. Cute little bikinis that allowed his imagination to fill in the not-so-difficult blanks.

"What about this condo?" he asked, glancing up from his phone to tap a listing.

"Nothing until spring, honey."

"Maybe the showroom is for sale or lease?" Emma could live and work out of the cabin and he'd take a condo, or vice versa. Distance, space. It would be perfect.

Kissing her in the lighthouse had not been a good idea. He'd thought he could brush it off, but the way she'd felt pressed against him just kept on slipping back into his mind like a boomerang.

The real estate agent was shaking her head and Luke set down his untouched coffee. Maybe he could buy out the developer. He could leverage the resort he'd built in the Caribbean as collateral.

"You didn't like your coffee?" Greta asked, her blue eyes large.

"It's fine, thank you. Is there a way to get my name higher on some waiting lists? I don't mind paying extra to get something immediately."

The idea of sharing a small cabin in the snowy woods with

the beautiful and irresistible Emma Carrington was starting to take a toll on his mind.

As a teen she'd told him they were a mistake when they'd made out behind a boathouse near Kiawah Island. And again when they'd gone to bed last summer.

He wasn't a man who liked to repeat mistakes, but he was fairly certain he would make a few more before the day was through if he didn't get them into roomier living accommodations. And what was that vow he'd made to himself back in the limo that morning? Something about staying focused on work. Too bad he couldn't recall why, exactly, only that it was important.

Kissing was still okay, though. Just nothing more than that.

Except kisses always tended to lead to more.

Greta had said something he'd missed. It didn't matter. Her expression told him everything—he was pushing his power and privilege just like his father did. Luke didn't want to be like Franklin and backed off.

"Sorry," he said softly. "I'm desperate."

The woman's tone was cool. "I'll call you if anything suitable comes available."

"I can't return to that cabin," he said in near panic. If he went back to Emma he would end up sleeping with her.

Greta quirked her head. "We keep a shotgun behind the door if bears become a problem, although you won't see any of them until spring melt. Watch for coyotes, though."

"What?" He'd been envisioning going back to the cabin, Emma stretched out in front of the fireplace in black lace lingerie, high cut over her toned thighs, looking lost and vulnerable and in need of a strong man to comfort her. He went to loosen his tie before realizing he wasn't wearing one.

"Some are becoming bolder, almost domesticated. How about a hotel?" she suggested.

"That's a great idea."

Now he was envisioning Emma on a hotel bed.

"There's one just up the road." The woman pushed him out the door. "Have a good evening, Mr. Cohen." She flipped her Open sign to Closed before throwing the dead bolt.

No. The hotel wouldn't do. He'd passed it on the way here and had already mentally crossed it off the list. It was small and the room would be too dark, too cramped. The cabin was small, but there were work surfaces he could spread his papers out on, and large walls where he could tack things up without worrying about housekeeping messing up his system.

The cabin it was.

He'd just have to figure out a way to keep it in his pants.

He rapped on the glass door. "Where can I buy a bed?" he called to Greta.

She pointed down the street to the hardware store. He turned and began striding toward it.

No matter what roadblocks Blueberry Springs put in his way, Luke was not sleeping with his wife.

No matter what.

Too much was riding on it.

EMMA TRIED to keep herself distracted while she waited for Luke to return. He hadn't left her. He was coming back. She knew that.

She paced in front of the fire, hands on her hips. Not securing the accommodations she'd promised made her think of all the other times she felt as though she'd led him on, only to leave him high and dry. As teens they'd kissed behind a boathouse near Kiawah Island. It had been heaven. An older boy. Discovery and passion. It was everything she'd ever hoped for. That night she'd mentioned to her sister how cute she thought Luke was, hoping to eventually tell her about the kiss. But instead, Olivia had announced that she had a whole life plan centered around her and Luke being together and taking over their respective family companies. She'd gone on to explain with excitement that their parents approved and were already talking to the Cohens about the possibility.

Emma had no plans, no argument to propose that Luke should be hers, other than she'd enjoyed every toe-curling kiss and wanted more. So she'd backed off, avoiding Luke and calling their kisses a mistake when he'd approached her to ask if she wanted to see the *Rocky Horror Picture Show* with him.

And then last summer there had been Aspen. They'd both been single and hurting, and Emma had let things get deliciously out of control. It had been a Band-Aid, a mistake. Nothing more.

But she felt guilty. Not just for swooping in and breaking the Sister Code by taking up with Olivia's ex for a night, but for seeming as though she always led him on, then pulled back.

Then again, why was she even worrying? She wasn't Luke's first choice and never would be—he'd made that clear by turning around and proposing to Olivia after their night together. And being in Blueberry Springs wasn't about romance, anyway, it was about business.

Luke was not going to be a problem. Emma wasn't one of those beautiful, smart, take-charge women he went for. She was just a former model hiding under a pretty convincing wig, and couldn't even secure proper headquarters for her own business project.

The front door of the cabin was kicked open, sending a brisk cloud of frigid air her way as Luke wrangled in a mattress. He came across the living room, dropping it against the far wall. He looked wild, strong and able to take on the world.

Emma felt the lift of hope. "What's that?" She shivered and hugged herself, moving to close the front door. It had grown dark outside despite it being not quite suppertime, and she'd built up the fire, turned on the lights and let her phone play music to keep her company. The place had eventually felt homey, cozy. But now, with Luke inside its four walls, it felt entirely too intimate.

"Welcome to your two-bedroom home."

"I'm sorry. If I had known…" She would have what? Not come until the perfect place popped up, in about five years? She had to be here. There was work to be done managing the greenhouses where her product's natural ingredients were growing, and so much more.

"I think this place is about as big as my old master bedroom," Luke said, surveying the cabin from his spot against the wall.

She'd never seen his bedroom, his bed. And yet she couldn't help but imagine what it might be like to wake up there every morning. Him by her side, a fresh day full of opportunity and optimism ahead.

"How about I pay for a hotel or a room at a bed-and-breakfast for you." She lifted her phone to make the call.

"This will do for now. We'll reattack accommodations in the morning and work out of coffee shops if necessary."

Emma put away her phone and tried to find something to busy herself with. She needed to act natural, as though she was comfortable with their living arrangements. Flirt, laugh, put them both at ease.

"How was driving the truck?" She knew he was used to flashy, nimble little sports cars.

"The truck is fun, believe it or not."

"You don't miss having a lineup of sexy cars at your disposal?"

"Well, I do, now that you're calling them sexy." He gave her a sheepish smile that made him look delightfully mischievous.

"I knew you only bought them to impress women," she teased, trying to hide the way his smile had reduced her ability to draw in oxygen.

He chuckled. "Busted. But don't forget, I have to prove to other men that mine is bigger."

Emma's gaze trailed south of his parka's hem. She remembered his size and it was just fine. She tried to find somewhere safe to direct her eyes as the silence between them grew awkward, no doubt both of them recalling pieces of Aspen in their minds.

"So, you have a bed now?" she said, her voice squeaking slightly.

"I guess we won't have to sleep together."

"Right." She straightened her spine. "No more mistakes."

"No more mistakes," he echoed, with what sounded like regret.

LUKE SHIFTED UNCOMFORTABLY. There was no doubt that the two of them were dancing around their past, as well as their attraction. That was inevitable, as inevitable as them coming together in passion once again. But the real surprise for him was how being newlyweds—if only in name—kept nudging his mind in directions it shouldn't go. Add in their wedding kiss and his thoughts were on fire.

His wife. His wife. His wife.

Hello.

Not his wife. Not like that.

They were trying to joke around the tension that had settled between them like a tissue-thin barricade that could tear at any moment, releasing them into each other.

He wanted Emma.

She wanted him.

She was unexpected, funny and sexy. That gorgeous hair. That generous smile and the way her curves looked tempting from any angle.

She was doing a number on him even though she wasn't his type. Was it the vulnerability stirring something inside? When he'd returned from his find-bigger-headquarters mission it was clear she'd thought he'd left her, despite the text messages between them.

Why would he leave? He'd lose 20 percent of the new product line's profits, as well as a chance to improve the image of Cohen's. Although she likely didn't realize just how much Cohen's image needed a lift. He'd worked hard to ensure that to the outside world everything looked close to perfect.

And as long as it stayed that way, everything would be good.

"Do I smell food?" Emma sniffed the air.

All he could smell was the scent of burning wood in the fireplace.

"Chicken?" she added.

"Oh, right." He turned to grab a bag he'd left at the door. "I picked up some supper, since neither of us cook."

Emma came over and began digging through the groceries. After selecting a mattress he hadn't been quite ready to admit defeat and return to the cabin for the night. He'd bought some whiskey, then hit the grocery store.

"This smells amazing." She pulled out a deli chicken, still warm from their rotisserie. She gently ripped a hunk of chicken breast off the carcass with her fingers, giving him a look of delight as she ate the piece without the use of utensils.

He blinked in surprise. He wasn't sure if it was sexy or disgusting to have the debutante acting in an unmannered way.

He made a point of looking away, not giving her the attention she obviously craved due to her act as he stood beside her at the counter. He poured himself a finger of whiskey and knocked it back, then poured another. He glanced up to see that she'd moved on to the veggie tray, slowly licking a trace of dip from her pink lips, instead of using a napkin, and leaving them moist and glistening.

No, he was pretty sure her lack of manners was sexy.

She'd added a sweater to her earlier outfit and it fit her like a glove, clinging to all the curves he remembered all too well despite the months that had passed since the last time he'd smoothed his hands over them, kissing his way up and down her form with revelatory delight.

Another piece of chicken disappeared between her plump lips and he felt his body react with a force that shocked him. He still had time to check into a hotel.

Instead of moving to the door, he found himself mesmerized by the way her tongue was slowly licking her lips, sending a pulse of testosterone through his system. He clenched his juice glass of whiskey, then set it aside as, without another thought, he pulled her close, his body reacting to the shock of having her soft form against him, and how contact was being made in all the right places. He kissed her. Hard. Once on the mouth before releasing her, one hand tangled in her beautiful hair.

Asinine.

He'd kissed her. Possessively. Passionately.

But there was something different about Emma today. Something intriguing. She was harder to dismiss. Harder to overlook and discount.

He wanted to kiss her again.

She snatched up his whiskey glass as though prepared to splash the drink in his face, fire in her eyes. He clamped his hand over hers, stepping back into her personal space.

"Emma."

He really didn't want to admit just how sexy she was to him right now.

She's your wife, whispered the devil on his shoulder. *You could consummate this thing like a real man. The two of you are good with secrets and it's going to be a long, cold and boring winter out here in the woods.*

Her cheeks were pink, her eyes searching his for answers.

He mentally scolded the devil riding on his shoulder. Emma and he were business partners, not lovers. Plus the angel on his other shoulder was whispering that Emma was flirting only because she was feeling vulnerable, and was worried he was going to abandon ship. She had a lot of baggage when it came to this cosmetic line and her emotional stakes were high. He should treat her respectfully and carefully.

"Luke." Her voice was low, torn between longing and anguish. "We can't."

"Why?"

She no longer met his eye. "It would be a mistake."

Shot down. Again. She was the only woman who'd consistently denied him. And she was the only woman who made him hate himself when she did. One day he'd figure out why.

He stepped back, giving her space, taking plates out of the overhead kitchen cupboard to keep himself busy. "Tomorrow I'll arrange for immediate high speed internet hookup and a cell signal booster so we can get some work done. There's a guy named Ethan who came recommended."

She nodded as he started carving the chicken, and then helped him set out their meals at the small table between the kitchen and fireplace seating area.

"Luke?" He looked up from the chair he'd pulled out for her. "Do you think the lawyers will give you the inheritance even if you don't carry out your marriage in the spirit your grandparents intended?"

Luke felt his groin tighten as he caught the meaning behind her words. He leaned closer, ready to act. She placed a hand tentatively against his chest as the devil on his shoulder began its frantic whispering and nudging, coaxing his libido to hit the brain-override switch and just take her already.

"Are you propositioning me, Ms. Carrington?" he asked, his voice husky with anticipation, his hope too fluid to contain.

She leaned closer, her perfume subtle, inviting, though her tone was serious. "I'm just saying that there may be more obstacles than we anticipated, Mr. Cohen."

"So we should consider each and every angle."

"We don't want to make any more mistakes."

That made it sound a lot like he was damned if he did and damned if he didn't.

LUKE'S CELL rang and he figured he might as well pick up the call, seeing as he wasn't getting any sleep in his makeshift bed on the chilly cabin floor. All he could think about was Emma's throaty words regarding the intent of his grandmother's marriage clause, and how sultry they had sounded coming from her lips. How intoxicating.

Even after asking if she was propositioning him, he still wasn't sure what she'd been getting at. Was she simply worried about receiving her promised cut? Or was she wishing to repeat past "mistakes"?

And the flirty act? She flirted with everyone. There was no need to think she was actually interested.

He reached for his phone, clearing his throat. "Luke Cohen here."

"We want to be paid tomorrow at eight."

The man's tone informed Luke this wasn't a call meant for the accounts payable clerk at Cohen's.

"I'm sorry? Who is this?" Luke tried to get caller ID to come up, but it simply said Unknown, the line echoey due to poor reception. "How did you get this number?"

"I have more than just your number. You know how much we need to be paid to keep our silence."

Luke sat up and rubbed his forehead. His guess? Another problem thanks to his father.

"I don't, actually, but say I refuse to pay?" No more being the street sweeper coming along after his dad. Franklin was an adult and no longer the CEO; he could clean up after himself instead of tainting the company with his bribes and overly generous donations that ensured he got what he wanted when he didn't find it beneficial to follow the rules.

"Then we play." The man's disguised voice held a note of grim humor.

"I'll trace your call. Have you arrested for blackmail." Luke glanced up to ensure Emma's bedroom door was still closed. The last thing he needed was for her to think Cohen's had an integrity problem that might cause her to steer away from the company as a launch partner.

His grandparents, who often took him for a few weeks each summer, had instilled a lot of their beliefs in him. Integrity. Honor. Gratitude. It had become even more important to him during his early teenage years, when he'd started making his own money as well as exerting his independence from his father. Their words had come at the right time, giving him something to strive for, showing him there was a different path to success than the one his dad had taken.

"Burn phone," the blackmailer said. "Untraceable. We need to talk delivery details. Your father assured us this debt would be paid."

"Cohen's is not paying you," Luke said through gritted teeth. *He* did not pay off people.

"You pay government officials. Sorry, was that actually extortion? I thought it was a well-timed bribe so the officer wouldn't inspect your improper labeling."

Luke shut his eyes and squeezed his cell phone to his ear. He stood so he could pace the room.

After the media fallout over Carrington's toxins last summer Luke had convinced the board at Cohen's to remove all toxins from their own lotions and other products. Not only was it the right thing to do—and one he'd long been campaigning for—but it was the only thing the company could do to survive some pretty poor publicity for him standing by their long-time family friends, the Carringtons.

His father had still been CEO at the time, and had just about fired Luke for bringing Cohen's into the media mess. But what had really sucked was a product labeling lapse that resulted in several thousand bottles of lotion from their Bliss line going out with the new ingredient list, but the old toxins inside. Luke had insisted they put out a recall for the mislabeled products, but his father had feared it would create unnecessary drama over what amounted to basically nothing. To save money and prevent wasted packaging, as well as factory downtime that would impact workers and their income, Franklin had allowed the lapse to happen. Then he'd paid off the inspector who'd noticed the discrepancy.

With money comes protection. That had been Franklin's offhand response to Luke's outrage.

And now someone outside Franklin's private circle had caught wind of it and wanted to be paid for his silence.

Luke inhaled sharply through his nose as his anger toward his father grew.

"The company paid a fine." His heart thundered at the lie. His father technically hadn't bribed the official, as the two men, according to Franklin's account, had settled on a "fine." Luke had kept calm, said nothing, then campaigned to have his father step into retirement.

Money hadn't protected him from that.

The blackmailer began to speak again, but Luke cut him off. "Look, Cohen's is helping Carrington Cosmetics to create a new—"

"Their products still have known carcinogens, which made Emma Carrington ill."

Luke felt a familiar tug in his gut. It had been awful watching her stand tall through the media storm, her family acting as though nothing was wrong, the women at the country club giving her a wide berth due to the bad publicity. Luke, not knowing what else to do, had sent her flowers from the executive team at Cohen's every week during her chemo, as well as quietly donated half a million dollars to the local cancer society from his own emergency fund—the one he strived never to touch.

"That's why we're creating a new product line," Luke said. "All-natural. Healthy. Safe."

"We expect immediate payment for silence. We know that this bribe isn't the only thing you're trying to keep secret."

Luke's blood ran cold.

"Take it up with Franklin," he said harshly. "Cohen's Blissful Body Care and I have nothing to do with his actions."

"You're CEO of *his* company."

It was true his father still had a controlling share.

"I plan on buying him out," Luke said, a new plan forming in his mind. If he ensured that the All You line launched high, he would be able to buy out his father's share within a year. "He doesn't make decisions for this company any longer. This phone call is over."

"We're watching you, Luke Cohen. We're watching you and that little town. And if you don't pay us—"

"Thank you for your call." Heart pounding, Luke hung up, hating his father more than he had in months. He grabbed a piece of paper and began doing calculations on how much it would take to buy him out.

The next morning Emma wound her way through the suitcases she'd left open all over her bedroom and hightailed it across the cold wood floor. She donned the wig she'd nicknamed Cousin Itt from *The Addams Family*, as well as the cap that went between it and her real hair. The fire was almost out in the main room, Luke all but vanished under his mound of blankets.

She struggled to shake off the awful helpless feeling her frequent nightmare had left behind. Since taking on the project she had a recurring dream where she was driving a large moving van laden with what felt like precious cargo. It would start to slip backward, the brakes not slowing the vehicle as it picked up speed, her attempts at controlling it futile until it went off the road, over an embankment, waking her up before impact.

The pile of logs beside the fireplace was gone and Luke was snoring lightly.

"Where's all the wood?" she demanded, loudly enough to wake him. "It's freezing in here."

Without moving the blankets off his head, Luke replied, "I

used it all, Princess of Carrington. Thanks for asking how I slept." He rolled over, going back to sleep.

She pushed at him. "Get up. It's morning. We need to chop down a tree or something. Can we order wood online? Right. We have crap for internet out here. We're stuck with only you to save us. Get out of bed and slay some dragons."

"I left my best sword at home."

Emma sighed and moved to the door, tugging on her parka and boots, skipping her mitts, since they made her gel nails rub against each other and she'd just had a mani before leaving the city. She didn't have time to deal with chipped polish and finding a new manicurist. Today was the first day of Luke taking charge and making things happen. No more panic, no more worries about failing. And hopefully, no more truck-out-of-control nightmares.

Although maybe a few more worries about whether or not their marriage was in the spirit of his late maternal grandparents' inheritance clause. She needed that small chunk of money.

Emma stepped out onto the porch, then right back inside again as the frigid air pierced her lungs each time she inhaled. It was difficult to even imagine the times back home when she'd felt too hot to move. That kind of oppressive heat and this kind of slicing cold didn't feel as though they could exist on the same planet.

"The air hurts!"

"That's because Blueberry Springs sucks," Luke mumbled from deep in his covers.

Emma felt a trickle of doubt.

No. None of that. She squared her shoulders and smiled, shaking off the negativity. She stomped over to Luke, whipping the blankets off his curled form. He looked grumpy and yet somehow utterly adorable.

"Gimme back my blankets."

"Come on. I didn't sell everything to let this place roll right on over us." She quickly caught herself. He didn't know how deep she was with this whole project. *Nobody* did. And while he might be less likely to abandon ship if he knew how much she was counting on him, she also didn't want him to think she was foolish or clueless for doing so—because who invested everything they owned in a project they weren't sure they could even manage?

She opted for some distracting quick chatter, hoping it would prevent that little slip from getting a proper chance to register in his mind. "We're Luke and Emma! Luma. Or EmmaLu. Whatever you want to call us. Team Rock Star!" She plunked herself on top of his side, using him as a seat. "You're not a morning person, are you?"

"Apparently cheerleaders are." He shoved her off him, sending her tumbling to the floor as he yanked the covers back up over his head, then rolled to his other side. "Cohens don't do manual labor. Call the landlord and tell him we need more wood."

Emma laughed, piling herself on top of him again. He was snuggle-worthy, all strong and firm under the thick blankets. She rested her head against his shoulder, her arms draped on either side of him. "Come on, sleepyhead. The world awaits."

"You're nice and warm."

It did feel pretty nice sprawled on top of him, but the room would only get colder the longer the fire burned down, seeing as it was their only source of heat. Plus it was dangerous snuggling with him, as it had been a long time since she'd been intimate with someone and last night's kiss had been a warning shot—get too close and trouble was sure to follow.

Yet she savored another few seconds before rolling off him. There was work to do. She could fantasize later at a safe distance.

She clapped her hands. "Come on, sexy man, get out of bed and take the world by the short hairs."

He lifted his head from the pillow to give her a bleary look of disbelief. "Did you just make a reference to—"

"Shut up and get up." She felt her cheeks heat. Luke had only ever really known her as the polite and proper Carrington, rarely seeing her goofier side. The woman who could curse like a sailor or do tequila shots with Mexican farmers off the beaten path of the fancy tourist resorts. The real Emma. The one who got The Look straight down the perfectly reshaped nose of her mother if she didn't toe the line with polite precision while out in public.

Luke sat, his dark hair sticking up off his forehead, his five o'clock shadow giving him a rugged look that made her mouth water.

"Fine, cruel woman," he said with a sigh. "You're not very ladylike for a Carrington, you know that?"

"And you're a typical spoiled baby of a Cohen."

He smirked, his eyes filled with amusement as he rose to his feet and stepped around her. He dropped his cotton pajama pants and exchanged them for a pair of jeans. He often rode his bike for miles along the city's bicycle paths and roadways, and the results were evident in his strong, muscular legs.

Heat immediately pooled in Emma's more southern regions and she figured if he kept stripping she'd soon be able to warm the cabin from the heat coming off her.

Luke caught her looking and she quickly glanced away.

"What?" he asked. "You've seen more than my underwear before."

"I think we need to establish some rules."

He winked. "I'll show you mine if you show me yours."

"You already showed me yours."

"Then you owe me another mistake." His voice was low and suggestive, but Emma's mood soured at the joking reference to her fallback excuse.

He acted as though the comment wasn't a dig, but it still felt like a warning. A warning about what, exactly, she wasn't sure, but knew it could reference pretty much anything that strayed past the business-partner line.

Luke donned his parka, letting out a bark of shock as he stepped outside. "That's brisk!"

Emma joined him on the porch. They needed to find bigger headquarters. And soon.

"Where's the woodpile?" he asked. Everything around them was white from a middle-of-the-night snowfall. It was gorgeous, quiet and unlike anything she'd ever experienced, even during ski trips with the family.

Luke, not waiting for an answer, began wading through the deep snow to a covered mound set between two trees. Emma tugged mittens over her hands. Manicure? Whatever. She was going to lose a body part in this chill if she didn't layer up every inch of her.

"Those are pretty big," Emma said skeptically, hanging back as he uncovered a stack of logs.

"I think we're supposed to split the larger ones. Have you seen an ax?"

"Behind the front door beside the shotgun."

Luke whirled. "Greta wasn't joking?"

Emma laughed at his expression. "Who's Greta?"

"The real estate agent. She warned me about bears and coyotes. Mostly coyotes."

Emma shivered and took a step closer to Luke, her attention flicking from forest to driveway to cabin.

They hauled several loads, trying to select the smallest pieces before giving up and grabbing the ax to split a few of the bigger ones.

"Do you know how to do this?" Emma asked, handing Luke the heavy ax.

"How hard can it be?" he said, hoisting the blade, sending a log flying instead of cutting through it.

Emma laughed at his confused expression. "We missed our calling. Someone should be filming us for a reality show. Wait until we try to cook or unclog the toilet."

"I don't do plumbing," Luke said with a shudder. He gave a serious nod of his head and contemplated the log before him. "I've got this." He adjusted his grip, then whacked the log hard, splitting it with ease.

He gloated, tossing the two pieces to the side, then lined up a new log. "Nothing to it."

Emma watched him work, finding herself wishing it was summer so he could work without a shirt on. She'd bet his muscles looked fine, rippling under all those layers of clothing.

"I knew I'd hired you for a good reason," she murmured as she collected the newly split wood and started carrying it inside.

When they had what they hoped would be enough to last a day, they covered the pile under its tarp again. Emma, feeling playful, swept a handful of snow at Luke, catching him in the face. He turned, giving her a shocked look. "Why'd you do that?" he asked.

"Haven't you ever played in the snow before?"

"I pay people to do that for me."

"Ha!" She threw more snow at him. He ducked and stomped away.

"Come on, you big baby." She tried to throw more at him but the snow wasn't sticky enough to form a ball.

"Baby?" He stopped to stare at her, his warm breath causing clouds of mist above his red scarf.

She taunted him. "Widdle baby Lukie. A widdle snow scaring you?"

He attacked, grabbing her low around the waist, hoisting her over his shoulder. She squealed as he ran to a big drift and dropped them into the fluffy snow. She giggled, securing her woolen cap over her wig as they tumbled.

She tried to cover him in snow, while he did the same to her, and he caught her arm as she moved closer in an attempt to try and knock him backward into a deeper drift. He pinned her lower half with his as they wrestled, trying to get the upper hand.

He was laughing, looking more carefree than she'd ever seen him, even on his sailboat back home.

Something sparked between them and their wrestling slowed, the clouds from their breath mingling. For a moment she thought he was going to warm her lips with his.

Then Luke quickly rolled off her as the crunching of tires on snow filled the air. There was a shiny red SUV creeping up the driveway, the driver staring at them through the windshield.

Emma stood, knocking the snow from her clothes. Whoever it was had the worst timing ever. Or maybe the best.

Definitely the best.

Her flirting had progressed from the safe zone straight into the danger zone without her even noticing. It seemed to be a common Luke-proximity issue and she needed to figure out how to rein herself in—then keep herself there.

Luke collected the ax from the snow and waved to the woman in the vehicle. She opened her door and stepped onto the driveway. She was tall and gorgeous.

"Emma, this is Haddie," Luke said quickly. "Haddie, Emma."

The woman gave Emma an appraising once-over with crystal-blue eyes. Her mascara was exquisite and definitely not Carrington's.

"I didn't expect you here so soon," Luke said.

The corner of Haddie's lips lifted into a perfect smirk. "I took the red-eye. When Luke Cohen calls in the middle of the night and says he has something, you don't sit around…" She glanced at Emma as though deciding how much to say in her presence. "I'm sure you know how it is."

Luke put a protective hand on the woman's lower back, ushering her to her vehicle after hefting the ax into Emma's hands with a, "I'll return soon."

And just like that, instead of kissing her, her husband went off with another woman.

LUKE SAT in a small sandwich shop and café in downtown Blueberry Springs. Haddie Goodchild, an investment reporter who'd been pestering him for a few quotes for a feature article on him, settled across the table, her bulky winter jacket hanging over the back of her chair. She yawned and took a sip of her coffee, then placed her pen, notebook and a digital recorder on the table, raising her eyebrows in question as her finger hovered over the record button. He nodded, giving his permission. He wanted to show that he had nothing to hide.

It was time for a preemptive strike against the blackmailers and any damage they planned to cause. Haddie's magazine had direct access to over a million subscribers, all big names in the world Luke lived in. What she said about him could combat anything anyone else said.

"I'm really glad you decided to give me a few quotes for my article," she said, after stating the time, date, location, as well as his name into the recorder.

"No problem. Thank you for coming all this way."

"So? What do you have for me?"

"I'd like to formally announce that Cohen's Blissful Body Care and Carrington Cosmetics have joined forces to produce Emma Carrington's new All You product line. Its ingredients are organic and all-natural. They're also locally and ethically sourced. Everything from the main ingredients to the packaging comes from renewable resources. Completely sustainable. But most of all, these new products are safe for women of all ages."

Haddie had lifted her pen to take notes but now leaned back in her chair. She had a shrewd way of looking at him that was unnerving, like she knew more than she was letting on and was waiting for him to slip up and confirm something.

"Okay," she said finally.

"Any questions?"

She heaved a sigh. "Honestly, I was expecting something a bit more personal, Luke."

Such as the fact that someone had tried to blackmail him last night? Not a chance.

"Cohen's is changing. Last summer we removed all toxins from our lotions. Even ones that fall under acceptable use and are considered safe when used in limited quantities. Now we're working to produce a product so safe I could eat it every day for the rest of my life without harm."

Emma's words from earlier in the week sprang to mind and he repeated them. "Women need this. The planet needs this."

Haddie's expression softened and Luke relaxed.

"So?" he prompted. "Will you add that to your article?"

"I'll give it a mention."

They stared at each other from across the table. Her blouse dipped low and the view wasn't bad. She was tall, intelligent, and had admitted on the drive over that she used to win local beauty pageants as a teen. Normally, he would ask a woman like her if she wanted to discuss the article over dinner, but there was something about her that just didn't get his motor running.

Maybe it was the way his mind kept replaying the look on Emma's face when he'd rolled off her delicious body to scoot away with Haddie. He'd been really close to kissing Emma, momentarily forgetting what was at stake.

"I've discovered a lot about you over the past few weeks of research," Haddie said, and Luke bristled at her tone.

"There's a lot to know," he said lightly. "The company regularly supports over twenty charities, for example."

"Right. Money brings power and favor."

"It helps those in need," he said pointedly.

"Helps the public overlook your company's past sins. Redirects their attention."

"Are you insinuating that Cohen's has something to hide?"

"Do you?"

"*I* have nothing to hide."

She narrowed her eyes as though noting the fact that he hadn't said Cohen's, but rather had referred to himself. She was sharp, that was for certain.

"There must have been a lot of mixed emotions with your father handing over the CEO torch," Haddie said. "Retiring, but still owning a controlling share. It must be difficult to fill his shoes and exert your own influence. Care to comment?"

"I think you summed it up adequately," Luke said simply. "Cohen's has always done its best to uphold current government regulations, and as the new CEO I take the safety and well-being of our customers—"

"'Done its best'—does that imply that you haven't always been successful?"

"I understand that drama sells, but I thought you came out here because you were interested in seeing Cohen's from a new perspective." He pushed his chair back from the small table, making it clear that he'd leave if she didn't play nice. She raised her hands in silent surrender.

Out of the corner of his eye, Luke spied Logan Stone, a man who looked like he could win any cage fight based on sheer size alone, enter the café. After the blackmailer's call last night, Luke had asked his security agent, Zach Forrester, for someone to shadow him. Just in case.

So now he had Logan, a rather obvious shadow.

The man stood at the counter, chatting with the blonde serving him, laughing about something as he placed an order. Logan lived and worked out of Blueberry Springs, which would hopefully help the fact that he didn't blend in well.

"I'm sorry," Haddie was saying. "It's simply that I've heard a few things I'd like to confirm."

"I'll answer what I can."

"Thank you." She smiled. It was a nice smile, but not sexy like

Emma's. "Your participation will help me write a more accurate and fair article."

Luke wasn't sure he liked the sound of that.

"In what ways is your managing style different from your father's?" she asked, consulting a page in her notebook.

"We're very different men."

"Would you like to expand on that?"

"Nope."

Logan had taken a seat across the small, narrow room with a take-out cup. He wasn't looking at Luke, but rather his phone. Was it possible Zach hadn't sent him and the man simply looked an incredible amount like the agent photo Luke had been sent? He couldn't imagine there being two men in town who looked as tough and as ready for a rumble as this guy.

"I heard a rumor…" Haddie began, and Luke returned his attention to her.

"There are a lot of them going around." But hopefully, none of them about his secret marriage. He needed that to remain under wraps for another four months so his father didn't try to road-block him.

"It's about Cohen's bribing the media to remain silent about Carrington Cosmetics," Haddie said.

Luke felt himself flinch in surprise. "I'm sorry?"

"Last summer, your company purchased several overpriced ads, with the agreement that those companies involved and their subsidiaries wouldn't run anything derogatory against Cohen's or Carrington or any of their owners for a six-month period."

Luke's pulse picked up speed. That had been a favor exchanged between his father and a golf buddy who knew all too well that a few negative articles could have pushed the family empire under at that point. Cohen's had purchased more ads from the media conglomerate, and in return, they didn't run anything negative. It was a fairly common practice, but it had left Luke feeling uncomfortable due to the lack of transparency.

"Can you explain the ten thousand dollar entrance fee you paid to attend a private party with several members of the Environmental Protection Agency in Palm Desert?" Haddie asked when he didn't comment.

"I like to stay abreast of recent environmental regulations, concerns and the like. It's important, and that fee went toward charity. An environmental one." There was absolutely nothing wrong with that. No way for her to spin that around and leave him with egg on his face.

"I don't think…"

"What?" he snapped when she hesitated. Logan looked up, his gray eyes slowly taking in both Luke and Haddie.

"I just don't…" She was hedging.

"What? You don't believe we can turn it around? That the new CEO is a good guy who cares?" Luke stood, drawing more attention to them with his raised voice. "I'm here to make a difference in the lives of women, Haddie. If you can't see that, then print whatever you like."

"I want to run a balanced article."

"It sure doesn't seem like it."

She was like the blackmailer. Dirt. Everywhere dirt. What about the good stuff? Didn't that count for anything? Why didn't anyone want to talk about that?

"I want to show the real man behind the CEO title." She stood as well, stepping toward him in her high-heeled boots. She wasn't as graceful as Emma, and he wondered what she normally wore when she wasn't trying to take down billionaires. Steel-toed boots meant for kicking?

"Luke Cohen is a man with heart."

She scoffed. "You wouldn't know a heart if it fell out of your chest. I'm tired of people like you thinking money makes you special, that wealth means relationships."

"I'm not who you assume I am," Luke said tightly. "I do good things."

"With your money?"

Why did she say that with such disdain? With financial status came responsibility, and he was definitely a cut above the spoiled trust fund babies who'd never earned a dime on their own. Since the age of nine he'd saved his allowance, investing wisely, doubling his money more often than not. He'd moved on to flip sailboats when the one his father had purchased for him for his eleventh birthday had come loose in the marina during a particularly bad storm and been dashed upon the rocks. It had been an insurance write-off, but Luke had bargained to buy back the wreck. He'd then worked through a charter service who helped him arrange to fix it, rent it out when it was fixed, then flip it six months later. He'd made seven grand. On the next boat he'd made twenty. The next one, fifty. Then eighty. He'd continued to flip boats and reinvest until at seventeen he'd decided to buy an old hotel in the Caribbean, miles from the more popular resorts. He'd had it remodeled. Bought up the surrounding land, sent in landscapers and now owned a bustling, billion-dollar property that was fully booked six months out.

He'd worked hard for that money and he used it for good. Each month, 65 percent of the resort's profits went toward supporting homeless shelters and food banks down on the islands, as well as a few back in South Carolina and Arizona.

"I do good things with my wealth."

Haddie poked him in the chest. Across the room, Logan stiffened, as though preparing to strike out in his defense. Luke gave a subtle hand gesture, letting him know he could stand down. He had this.

"Without money you'd be nobody, Luke Cohen."

Luke repressed the urge to shudder at the truth of her statement. He knew what it was like to depend on social services to feed you, keep you safe. He had an untouched, decent-sized emergency fund for that very reason.

"There's nothing wrong with how I use my wealth," he said to the reporter. "And I won't be made to feel guilty because I have enough that I'm not worried about feeding myself or keeping a roof over my head."

"The article runs in three months and all I've seen so far is a typical, untouchable man who uses his money to win people over and create his own rules."

"Then try taking a closer look."

She smirked. "What does it matter? I know men like you and I've never had to rewrite an article."

"Then get ready for me to pop that cherry, because you've yet to see what happens when Luke Cohen takes charge."

EMMA HAD STAYED clear of Luke since he'd come back from his little date with the tall woman in the SUV. He didn't say anything about his sudden "appointment" with Haddie, but Emma could tell it hadn't gone well.

Lovers' spat?

Business deal fallout?

What was it?

She itched to ask, but knew better than to dig into his private life. They were family friends, business partners and legally spouses, but she still felt as though none of it gave her the latitude to pry. Plus she didn't want to give him the impression that she thought their new relationship was anything more than professional.

As the one in charge of All You, she'd learned quickly that less talking was better—especially out in the greenhouses where engineers were constantly tinkering with the setup as the scientists tried to find the optimal growing conditions for the line's much-needed natural ingredients such as the valerian plant. There had only been once where she'd known what needed to be done and had dived right on in and gotten her hands dirty.

But generally, she spent a lot of time listening carefully to various team members, taking a moment to pause thoughtfully when they asked for her input. Especially with Vintra, her head scientist, as he explained things such as proposed formula tweaks or water pH levels before asking for her opinion on a change. She'd try to nod intelligently and as though she understood before saying something such as, "I can see you've put a lot of thought into this and weighed out the possible implications. I think we should go ahead with your plan. Please keep me apprised of the results." Then she'd follow up in an hour or a week, depending on what felt appropriate, trying not to panic in the meantime over possibly having made a choice that would set them back instead of move them forward.

She would do the same with Luke. She'd listen, stay out of the way, and be a good business partner who didn't let her personal life slip into the workplace. The more she kept it about business, the more everyone saw her as focused and outcome-minded, and the less she received cracks about being an airhead model.

Still, she couldn't help but bring up the mysterious, beautiful Haddie.

Emma smoothed her hair, then gently cleared her throat. "How was your meeting?"

"What?" Luke looked up from his phone, as though surprised to see her there in the cabin's small sitting area.

"With Haddie? She's pretty."

"Yeah. She used to win pageants." He went back to his phone. "She's writing a piece on me."

Between the Sheets with Luke Cohen.

Emma gave herself a mental shake. Internally, she was acting like a jilted lover, a jealous spouse, and she had no right to. The woman was merely a reporter, a part of the overall Luke Plan that would get them the kind of publicity that would help All You rise high. Just like she wanted.

"Do you want to see the greenhouses?" she asked. "The valerian is coming along well."

"I'm waiting for the internet guy to come."

"Maybe later?"

He nodded.

"Luke?" She waited until she had his attention again. "I just want to say that I'm grateful you're here. And I'm sorry if my playing around earlier made you uncomfortable."

He blinked slowly, as though processing her words through a translator. "It's fine."

"I want you to know that I can and will be professional and that I'll do my best to help with everything."

"I know."

"Okay." She went back to her task of planning her next beauty video for her blog, squelching the urge to keep talking. Normally, she could prep, record and upload a video in less than thirty minutes, as she let most of it flow naturally, giving her videos a chatty feel that her subscribers seemed to like. However, Luke wanted her to do more editing before uploading, splicing in images of the upcoming products and making it more focused in terms of marketing.

She wasn't sure how to do that. She'd originally started the blog as a somewhat vindictive form of therapy after one of her nasty breakups with Vaughn, a photographer who used to do many of the company photo shoots that involved her and her sister. It had been a ridiculous relationship, with enough fights and near breakups that should have clued her in sooner that he wasn't the right man for her. But he'd always return with kind words and promises about spending more time together. He'd bring her something nice, like a new dress, telling her how ravishing she was before taking her out to some fancy restaurant and showing her off, making her feel special and loved.

She knew now that he'd simply been using her and that love hadn't had a thing to do with their relationship.

But the blog was a keeper. A fun outlet for her to talk about beauty, as well as share her knowledge.

Maybe she just didn't have the right kind of business mind, because Luke's basic request felt impossible. Then again, it could simply be her lack of mojo, seeing as she hadn't felt particularly inspired to record videos since her illness. Part of it was that she'd felt ugly, thanks to water retention and rashes during and after her cancer treatments. Part of it was she didn't want to wear a lot of makeup any longer. And finally, her luscious locks were actually a wig she took off at night so it didn't tangle.

Hypocrite. Poser. Fake. Liar.

Any of those words could be accurately used to describe her.

Emma fingers slipped to Cousin Itt and the knots that always seemed to form at the nape of her neck, absently working them out while she thought.

What kind of pageants had Haddie won? State-wide? National? She still looked like she could win a few.

"Do I…?" Luke paused and shook his head. "Never mind."

Emma abandoned her detangling task and pushed away her notebook, giving him an encouraging, I'm-listening smile. "Do you what?"

"Do you ever find that people perceive you as being insincere when you donate money? Because you're rich?"

"Like I don't actually care and it's just another photo op and tax break?"

"Yeah."

They often were. A little positive publicity and an easy way to get the company's name in the papers, often at carefully strate-gized, optimal times.

Luke hooked an ankle over his knee, arms crossed, as though he was truly considering her and the topic. Nuts. When he looked at her like that—as though her opinion mattered—it nearly undid her.

She cleared her throat and licked her lips, determined to be a serious businesswoman worthy of consideration.

"Do I—or Cohen's—seem insincere?"

"Your dad does," Emma said with a laugh, before catching herself.

"I'm not my dad," Luke said quickly.

"That's true." She curled a strand of hair around her finger. "I appreciated the way you donated to the local cancer society back home. When I was sick."

Luke's eyebrows lifted in surprise. "You heard about that?"

Of course she had. How did you not notice such a handsome, supportive man, even from afar? He was the kind of person women swooned over, and his kindness had pretty much cinched it.

Emma got up and moved closer, taking a spot on the other end of the couch in front of the fire. "You didn't mention it to me, which leads me to think it wasn't a publicity stunt. It was something you did because you wanted to make a difference in the lives of others, and it was a way of showing support." She swallowed over the lump that formed in her throat, making her unable to add that she appreciated he hadn't made her illness a way to draw more attention to himself, like some of her so-called friends had.

Luke's tense look faded and he reached over, squeezing her hand.

"Thank you for the flowers, too." Every Monday, before her medical appointments started for the week, a new bouquet would arrive from the executives at Cohen's—which, she knew, was actually Luke. They'd brightened her mood and made her feel less alone in her battle.

"That was my assistant, Alexa," he said uneasily. He got up and moved about the small room. "Does Carrington have anything to hide? Anything I should know about?"

Emma shook her head. "Everything came out in the open last summer."

She'd been impressed with how calm Luke had remained through it all, how quickly Cohen's had changed their lotions to ensure they were safer. It was one of the reasons she'd asked Luke to help. Besides the fact that nobody else would take her calls, and if they did, hadn't bothered to hear her out once they'd learned that she was the one in charge of it all and not simply the public face for the products.

A model? Ha ha ha.

At least Luke hadn't laughed.

"Haddie believes that money I've donated was given with the intention of influencing others."

"Isn't that called wise marketing?" Emma asked with an uneasy chuckle.

Luke gave a huff of laughter that had a slight edge to it. "If she's thinking it, Emma, everyone is, or soon will be after she publishes her article this spring. The past behavior of our families and our companies could overshadow this project. We need to come up with a counterplan to combat any possible attacks. Beat them to the punch by hitting the press with it first. This new line is not a publicity stunt intended to appease the public. We need to illustrate that it's a sincere attempt to improve the world and the products our loved ones use."

Emma's heart thrummed faster and she wondered if she dared think he might consider her a loved one.

No, she was being silly. This was business. He knew the right phrases and was talking strategy, not making some sort of confession of undying love.

"We need to combat the fact that you haven't been a poster child for good health. We need to emphasize that All You isn't a pet project meant to make a spoiled debutante feel better after a health scare."

"It's not a pet project," Emma said, feeling the cut of his

words. Her fingers found the thin, gold chain bracelet she wore, and she rolled it in her grip as though gathering strength from it.

"A safe, sustainable product doesn't shift perspectives. We need something bigger, a campaign people can get behind. A social movement."

She swallowed the emotion swelling in her throat. "We're helping a small town, creating jobs and supporting their infrastructure through business taxes. We're also keeping it natural and local."

"That's not big enough," Luke said decisively. He caught her expression and his tone softened. "I'm sorry. I didn't mean to sound callous. It's just strategy. I want this to do well."

Emma stood, tipping up her chin as she straightened her shoulders. Luke was watching her, a shadow of doubt in his gaze.

She planted her hands on her hips, giving him a sassy look. "We're going to work this problem like a model works her daily calorie allotment. We'll find something."

A warm current passed between them, the tension that had been riding in Luke's shoulders easing away, a hint of amusement making his eyes twinkle. "Thanks, EmmaLu."

She held back the smile that formed at the new nickname, which hinted at solidarity. She sashayed closer and said coyly, "You want to know the secret to success, Luke Cohen? Trust your wife."

He burst out laughing, wrapping an arm around her shoulder and drawing her in for a brief hug. He smelled wonderful, his body a haven of comfort she could get lost in. "Wives are the best."

"No, not all of them, Luke. Just this one."

LUKE WAS STANDING knee-deep in a drift, looking at what amounted to a big pile of snow. Somehow Emma had not only flirted him out of his earlier mood over his worries about Haddie and her article, but had also convinced him to come out to the middle of nowhere to look at snowbanks. Correction, where more greenhouses were going to go in spring once the snowbanks melted.

His feet were cold, and staring at snow was a waste of time. He still had to figure out how to get his dad to handle the blackmailer, as well as come up with a plan for reporters like Haddie. How could he turn their heads to see it the way he did? No conspiracy. Just a corporation trying to do good things.

He'd let himself believe that coming to Blueberry Springs on a company-image-enhancing mission would be easy. Simple. Straightforward. In a few months time he'd appear back in South Carolina with deeper pockets, a big smile and a company everyone was clamoring to feature in their news pieces.

Whatever happened, he'd make it work. He always did, but he was still worried. He'd been here for less than twenty-four hours and was currently fearing frostbite, had a hankering to kiss his secret wife and was fending off blackmailers, while a reporter was hoping to turn him into the Big Bad Wolf of the skin care world. Not exactly a wonderful start.

And it turned out Emma wasn't just some flaky model, which was making it more difficult to disregard her.

She had taken several steps away while Luke was lost in thought, her phone screen aimed at herself. The open meadow was behind her and she was video chatting with someone.

"This is where we plan to put three more greenhouses. They will be nice and close to the plant source, which will mean fresher products for our customers, as well as lessen the environmental impact of shipping ingredients and products all over the planet before having a finished end product. We at Carrington are keeping everything local."

She was recording a video with more of a marketing angle, as he'd requested. He smiled, pleased she was taking his requests and ideas seriously.

Emma paused, her tone becoming less formal. "And can I just say that these plants like a really cold winter?" She gave a small laugh and a dramatic shiver. "Oh, I almost forgot to mention that Luke Cohen of Cohen's Blissful Body Care is partnering with Carrington for the All You launch. Not only is he a total hunk and business brain, but he sent me flowers every week when I was unwell last fall. Total swoon!"

Luke cringed at her mentioning cancer and the new products in practically the same breath.

She turned her phone's camera to him. "Say hi to Luke."

He gave a small wave, hoping she wasn't broadcasting live. She laughed and turned the camera back to herself, her face lit up, her spirit fully alive. She was candid and personal. Appealing. He made a mental note to watch more of her videos.

"That was a bit lackluster," she said to her phone. "I think Luke must be camera shy. We'll have to work on that." She gave a conspiratorial wink and ended her video, pocketing her phone.

"Don't mention your illness in videos."

"Everyone knows."

"You don't need to remind customers that Carrington made you sick. We're trying to overcome that black mark."

She nodded slowly and pulled out her phone.

"What are you doing?"

"Deleting it."

"Don't delete it." Luke immediately felt contrite and came closer. "It had potential."

She shook her head. "I wasn't wearing makeup."

He found himself taking her in. Just like when they'd wrestled in the snow earlier that morning, her cheeks were rosy from the cold, her face clean of makeup. Just like then, it felt as if she was bared before him, with nothing to hide.

Which was ridiculous. But it was how he felt.

It made him want to kiss her.

"Do you really think there could be an issue with not carrying out our marriage in the spirit my grandparents intended?" he asked.

Emma jerked in surprise, her cheeks flushing. "I'd ask a lawyer."

And risk his father hearing about it? No, thanks. He'd rather his dad kept busy buying his mother pretty gifts to keep her at his side, his attention on her.

His grandmother would be ashamed and disappointed in Luke for the fake marriage, but he hoped that if she were still alive she'd understand that he was doing it for the greater good—for the good of her own daughter, so she could use the inheritance to better her life.

Emma had moved along to show him something else, and Luke took large steps to catch up with her. She was stomping through the heavy snow, pointing out this and that, discussing details most individuals would have to refer to their notes about, rather than rolling them off their tongue the way she was. She was into it, knew what she was doing, and the longer he was silent, the more confident and animated she became.

He cleared off a stack of wooden posts and sat on them, studying his business partner. "Why is it you really need my help?"

She stared at him blankly. "Excuse me?"

"You know what you're doing."

Emma, the pretty model, had a good brain in her head. And that did little to ease the attraction that had been growing between them.

She was taking a risk, partnering with him. The blackmailers could turn nasty. Haddie could release a mean article at the worst time. It was starting to look as though Emma would do better without Luke's help.

"No, I can't do this without you." She was shaking her head, her curls somehow seeming less bouncy and shiny than they used to. Was it simply an effect of the dry mountain air?

He stopped studying her hair and met her eyes. She looked a bit freaked out, as if thinking he was about to hail the first cab out of here—assuming there were actual taxis in Blueberry Springs.

She had that same uncertainty he'd seen back in Charleston. The one that made him want to take charge and fix things.

"I've never launched something before," she said.

That was true. And from what he gathered, she had little support from Carrington.

"You're different than when you're around your family," he commented.

She looked surprised, then brushed her cheek with a mittened hand, as though feeling self-conscious. "I don't tend to wear makeup when I'm with…well, I just…"

"You're pretty without it." He liked the idea that she wasn't wearing makeup because she might think of him as family.

"Oh." She seemed bashful, almost unsure as to how to accept the compliment, and took a hesitant step backward as though preparing to flee. "Not really."

Back home she was always done up, looking proper and effortlessly elegant. Exactly what he'd always found attractive. But her natural beauty and the way she seemed so exposed now was compelling in an entirely different way.

"I can see the nuances of your expressions, a couple freckles over the bridge of your nose, a hint of smile lines…" She was real. Natural.

She covered her face. "I have wrinkles? Already?" She sounded distraught.

He chuckled. There was the Emma he knew. The one he didn't find as intriguing. Thankfully.

EMMA RODE back into town with Luke. He was so business-serious sexy today she didn't know whether to lick every inch of him for being so darn intelligent and appealing, or to fear he'd toss her aside so he could get things done even faster.

But she was taking mental notes on what he felt was important, and was going to prove herself to him. She could keep up. She could learn from her past mistakes and do better.

She felt herself smile. He'd called her pretty—without makeup.

He'd also said she had laugh lines. Wrinkles, in other words. Did that mean she was getting too old to fall back on her trophy-wife plan? Not that she ever wanted to be one, but it had always been a reassuring safety net.

She sighed and adjusted the seat belt across her chest as Luke pulled up outside Mandy's little café on Main Street.

"This the place?" he asked, putting the truck into Park. They'd planned to stop to warm up and grab an early lunch. The sidewalks seemed extra quiet due to the cold.

She nodded, hoping Luke's discomfort over seeing Olivia yesterday didn't extend to members of her new family, seeing as the café's owner was now her sister-in-law. Mandy made the best brownies and Emma had been jonesing for one ever since she'd left Blueberry Springs before Christmas. Mandy distributed her whiskey-and-gumdrop brownies to grocery stores around the country, but Emma had discovered they weren't the same as having one still warm from her oven.

"Have you got a crew hired to put up the greenhouses in the spring?" Luke asked, before she could jump out and get her chocolate fix.

"I have a tentative commitment." She handed him a notebook with the information, feeling a fizz of uncertainty.

"We need something firm so it doesn't impact production. They need to be out there building as soon as the snow's gone or we'll have a supply lapse." He pulled out his cell phone, his take-charge persona fully in gear. "We want you on-site as soon as the snow melts," he said into his phone moments later. "When will that be?"

Luke sighed.

Emma already knew Mother Nature was a pain in the butt when it came to scheduling and that the construction company was likely giving him the runaround about how long it would take for the snow to clear.

Luke's tone took on a new firmness that sent a tremor of anticipation down Emma's spine. It was sexy and commanding. "We'd like a plow to clear the snow from the proposed greenhouse areas the first week in March, to speed things up."

He paused, then winked at Emma, who smiled.

"As soon as the snow is gone and the ground is firm, we want those buildings up. Timing is *very* important." Luke frowned. "Not good enough. We've hired you for the job and will go elsewhere."

Maybe too direct and firm.

"There's nobody else," Emma whispered.

"I'm willing to go outside Blueberry Springs."

She began shaking her head vigorously. "We have a contract with the town to hire locally."

Luke gave her a look as if to say she had to be kidding. She wasn't. It was part of a deal Olivia had made early on with Devon, when he'd been running for mayor.

"But what we're willing to do," Luke added smoothly, "is give you a retainer. You're ours from March 1 through to May 30. No other jobs."

And that, right there, was why Emma knew she'd done the right thing in hiring Luke.

He was nodding and Emma held out her hand for a high five, but Luke switched his phone to his other hand, looking out his side window instead of at her. Mr. Serious Businessman was in the house. Or truck, as it was.

She eyed the café with longing. Would it be rude to leave him to hash things out and for her to go get a brownie? She didn't believe a true businesswoman would, so she stayed.

"First of March," Luke repeated firmly, before placing the phone in his coat pocket. He was silent for a long moment and Emma didn't dare speak.

"What is wrong with Blueberry Springs?" he finally commented.

"What did he say?" Emma asked tentatively. She'd had to flirt like crazy with the owner even to get the contract on his wait list, and it sounded like Luke had gotten further, but not to his expected end point. "Did he take the retainer?"

"He said he has regular customers and can't drop them for a one-off job. He laughed when I offered extra."

And Emma understood why. Blueberry Springs didn't like people walking in and waving around their wealth. Relationships came first, and she and Luke were outsiders.

"Let's get some lunch," she suggested, climbing out of the truck and hoping she could figure out how to teach Luke how to work with the community before he did something rash, like get them ousted.

Luke joined Emma on the sidewalk, a bitter wind chilling him in seconds. He got the feeling this was a town where it mattered who you knew, not how much you could pay, and that could be a sizable problem for them.

"How much sway does Devon have? He's mayor, right?" If worse came to worst maybe Emma could ask her new brother-in-law for some favors. Luke nearly laughed. Like he'd ask *him* for help.

No, they were doing this on their own.

"How does this place work? What do we need to do?" he added.

"We have to win them over," Emma said simply.

"Kiss babies?" He didn't have time for that. He needed to pay people to do their jobs and move on to the next item on the list.

She gave him a soft smile that told him kissing babies was exactly what he was going to have to do.

Great.

"How many babies are there?"

Emma giggled in amusement. Snowflakes were gently drifting from the sky, landing in her long locks, and he found himself becoming distracted from his worries.

"Just…relax. Be approachable. Real. Take a bit more time with people."

"I'm not real?" Luke rocked back on his heels, burned by the comment.

Emma sighed.

"Emma, you're asking me to be insincere. We're coming in, making money and then leaving. Neither of us is staying here any longer than we need to."

She tucked her bottom lip between her teeth and stared off down the sidewalk.

"You're good at that socialite stuff, and have connections to the town. You infiltrate. I'll deal with the fact that this guy only has one machine to plow the meadow."

"Why don't you just buy one and clear the snow yourself?" she suggested, walking into the café as he held the door for her.

Luke paused for a second, the restaurant's warmth and welcoming, mouthwatering scents hitting him. That was a great idea. It could save him a ton of time and worry, because if there was anyone he could count on, it was himself. And how hard could it be to clear a bit of snow?

It was perfect.

"Close the door!" someone called. Luke quickly stepped in and let the door shut behind him.

He pulled out his phone to do a quick web search on heavy machinery while he followed Emma up to the counter.

"Hey, Mandy. How's Axel doing?" Emma asked the blonde woman standing behind it. She added for Luke's benefit, "Last summer she adopted the cutest baby boy."

"Congratulations," he said automatically, going back to his phone.

He glanced up again. Wait. Was there a baby present that he was supposed to kiss? He blinked and gave his head a small shake. No. Emma was doing the relationship stuff. He had a snowdrift issue to resolve.

"He's fabulous, and busy!" the woman was saying of her little boy.

"Like his mom and dad," Emma said. "Mandy runs a multimillion-dollar brownie company, as well as this café. Her husband, Frankie, has his own auto body shop. Does some amazing custom work and was on a reality TV show."

Again Luke offered his congratulations, but his attention had been snagged. Multimillion-dollar brownie business. Out of Blueberry Springs? He'd bet she had some good tips on how to handle this place, its perks and pitfalls. "Do you bake the brownies here in town? How's distribution? Any issues with weather and road conditions?"

Mandy shared a small smile with Emma and replied, "I have a commercial kitchen here in town, and so far distribution has been fine other than the odd delay due to road closures. Avalanches tend to be bad."

Luke handed the woman his card. "If I have questions about running a major corporation out of Blueberry Springs, can I call you?"

"Sure." Mandy wiped her hands on her apron and pulled a

business card from the small tray in front of her cash register. She handed it to him.

"Can I get your cell?"

"It's on the card."

"I mean your direct line."

"It's on the card," she repeated. Again that small, knowing smile.

He glanced at the card. He'd messed up again, hadn't he? He was being denied direct access for not asking about her kid—because honestly, no businessperson worth their salt let anyone have their main number.

"Thanks." He turned to Emma. "These heavy duty machines are expensive, but not prohibitively so. I'll arrange to have a new backhoe delivered."

Emma gave him a polite, patient smile. "Luke, this is Mandy Mattson-Smith. Mandy, Luke Cohen."

He felt the earth tip. "Mattson? Any relation to Devon?"

He hated that he had reacted to Olivia's new last name. It shouldn't matter. Not any longer.

"I'm his sister," the woman stated.

Emma placed a hand on Luke's arm as though expecting to have to hold him back. "Mandy, Luke is working with me on the All You line. He's an old family friend."

Mandy's eyebrows lifted ever so slightly, but she smiled and extended her hand across the counter for a shake.

Luke politely complied, ensuring his expression was warm and open. No wonder she hadn't given him her direct line. She'd known who he was. "Pleasure to meet you."

The café door opened and a large woman entered, booming a hello to all as though she was the mayor of the town, and not Devon Mattson, the man they'd just been referencing.

"Hello, Mary Alice," Emma said politely, moving closer to Luke so the woman could join them at the counter.

"I heard you were back in town," the newcomer said, unzipping an orange parka that reached her knees. "Who's this hunk you've brought with you?"

"Luke Cohen." Luke offered his hand. The woman pulled off a mitt that went as high as her elbow and gave his hand a hearty shake.

He shot Emma a look as if to say, *See? Totally doing relationships right now. Not ordering my lunch so I can sit down and get some work done sometime this century.*

"Ah, yes," the woman said. "You landed a helicopter in the soccer field. I'm Mary Alice Bernfield."

"That was Olivia's father—Emma's father," Luke stated.

"Cohen's Blissful Body Care is carried in our local drugstore now because of your large donation toward replacing the roof on the continuing care center," she said.

Luke gave a polite nod of acknowledgment. "Thank you. We do what we can to help communities."

Mary Alice chuckled. "You're a very serious type, aren't you? Always saying the right thing and all about the business." She tapped her chin thoughtfully, casting Mandy a sidelong look. "Say, these two would be perfect mentors for our new outreach program, wouldn't they?"

Mandy's face lit up. "You two should join us!"

"I've got a lot to do with this launch, but if you need financial support Cohen's likes to assist the communities we work out of," Luke replied.

Emma elbowed him hard enough that he felt it through his thick coat. "Tell us more about what a mentor does."

"We pair you up with an at-risk child or teenager who needs a mentor or role model, and once or twice a week you spend some time together after school."

"I'm in. Luke?" Emma turned to him, her expression full of hope and expectation.

"What's the actual time commitment?" he asked carefully. "Is there a curriculum?"

"Only an hour or two a week," Mandy said. "You just spend time. Listen, advise. Hang out."

"Are you two married?" Mary Alice asked out of the blue, and Luke nearly choked on a swift inhalation.

"Mary Alice likes to make relationship bets with her sister," Emma said. She asked the woman, "Have you won any lately? I know there have been a few recent surprises."

"Tell me about it. Ethan and Lily already being married. I didn't see that one coming." The large woman shook her head. She reached into her open jacket, her hand disappearing down the front of her shirt. Luke politely looked away. Moments later she was waving her phone. "You two have something. I can feel it." She narrowed her eyes. "I say married by..." She flipped through a few months on her calendar app, humming thoughtfully. "...July. No. August 28."

"Well, that's a good date," Luke said in surprise. "My mom has the Portia House ballroom booked back in South Carolina for that day."

"I must meet your mother," Mary Alice insisted. "Are you two engaged then?" Her gaze trailed to Emma's ring finger. "Because that would be interesting, with you chasing after Olivia only a few months ago."

"We're not," Emma said sharply.

"Not yet, hmm?" She tucked her cell phone back into her bra and nudged Emma out of the way. "Mandy, an extra large coffee, please. I have a lot to do this afternoon."

Mandy passed her a coffee as Emma gave Luke a strange look, asking quietly, "Your mom still has the Portia House booked?"

"She couldn't bear to give up the date," he muttered. His mother had originally placed her name on the three-year wait list in the small, ocean-side town of Indigo Bay in anticipation of upcoming nuptials between Luke and Olivia, as it was The Place in South Carolina when it came to weddings. Then last summer, when the two had broken up, Charlotte had decided to keep her spot on the list in the faint hope that Luke would find someone new by August. Truthfully, he didn't see himself ever using the booking, whether it was next summer or twenty summers in the future. He wasn't against marriage, but he'd had a front row seat to his parents' fights, and their inability to let go and live a happy life apart from each other. Plus he didn't need more people to worry about or feel responsible for. He had enough on his plate. And as for the perks of marriage, there were always women willing to join him at a gala or for an evening or weekend.

"Mandy will get in touch with your mentor match-up," Mary Alice said, hustling out with her coffee, holding the door for a young woman with two small babies in a stroller as large as Emma's old moped.

Emma and her moped. She'd always looked so adorable on the powder-blue machine, with her matching helmet and big grin. What had she said that morning when he'd been wanting more sleep? Something about selling off everything to come out here and give All You a big push? Whatever it meant, he knew he'd likely never see her on the moped again with that big, free smile of hers.

Realizing that Mary Alice was escaping after signing him up for a responsibility he didn't want or need, he opened his mouth to call out a "let me think on it," just as Emma said, "Sounds wonderful. Thank you for thinking of us!"

Relationships, Luke thought with a sigh. He had a feeling that Blueberry Springs was going to keep him very, very busy.

4

*E*mma had been working on the launch plan with Luke for almost two weeks straight. Currently, he was in town going over something with the head scientist, Vintra, as well as chatting with a reporter—he'd been working hard to make sure the world knew what they were doing out here—and Emma was at the cabin, wrapping up her to-do list.

She was exhausted. Mentally and emotionally. Not just from keeping her hands off Luke as he worked by her side, taking charge of things left, right and center like her own personal savior, but also for trying to be a real live businesswoman who could keep pace with someone like him.

Over the past few days she'd lined up product reviews with some of social media's biggest names in the cosmetics world, as well as interviews with scientists and some of Carrington's harshest critics. All part of Luke's counterpublicity plan.

The first time she'd managed to convince a critic to give their new products an honest review she'd wanted to squeal in delight. It had been an empowering boost, but different and stronger than being able to turn a few heads of the opposite sex, something she was used to. This was bigger. More addicting. It made her want to reach further and never stop.

It also made her want to resurrect her old plan for a Carrington lingerie line, as well as a darker, sexier makeup that pushed the company's usual boundaries. Sure, it didn't quite fit the pure image for the tween market she was currently cultivating with Luke's assistance, but it sure would wake up those pinched-mouthed women at the country club who feared rule-breakers. Prim and proper and better than anyone else. The ones who were there when you were at the top, then looked the other way when you were sick and in need.

Emma toyed with the thin gold bracelet her grandmother had given her the first and only time she'd somehow stumbled onto the honor roll in high school. Grammy had been proud, but Emma had felt like she was lying to the world and that someone would find the error in her placement and laugh her out of school. Yet Grammy had believed in her. Emma just needed to remember to believe in herself—not always an easy task.

She woke up her laptop and opened the old lingerie file. She flicked through the proposal, surprised that it was better than she remembered. How had the board said no? She looked sexy in those garments and it was so much more interesting than the boring old cosmetic lines that Carrington insisted weren't dated.

Vaughn had done an amazing job with the photo shoot, making her look demure and tantalizingly sensual. And even though things had gotten a tad out of hand after a bit too much champagne, he'd been a gentleman and deleted all the risqué shots. What she had in this file was good, and she decided that after she launched All You she'd use the profits to start a pure lingerie line. Organic cottons, soft blends from renewable resources.

She'd hire a designer to make them as sexy, flattering and comfortable as possible. She'd give women a reason to believe in themselves and their beauty. Real beauty. Lingerie that enhanced what they had and didn't make them feel as if they needed to lose twenty pounds and do eighty crunches before breakfast in order to look good in it.

It was going to be different.

All of it was.

Feeling a renewed sense of purpose, Emma closed her laptop, noting her chipped nail polish. She needed to pare down her nail regime to something lower maintenance, especially with hauling wood once or twice a day, since it didn't look like they were moving out of the cabin anytime soon.

She rolled her shoulders, reopened her computer and sent off three queries to bloggers about testing and reviewing the new products, then settled in to plan a much-delayed beauty video.

Her cell phone rang and she attacked it, expecting it to be Luke. He'd been working long hours, poring over contingencies, timelines and schedules, making sure the production details were perfect. The man was a lifesaver, but he was going to burn himself out. She needed to institute more breaks, since she'd read in one of his business magazines that downtime enhanced creativity and productivity, which would always come in handy.

"Emma? It's Franklin Cohen."

Her father-in-law. Well, he didn't know that. "Hello, Mr. Cohen. How are you today?"

"Fine, fine," he said hurriedly. "I'm trying to get ahold of my boy. Is he around?"

Emma had noticed Luke silencing a few calls lately—now that they were coming in crisply, thanks to his recently installed cell phone booster, due to help from Olivia's brother-in-law, Ethan Mattson. She wondered if Franklin's was one of them. Or all of them.

"He's out right now. Have you tried his cell?"

"He isn't picking up." There was a slight judgmental tone to his voice that suggested Luke must be pulling all the weight, since he didn't have time to answer his phone but Emma did. Although maybe that was only her own sense of guilt over how hard Luke had been working.

"He was doing some interviews and talking to Vintra, our scientist. I'm sure he'll return your call at his next available moment."

"I've been leaving messages for days. It's urgent."

"Anything I can help with?"

"No," he said quickly. "His assistant said he canceled his Friday flight. When is he coming home?"

"I'm not sure," Emma hedged. Luke had canceled his flight home? Why? Crisis here? No crisis there? He was enjoying being trapped in a tiny, wood-smoke-scented cabin with her? "I'll tell him you called."

"You do that, sweet pea. Tell him between six and seven Eastern is best for me and that I'll be awaiting his call."

Emma sat back as the line went dead. She wondered why Luke wasn't returning the calls. Was there conflict between them for Luke splitting his time and leaving Cohen's hanging?

She flipped through the mail, looking for something that might inspire her video. She'd already done mascara and foundation lately, and hair was out of the question. What was next? Lipstick again? She found one of her gossip magazines and decided to indulge in the guilty pleasure of diving into the world of the beautiful and famous. Even project managers got coffee breaks, right? And she could argue that she was actually studying the market.

Sometimes she loved her job.

Sitting in front of the fire—the scent of wood smoke seemed to have infiltrated her entire wardrobe—she began flipping the glossy pages, pausing here and there to check outfits as well as a few ads. Emma turned another page and took in a familiar face. Her happy, pregnant sister was gorgeous, spliced beside a dull-looking woman whose smile wasn't real. Emma fell back against the couch cushions. The woman was her.

Her.

For years Emma had outshone anyone on the page, but no more. She was lifeless, unhappy and no longer beautiful or glowing.

Tears pricked her eyes as she struggled to read the blurring headline. The caption referred to the sisters as having swapped places, suggesting that Emma's recent illness had taken a toll on her, along with the burden of running the doomed, too-little, too-late new Carrington line while Olivia moved on to new things, living a new life away from Carrington and its mess.

She was breathing hard as she slammed the magazine shut. Was that how she really looked these days? Surely they'd altered the photo. Emma opened the magazine again, confirming that what she'd seen was real.

She was the swan who'd turned into an ugly duckling.

She walked to the fireplace and shoved the magazine into the flames, as though burning the pages would make the truth vanish.

Because if she wasn't the beautiful one, then who was she?

And how was she supposed to create a video blog about making women feel beautiful when she looked like that? Nobody would trust her advice.

She was done.

She glared at the burning magazine.

She had to get out of the cabin and find a way to quiet her mind, which had put on its boxing gloves, ready to battle her self-esteem.

Emma snatched the snowshoes that hung above the cabin door and strapped them to her boots, prepared to walk until she found a reason not to quit the entire project.

Luke called into the cabin once again, hearing no response. Where was Emma?

He walked through the small abode, wondering where she could have gone and if he should be worried about her.

His heartbeat accelerated. What if something had happened? What if the blackmailer had taken her?

He gave himself a mental shake. He was being dramatic. Talk about an overreaction. Olivia had likely come and picked her up for some girl time. There was probably a note or a phone message waiting for him.

He wandered through the cabin, finding nothing but her phone abandoned on the kitchen counter. The fire in the hearth was roaring, so wherever she was, she hadn't been gone long.

The place felt empty without her. Quiet. Too quiet.

He opened the front door and looked out toward the wood-pile, thinking maybe he'd walked past her when he'd arrived moments ago. He didn't see her. He called from the front step, his voice echoing in the mountainous terrain, seeming louder than it should. On impulse, he glanced up over the door and saw that the wooden snowshoes were missing.

He smiled, thinking that was like Emma to go snowshoeing for her break.

He'd noticed that the workload seemed to be wearing on her, and he was glad she was taking care of herself. He should really start doing the same, now that he had a handle on the project. They'd made a lot of progress over the past two weeks, with Emma really stepping up. She'd dropped the flirty model act in favor of facts and charm to convince quite a few critics to give All You a chance, exceeding his expectations. She'd invariably been grilled about Carrington's past products and mistakes, but she'd been unfailingly polite, open and honest. She was winning over some powerful voices and that would help them immensely.

But that didn't mean All You still couldn't fail. Good products did all the time, with less against them.

His cell rang and he answered, expecting it to be one of the reporters he'd met with in town. He'd spent three hours being grilled by various media types about the new project—a little something to go out against Haddie's possible attack.

"Luke Cohen here."

"Luke, my boy." It was his father. Great. He should have checked caller ID. "You got a hole in your pocket? I've been trying to get ahold of you and was thinking your phone had fallen out somewhere."

"Why are you calling?" Luke's tone wasn't exactly friendly.

Franklin's voice lowered. "I've got a problem."

"Does it have anything to do with not taking my advice about the recalls?"

"It might," his father said carefully. "I need you to authorize Cohen's to—"

"Don't you think it's time you truly stepped down and stopped causing problems?" Even though Luke knew Emma was out, he couldn't help but glance around as his voice grew louder.

"Son," his father said sharply, "this is an ongoing Cohen's issue. I have spent my days—and money—protecting this family, protecting this company."

"Your money? That's a great idea."

Luke knew his father didn't have money. His mom had revealed that fact some time back. It came in, it went out, leaving her on a very restricted budget, causing explosive fights when she spent time at Sotheby's auction with her friends.

Luke had tried to convince her to leave Franklin before the inheritance came through so she could have it, but she refused. It was as though she was too worn down from fighting him all those years.

"Luke...!" His father was using his impatient tone, which Luke knew was intended to inform him that he had the wrong end of the stick. It seemed his dad always felt that way, and as though

Luke was too naive to see what Franklin thought was a big secret about his marriage.

"I'm not paying to hide your easy-way-out decisions," he stated. "I have honor and integrity, and so will Cohen's while I'm in charge."

"Son, I did it to protect the company. To protect you. Our employees. Our family."

"Nice speech. How about you try asking the board to free the money?" He knew his father was hoping for him to quietly push things through, cover up, make the situation right again.

"The board doesn't see things the way you and I do," Franklin said, in a tone meant to be confiding.

"You took a gamble. An illegal one. I want no part of it." Luke went to end the call.

"I made you who you are, so don't get high-and-mighty on me. We're the same man."

"We're *not*."

"You'd be nothing without me."

"No, actually, I would be just fine."

"You think you would have had the motivation to flip boats, buy up resorts and the like without me? I don't think so." His father's voice was low, knowing, and it ticked Luke off.

"You can't take credit for who I am. You showed me just how little family meant to you when I was nine."

His father was quiet for a moment. When he continued, his tone was patient, firm, angry. "You ignoring the reality of this situation is going to impact your mother and that new wife of yours."

"What?"

"Learn from what I have already. Pay to make it go away."

His father hung up and it was all Luke could do not to send his phone through the nearest window in a fit of helpless rage. Instead, he covered his mouth with a hand and paced. Franklin knowing about him and Emma could really push things back in terms of setting up his mother's safety net—the one that would be just for her. Not the nest egg he left untouched and had promised his mother she could dip in to if she ever left.

If I had money, Luke, my life would be very different. My relationship with your father would be very different.

Franklin would interfere with Luke's claim for the inheritance, and likely already had guessed that they weren't carrying out the union in the spirit his grandmother intended.

Luke sat heavily on the couch, trying to predict his father's next move.

He truly didn't know.

Instead, he sent a text to Haddie, linking to an article from the Caribbean about him. A little research for her before tomorrow's follow-up interview here in town. She'd frustrated the Dickens out of him that morning when she'd texted for clarification on a point. She was so insistent she thought she knew who he was. The article would help. It wasn't widely known that he owned a resort down there or that he'd opened and supported several social assistance programs. It was time to show off everything good he'd done over the years before it all went to seed on him.

He tipped his head, resting it on the back of the couch. He needed to know who that blackmailer was.

He needed to shut him down.

He called Zach Forrester. "I want you to look into something for me." He sent the man on the trail of the blackmailers, embarrassed by how little info he had. It didn't seem to dismay Zach, who sounded intrigued by the challenge.

One more problem successfully delegated.

Luke stretched out on the couch, sliding his feet onto the armrest as he stuffed a cushion under his head. Often when he sat down, Emma would swing her small feet into his lap and he'd more often than not give her a gentle foot massage as they discussed aspects of their launch strategy. She listened without interruption, which was a nice break from the board back home, who often jumped in before he finished.

Had he called the real estate agent today? He reached for his phone and sent off a halfhearted text, tired of nagging Greta. The cabin wasn't so bad. A bit small, but sufficient. And he kind of looked forward to Emma throwing herself on him every morning so he'd trek out into the snow for more wood. She liked the cabin warm and cozy, he'd discovered.

He shifted position, feeling bored. How had he spent so many nights alone back in Charleston? He hadn't felt lonely there and he wondered if he'd just become accustomed to being crammed in here with Emma and her chatter.

He checked the time. He'd been home alone for a whole twelve minutes. If he didn't know better he would say he missed Emma's companionship.

He should do something productive, like research condos for his mom, as she'd no doubt want to move out as soon as possible once the inheritance was secured—assuming Luke's father didn't mess things up.

When Luke was nine his mom had left Franklin, taking Luke with her. They'd suffered a long, hot bus ride to Arizona, where she'd planned to stay with a cousin who had several kids. Her relative hadn't been home the first night and Luke's mom had decided to try and multiply their meager cash into enough for a suite at a five-star hotel. While Luke waited outside the casino, she'd lost it all. They'd slept in the hallway of the cousin's apartment building, waiting for her to come home. The next night they'd stayed at a homeless shelter. Finally, the woman had returned, telling them she couldn't afford more mouths to feed in the one-bedroom apartment, and that Charlotte should ask her rich husband for money, not her.

Luke had suggested they go to their grandparents', but his mom had simply shaken her head, eyes averted in shame.

They'd returned home several days later.

The whole week had been confusing to Luke and it hadn't ended when they'd come home. His dad had pulled him into his main floor office, a stereotypical room with leather, dark wood, cigars and whiskey. Luke hated it. It was stifling and he always felt as if the walls were closing in.

"If anyone asks, you and your mother went to visit a cousin last week," his father had said.

"But we did."

"That's my good boy."

Funny how he'd forgotten about that conversation until now. As Luke got up to pour himself a finger of whiskey, another memory slipped through his mind. A conversation that would change the course of his life.

His father had sat him down when he was nineteen.

"We think you and Olivia would be a good pair."

"Olivia's all right. Emma's cute and funny." She had been too young at the time for anything romantic, but she'd had a spark he enjoyed, whereas Olivia was always so serious.

"Emma is too immature, too flighty. If you're going to be CEO one day you need a reliable woman. I've arranged for you to take Olivia to the next gala."

Luke, having seen what marrying for love had done for his parents, understood it was sensible to choose a wife based on your career and life goals, and Olivia was a partner who would fit that life. So the two of them had started what would ultimately be an ill-fated courtship.

Funny how he'd forgotten about that conversation and his old interest in Emma. He'd liked how she'd always put a smile on his face, brightening any social gathering.

He looked up in anticipation as the woman he'd been thinking of came into the cabin, knocking the snow off her shoulders. She grinned at him, looking an awful lot like someone with whom he could fulfill his marriage in the spirit his grandparents had intended.

EMMA HAD HAD an amazing hike through the woods. Everything out there was gorgeous and snowshoeing had been exactly what she'd needed to clear her mind.

As she let herself into the cabin, she found Luke sitting on the couch, one arm slung across the back as he faced the door. Waiting for her.

"You're home," she said happily.

"I am. And so are you." His voice had a warmth that sent shivers through her. "How was it?"

She carefully took off her woolly hat and tossed it onto the kitchen counter along with her mitts, trying to play it cool. Something had changed while she'd been out. Luke was intense, but…also focused. On her. Not distracted like usual. Not eager to start spouting off more orders for them to follow.

"It was amazing. We need to get a second pair so you can come out next time." Exactly what she'd been thinking he needed, to take his workaholic tendencies down a notch. "Oh, and your dad called."

"Yeah, I talked to him." He turned, facing away from her, his movements stiffer.

"Everything okay?"

"We should secure some celebrity endorsements, as well as a few quotes from the scientists saying the new line is great. We also need to address the toxin issue. Maybe educate your video blog followers about guidelines."

There was the Luke she knew.

"My followers don't really…" She caught his expression and caved. "I'll try." He was the one with the experience, after all.

Emma unzipped her parka, tossing it over one of the chairs at the table. "How's your mom?" *Still spending up a storm?*

"What?"

"Your mom. How is she?"

"Oh." He seemed to catch himself. "Fine. I think. I didn't talk to her."

"You two have always seemed close. You must miss her?"

"Sure. We need to predict where our critics are going to go and get there first."

"I know," Emma said, trying to hide her exasperation. He kept harping on this part of the plan.

"It's important."

"I know."

"I have a lot riding on this."

"So do I, stress monkey. So turn off your phone and your laptop."

"Sorry?" Luke looked surprised at her order.

"We should mute our phones and close our laptops at seven every night so we can unwind. We'll sleep better and be more productive if we take a few hours off each day."

"I have a business to run on the other side of the continent. I can't just unplug."

"You work evenings because you're a lonely, bored bachelor. Do you want to look back on your life when you're..." her voice began to waver and she tipped her chin "...however old and realize you wasted most of it in front of a screen? There's lots of life here. We should taste it." She found her phone on the counter and began a new online search.

"I thought you said I have to turn off my phone," Luke said, eyes narrowed.

"After seven. Right now I'm ordering you snowshoes. Mandatory physical exercise, and coffee break instituted every day at three."

"Emma." His tone was sharp.

"I know what I'm doing. This is for your health. No project is worth dying over."

He'd come to stand near her, to face off with his fierce need to dominate and exert control over every aspect of his life, no doubt. But his body language softened and he reached out to stroke her cheek.

"Are you okay?"

Thrown off by his sudden gentleness, she turned so they'd break contact. "I'm fine, and before you go there, I can keep up. I only want us to work smarter, not just harder." She turned and poked him in the chest. Wow. He had really firm pectorals. "Plus I'd like to see you keep up to me on snowshoes."

She could feel the heat coming off his body and soon found her head feeling a bit light.

"I'm the boss. I decide."

"Challenge accepted then? Great." She tapped the buy button. "Because I just bought you snowshoes from the store in town—Wally's. You can pick them up tomorrow when you go in for your date with Haddie."

His eyes narrowed. "How did you know we're meeting?"

"I'm your wife."

He didn't look impressed with that answer. So much for humor. But there was no way she was going to admit she'd peeked at his notification screen when he'd been in the bathroom that morning. He'd been in a furious text conversation with someone, becoming more and more agitated. Of course she'd looked. What if it was about All You?

"You're going to have to get up a little earlier in the day to slip one past me," she said. "Now turn off your phone. You're mine for the evening, starting now."

His eyes blazed, hinting that he surely thought she'd just given him some grand come-on.

"It's not seven yet."

"Listen to your wife."

"Yes, Mrs. Cohen."

"I haven't taken your name and I never will," she said simply. She threw in a flirty smile to lessen the sting of her rejection.

"I'm not one who likes to sit around and be bored in the evenings, Emma. I also don't like games."

She picked up a black bag resting near the front door. "I had my sister run me into town earlier and I got this at the library." She unzipped the bag, revealing a projector that hooked up to a computer.

"I thought you said we weren't working tonight. We're still weeks away from going over the commercial pitches."

He actually looked a tad disappointed by the thought that she might be proposing work.

She pulled a DVD case from the bag with a flourish. "Movie night!"

"*Rocky Horror Picture Show?*" He walked over to where she was standing, taking the DVD. "I've always wanted to see this." His eyes narrowed in thought. "We were..." He shook his head, handing the movie back to her.

"Anyway," she said brightly, at a loss over how to respond. She felt foolish. She was trying too hard and this movie—the one he'd invited her to go see all those years ago—was like her saying, hey, let's date.

They shouldn't date.

She busied herself rummaging around in the kitchen, then pulled a bag of popcorn kernels from the cupboard.

"We don't have a popcorn maker," Luke pointed out.

Emma went over to the fire and held up what looked like a covered metal mesh bin on the end of a stick. "We do. It's a popcorn maker for the fireplace. I got it at the hardware store for a buck because the lid was bent, but I fixed it with a butter knife." She slid the grated lid open. It took a bit of wiggling but worked now.

"Resourceful. But I don't know, Emma. We have a lot of work to do."

"We've only taken time off to sleep over the past fourteen days. I read a productivity article and we're destined to crash soon. A tiny bit of time off will increase our creative problem-solving as well as out motivation to get things done."

"Where'd you read that?"

"Your business magazine."

He glanced over at the small coffee table in front of the fireplace. She knew it was an issue he hadn't yet taken time to read.

"Fine. You win, Emma Carrington." He gave her a look as though he'd underestimated her and she tried to hide her smile.

"Good."

The air between them stilled, the room quiet other than the crackle of burning logs.

"You're the only woman I'd ever want to partner with in the woods, EmmaLu," he said softly. "The only one."

She placed a hand on either side of his face and rose up on her tiptoes, her lips an inch from his, before catching herself and dropping the kiss on his nose.

"You, too, Luke."

He looked disappointed that she'd caught herself in time. Just like she was.

But relieved, too. Of course.

<hr>

EMMA, wearing a fitted sweater that highlighted the curves that had kept her a successful model for so many years, had nearly kissed him.

They weren't doing that, right? No meaningless sex. Not even as a form of stress relief after two hardworking weeks. Emma's proposed movie night was innocent.

He needed to remember that.

But with her lined up beside him at the kitchen counter, puzzling out how to make pizza dough from scratch so they could have a pepperoni and mushroom pizza for supper, and she was all he could think about. From the enticing way the scent of the outdoors layered over her individual Emma aroma of spicy and sweet, to the way she laughed and how her long, delicate fingers worked the sticky dough.

Why was he working so hard? Why was he resisting following Emma's shapely form through the woods each day? He could sell off his old life and live quite comfortably in Blueberry Springs for the rest of his days. Why not do that?

Luke gave himself a shake. There was definitely something wrong with his brain. He was a Cohen. He worked hard, made money.

"There was this hare camouflaged in the snow and when it moved I nearly fell off my snowshoes, I was so startled. It was so cool to watch it hop away from that close up."

Luke chuckled at the image of Emma being startled by a rabbit.

"You won't be laughing if I don't share my popcorn with you after supper."

"You're not that mean."

"Maybe I'll surprise you." She gave him a saucy look that made him smile.

Luke stood back from the counter. "Sprinkle on the mozzarella."

"What about the Parmesan?"

"Already mixed with the mozzarella."

Emma complied and he marveled at the team they made. Neither of them knew how to cook and yet their hand-tossed crust looked close to edible.

Maybe they could open a pizzeria. Call it EmmaLu's.

"Pizza and a movie," he said, thinking of the quintessential first date most teenagers had—something so casual and normal that he'd longed to try it, instead of taking his dates to stuffy, formal affairs his parents had always insisted was the proper thing to do.

He detected a hint of wistfulness in his voice and quickly cleared his throat. "Date night for married people."

Great, he was turning into a sap. He should zip his lips before she thought he was falling in love or something.

"Married people don't date," Emma said seriously. "At least my parents don't, unless it's with a few hundred other people at a gala."

"It makes you wonder what real people do on a night out," Luke said.

"Our parents aren't real?" Emma teased.

"Their love isn't."

She quirked her head and Luke sought to change the subject. "You've got cheese…" he reached for Emma's hair, pressing closer "…right here."

"Mind the hair!" She wrapped her hands over his, finding the shredded mozzarella on her own and removing it.

He stepped back, taking the hint, then joked, "Women and their hair."

She flashed her blue eyes as though exasperated.

"It is gorgeous, you know. How have they not married you off yet? Aren't you approaching old maid status?"

"Luke, are you cracking a joke with me?"

"Appears so."

"You telling jokes is like an elephant trying to skydive without a parachute." She made a whistling sound, followed by a crashing one.

"Thanks."

She brushed her hand through the flour he'd spread over the counter so the dough wouldn't stick, and smacked him gently on the back of his black cashmere sweater, certainly leaving a handprint.

He gave her a dark look and resisted retaliating. She was flirting, but he didn't know what she wanted. She wouldn't let him touch her hair, and yet she stood close. It was time to figure out exactly what she was angling at.

He snagged the back of his soiled sweater, pulling it over his head, leaving his torso bare. He tossed the garment on the counter. "Guess I need a clean shirt."

Emma's gaze was trained on his chest. "Yeah," she said softly. "I guess so."

He leaned closer, but didn't touch her, waiting for her to make the next move. Her eyes slowly trailed up to meet his. He gave her a questioning look and she spun to face the pizza waiting on the counter.

"Is it ready for the oven?" she asked, the tightness of her voice a telltale hint that he'd affected her.

Wordlessly, he opened the oven door while she slid the pizza pan inside. They'd loaded it with pepperoni and fresh mushrooms. Even uncooked it smell heavenly and delicious. Just like Emma.

"I wonder if you can cook something like this in a fireplace," she said.

"I heard one of my friends' wives mentioning having an outdoor pizza oven. Maybe we could have one made for our yard."

She smiled, her expression reflecting back what he was feeling. They were making plans as if they had a real future. He found that he liked it.

Her attention had drifted to his chest again and her teeth gently worried the corner of her bottom lip. She took his discarded sweater and handed it to him. "You'd better put this on. I hear it's bear mating season and that chest of yours might attract some unwanted attention."

He gave a light chuckle and ran a hand through the sprig of chest hair between his pectorals. "I don't think this is going to attract any bears—which are hibernating—but if it helps you keep from burning our supper out of sheer distraction due to my impressive man powers, I'll put it back on." He made a show of sliding the fabric back over his torso with a lazy, satisfied smile.

She shook her head at him. "You're so full of yourself."

He gave her a cheeky grin, loving how they could banter. She was quickly becoming one of his favorite people.

"I like where we're at," she said, and he wondered if she felt that connection—as if their minds were at times on the same frequency, like a radio station. "I never felt like I had this with Vaughn. There was all this drama that left me feeling as though I didn't know which way was up any longer."

Luke had never thought much of the photographer, mostly because Olivia had made it clear he preferred Emma in their photo shoots and left Olivia feeling fat and unwanted.

But the fact that Vaughn hadn't been that nice to Emma, either, made Luke's blood boil.

Emma caught him studying her and quickly added, "Not like this is the same. Not at all. I mean, we're *married*, but not…you know."

Her hands were fluttering nervously and she began sweeping up the flour covering the counter. He took a step back as she gathered it up. "You're not going to throw that at me, are you?"

She gave him a mischievous look, but dumped it in the trash.

As she busied herself with the cleanup, Luke pondered what she'd said about Vaughn. Her tone had suggested there would be no further lovers-reunited scenarios, as there had been in the past, but by his count—and he wasn't counting—Emma had taken the guy back at least four times. Four times too many, as far as Luke was concerned.

"Where did things end with you two?" he asked casually, opening the fridge for her as she put away the cheese. "Any chance of a reunion?"

He didn't think he had to worry about the man reappearing, but the possibility could explain some of Emma's hesitance and mixed signals.

Her expression darkened. "We're over."

"Are you still in touch?"

"I have nothing to say to him," she snapped. She went to the living room and put her sudden fury into turning the sofa to face the wall between the bedroom and bathroom, as it was the only flat surface in the log home.

Luke silently joined her, taking down the tacked-up, four-foot-wide calendar that included their launch's to-do list time-line, so they'd have a blank piece of wall to use as their screen.

"I can't believe Luke Cohen, CEO of Cohen's Blissful Body Care, has a computer old enough to actually have a DVD player in it," Emma teased as he slid the disk into its drive.

For a second he felt affronted, but then let the comment roll off him with a shrug. "There's a lot about Luke Cohen the public doesn't know."

"Such as he's currently living in a cabin heated only by wood?"

"That," he agreed.

"Driving a pickup truck and doesn't have a sports car in the driveway?" She pretended to gasp as if it was shocking news.

"A secret wife," Luke added.

"Watching movies *borrowed* from the *library*."

"Okay, that's enough." He spun on his heel, stalking to the oven to check on the pizza.

Emma held in a chuckle. "You're not all bad, Luke Cohen."

He had a feeling she was thinking about their friends back at the country club, and his competitive side rose inside like an underground spring. "I have a screen in my private home theater bigger than this room's floor plan."

"It'll still be there when you return."

He found himself taking in the shared cabin. The walls were covered with various colored papers outlining their business plans. His mattress on the floor, his phone charger and reading light resting beside it, oddly felt like a real bedroom. The whole place felt like home—unpretentious and real. It had been only two weeks, but they'd been intense.

He settled on the couch, and Emma joined him, sitting shoulder to shoulder. He could feel her body heat through their sweaters. She shifted, lifting her knee onto the cushions as she faced him, resting her elbow on the couch's back, hand tucked behind her ear for support. She looked so genuine and pretty without makeup, and he was surprised how comfortable he was just hanging out with her.

Like friends.

He wondered if they'd still be like this when his contract was completed, or if they'd revert back to their old selves, treating each other as acquaintances more than anything else.

"We need to get out and have more fun," she said. "I feel like my life…" She cleared her throat in a way that made Luke think she might be struggling with emotion. Likely worries borne out of last summer's illness. She popped up suddenly, pulling the pizza from the oven even though the timer hadn't gone off, placing it on a cooling rack before returning to the couch.

She was studying him, still seeming to struggle to put her thoughts and feelings into words. "I feel life is passing me by sometimes. Like I'm focusing my time and efforts on the wrong stuff. I'll look back and…"

He sat in silence, letting her put a voice to her feelings. She paused for a long while and he found himself mulling over his own recent choices. How many would lead to regret, how many to celebration?

"Ever curious about how your life will look in half a year?" she asked quietly. He found his attention drifting to her hair, certain it was indeed different than it had been in the past. Surely he'd know if it was a wig?

She was waiting for a reply and he tore his focus off what he was becoming more and more certain wasn't her real hair.

He shifted uncomfortably. "We'll be rich," he said simply.

"Beyond that."

"We'll have it all, Emma. We'll have everything we want. Everything on that goal list over there on the wall."

She rested her right hand on his shoulder, playing with the fabric of his sweater, leaning close. He wasn't sure if she was seeking comfort, companionship, a reassuring hug, or if it was something more intimate. Something more in line with the undeniable attraction that kept buzzing in the background of his mind.

He leaned forward, pausing before kissing her softly.

"What was that for?" she asked, her lips a breath from his.

"It just felt right."

"With you, it always does, Luke." Her clear eyes met his. "And that's the problem."

LUKE KNEW he should resist the urge to kiss Emma again, especially after her stating somewhat unregretfully that the two of them together was problematic. Good, but still problematic.

And yet he pulled her closer, into a lingering kiss.

He felt connected to her in a way he hadn't with anyone else, and he wanted to explore how deep it went. Maybe it was false, with both of them just satisfying an innate curiosity.

She scooted closer and he felt his need increase. This couldn't be just an in-the-moment thing. There was too much power, too much need.

He pulled away for a second, hoping to catch his breath and get his head back on straight. He felt alive and liberated, and it was all he could do not to draw her into the bedroom and make love to her.

She deserved more than just a night, though.

He kissed her again, exploring her intent, his hands weaving their way under her sweater and up her back. Why wasn't he taking her to bed again?

It was only sex. They were adults who could do this without either of them expecting more. Sex hadn't complicated anything in Aspen despite the situation they'd been in. There was no reason it should now.

"I want to take this further," he whispered, his lips grazing hers, unable to fully pull away.

Emma leaned back, her blue eyes bright and inquiring.

"We're married," he said casually, linking her fingers with his, drawing her into his lap for another kiss.

He didn't want to talk, as his usual smooth words felt stuck behind a barrier. He'd never been shy around women before, and never cared whether or not he got shot down. He supposed his awkwardness now was due to their business arrangement, and that he was knowingly breaking a rule they'd both agreed to heed.

But his past encounters with Emma had been accidental and brief, a flash of fire in an otherwise mundane acquaintanceship, and tonight he saw no reason not to explore that further and see what happened.

It was risky, though.

Emma was watching him wordlessly, no doubt weighing out the pros and cons.

"I'd like to take you to bed," he said, nuzzling her cheek. "Not as a..." He kissed her neck. "But, you know, as a..." He didn't know what he was trying to say, so he lifted his head and gave her a cocky wink and smile that usually worked with women.

Though still in his lap, warm and right, she leaned away, giving him an unimpressed look. "I'm not someone you're picking up in a bar, Luke Cohen."

"No, you're not."

She crossed her arms, waiting for more. Was she going to make him beg?

"I've never asked my secret wife to bed before and I'm not sure what the protocol is. My parents didn't teach me the social niceties of a situation such as this one."

One of Emma's hands lightly tagged his shoulder as she laughed, rich and pure. "Was that another joke, Luke Cohen?"

He gave a faint smile.

She stood and took his hand, pulling him to his feet. "I believe you simply do this. No words required." She wrapped her arms around his neck, kissing him in a way that made him think there might never be another woman in his life who reached him in the way his wife did.

5

*E*mma opened her eyes, finding the weight across her ribs was Luke's arm. She smiled before the internal freaking out began. Last night had been amazing. Even better than their Aspen hurt-and-angry sex. And that had been pretty darn good.

But last night was worrisome, because now she knew what they could truly have when they weren't using each other to quell the inner noise and pain. How was she going to resist next time? They had work to do and he could become a serious distraction.

She stared up at the ceiling of her small room, wondering what it meant that Luke hadn't returned to his own bed last night. She reminded herself that this would come to an end in a few months and it wasn't meaningful—it never was with Luke.

She lifted a hand to her forehead, making sure Cousin Itt was still secured in his proper place by readjusting a few of its pins. She wasn't supposed to sleep in her wig, but wasn't going to reveal the scrub brush that lay underneath to Luke. Especially not now. He thought her old hair and its replica were beautiful.

She'd foolishly told Vaughn about her hair shortly after her hairdresser had kept her salon open late to trim up Emma's patchy locks and fit her with a wig. He hadn't reacted well.

Emma swallowed the old emotion. She wouldn't tell Luke. Last night had been a mistake.

She huddled under the blankets, avoiding the chill in the room's air, sliding closer to the handsome man gracing her bed, determined to enjoy the comfort of his presence while it lasted.

She woke later to find Luke propped up beside her, the blankets tucked around him as he read emails in the bright sunbeam that hit her bed around nine. The stubble shadowing his jaw gave him a rugged appearance that felt foreign, novel, and like a secret. Her guess was that not many people had ever seen Luke unshaven.

She propped herself on an elbow and blinked, trying to sort out why he was still in her bed. Working. He hadn't gotten up, showered, started his day? Instead, he was hanging out like they were a real couple enjoying a lazy Sunday morning.

"Did you get this email?" he asked.

Emma tried to focus on it as Luke held his phone in front of her. "Is there coffee?" she asked, rubbing her eyes.

"No. Power just came back on. We got hit by more snow. I threw a log on the fire and hightailed back in here where it's warm." He was back to his phone. "I'll reply to this guy."

So he was in her bed because it was warm, no other reason. She should be relieved. No, she *was* relieved.

She burrowed deeper under the patchwork quilt. They were still friends, still in business together. Just like before, they were acting as though it had never really happened. Except he was still in her bed.

Because it was warm.

"We broke our no-sex rule," she said, unable to resist bringing it up to see what he was thinking.

His lips curled in a satisfied smile. "Twice."

"This isn't going to become weird, is it? Working together and…everything."

Were they going to break their rule again? Or was it a one-off? What if he slipped into her room in the middle of the night, looking for action, and found her sleeping without her wig?

"Emma, how long did you actually think we'd be able to hold out, given our past?" He continued to scroll through emails on his phone. "You. Me. A remote cabin in the snowy forest."

For some reason his offhand manner stung, but she couldn't pinpoint why exactly. He was acting exactly the way she'd hoped —like it wasn't a big, complicated deal.

"It'll only get weird if one of us makes it weird," he added. "Which I have no intention of doing."

She relaxed into the pillows. "Me neither."

Luke climbed out of bed, stretching. His chest was bare and glorious. He could probably do a million chin-ups without tiring.

"Like what you see?" he asked, as he shook out yesterday's sweater, his boxers already donned.

She knew she should probably look away, act demure, instead of drinking him in so brazenly. The duchess would be freaking out about proper decorum, but Emma found she didn't care.

"I showed you mine last night," she said slowly. "It's your turn again."

She knew she was flirty, bringing them closer to repeating last night's mistake once more. But he was too tempting only half-dressed, acting as though nothing had changed.

He smirked, sliding the sweater over his head. He leaned close to the bed and whispered, "I like the new tattoo, by the way."

"It's a celebration of life. And if you want to see it again, just knock twice or make me more pizza from scratch." She gave him a slow smile. "But next time don't overwork the dough. It was a bit too chewy."

"I had some…tension to work out." His gaze, hot and wanting, trailed over the blanket that covered her, as though engaging X-ray vision. "But a woman I know helped me release quite a bit of it."

"All of it?"

"Not quite. Think she could help me out? We could act like we're snowed in."

She lifted the covers so he could dive back under them as she said with a welcoming smile, "Maybe we should."

LUKE HAD TAKEN his time pleasuring Emma, allowing her to trust him, trust them. They were good together in ways he was still discovering. And yet he'd seen flashes of uncertainty in her eyes as well as the questions. Should they do this? Should they take their one night and build on it, create expectations, push their boundaries? Or should they quit while they were ahead? He hadn't wanted to sink back into spouses-without-benefits mode and he didn't think Emma did, either. Being with her stirred up something within him that he was starting to believe was insatiable.

Together, they'd explored the edges of their hesitations and doubts, slowly building toward the inevitable, until the shift, the flare of longing in their locked gazes, the passion that broke past their barriers and doubts hit a frantic, powerful thrusting release that left them both dazed and panting.

Emma's habit was to be quick, as though she'd been trained by impatient lovers. As a result, Luke had taken his time, driving her to the edge before backing off, ensuring her moments were of a Richter-scale-worthy quake that left her legs quivering and her chest heaving as she collapsed in his arms, spent. Nothing hurried. Every moment sacred.

It had been noon before they'd finally pulled themselves out of bed on weak legs, declaring the day a write-off.

Uncharacteristically, he hadn't wanted to work or even allow his mind to venture there. So they'd put the truck into four-wheel drive and made the slow and snowy journey into town for supplies. Emma had noted a winter festival happening in the square and had begged him to go.

He'd said no.

She'd tipped her head and patiently explained that this was a perfect way to become part of the community, and before he'd known it they'd spent an hour watching lumberjacks carve ice sculptures out of lake ice with their noisy chainsaws.

He'd been mystified with the precision of their carving and, when offered, had tried his hand at it. He'd attempted something simple—an ice snowman. It had been pretty decent until he'd caught Emma flirting with the lumberjack out of the corner of his eye and had accidentally sliced the snowman's head off.

That had been hours ago. Now it was just past supper and the call of adventure—or rather the festival—had brought them out to the middle of Blueberry Lake, where he felt as though he might be finally getting a handle on skating. After all, he *was* still upright on the cleared patch of ice.

"Luke! You skate like a Southerner!"

He wasn't sure which of the various people gathered around the skating area had called out to him from their lawn chairs. It seemed as though most of the town knew of him already and had no qualms about offering tips, pointers and laughter from the sidelines.

Even Logan, who'd been popping up here and there as he tailed Luke, gave a faint smile. Luke happened to know the man was an Aussie who'd spent a lot of time in the South, and was likely no better on skates than he was. An Aussie ex-spy married to the owner of Veils and Vows—a woman who dolled up brides. Quite the unlikely couple.

"I *am* a Southerner," Luke replied. "The only ice we deal with is in our sweet tea."

The group laughed, but unlike back home it wasn't derisive. Rather, it was joyful laughter borne out of watching him be brave enough to try—and fail—at something new in public.

Stupid, really. He should have hired someone privately to give him the shakedown on how to balance and glide on these thin metal wedges before venturing out. No one in town would take him seriously after this.

"Straighten your back," someone called. "There. Now put your weight on your right foot and glide."

"I think I'm done," Luke grumbled as he wobbled across the ice. He felt he had the logistics of the new sport figured out mentally, but communication between his brain and legs seemed to be a little off.

Learning to ice fish hadn't been like this. He'd been able to sit in the crowd, surrounded by white, craggy mountains under a perfect blue sky, shooting the breeze, nobody being any wiser that it was his first time dropping his hook down a hole carved into a frozen lake. But skating? It was obvious he was still wet behind the ears.

Beside him, Emma was giggling, thinking it hilarious that they had to hold on to each other to remain vertical. He didn't mind that part, even though it often threw them into a scramble to stay upright when one of them moved.

Someone had flicked on floodlights an hour ago as darkness closed in, and a car stereo filled the air with music.

He was in the middle of beauty, a large expanse of frozen lake with fishing shacks scattered around them. The whole scene was picturesque, something from a travel guide that many would pay thousands to experience, yet it had cost him only a few bucks.

The festival was casual but fun, and he felt as if he should pay admission to someone for the effort they'd put into making all this happen. He'd spent a whole eight dollars the entire after-noon, to get two hot dogs and a beverage for him and Emma. Today was shaping up to be one of the more memorable days of his adult life, and he felt he shouldn't be able to just waltz in and have it, with someone plunking a fishing rod in his mittened hands when he'd needed it, skates on his feet later.

"You two make a sweet couple," an elderly man called out, and Emma turned to smile at him. Her lashes were thicker today, darker. She'd put on makeup to come into town, and after seeing her without it for a few weeks, Luke found it felt odd, not quite her.

At first, seeing her without makeup had made him feel as though he'd been demoted in importance, as he no longer warranted her making an effort with her appearance. But now he felt as if he was part of her inner circle, and seeing her dolled up was a bit of a shock.

They started to tip over and Luke corrected himself, taking Emma with him. She was concentrating, every once in a while peeking up at him, her stern mask of focus breaking. Then, inevitably, she'd lose her balance, rocketing backward, and he'd have to throw his arms around her to catch her. That part wasn't so bad, actually. Even if half the time he ended up with her loose, golden curls in his mouth. It always made him think of them moving together between the sheets, how her hair would brush his chest, heightening his anticipation.

They slipped again, their balance precarious as they clung to each other. Emma was laughing, the sound the only thing he heard. He held her tight, wishing to be her hero, which was proving difficult when someone kept tipping the world beneath his feet. Up. Down. Sideways. Although maybe the instability wasn't due to trying to balance two thin metal blades on a sheet of ice. Maybe it was the effect of holding Emma, but not being able to kiss her, snuggle his face into that warm, sweet-smelling spot just below her ear.

"Anyone know of a certified instructor who can get me skating like a pro?" he called to the audience. Someone had to be able to teach him, so that the next time they came out he could be her rock.

The group watching them skate laughed, taking his request as a joke.

"Seriously," he called. "I'll pay good money."

More laughter.

"What's with these people?" he whispered to Emma. Did nobody want to earn an extra few hundred on the side for a private lesson or two?

"They like you. Think you're funny."

"Know what they call a pop—no, a father—who falls into ice water? No, off an iceberg?" he said loudly and to nobody in particular.

"Popsicle!" Emma replied.

His botched joke drew a few chuckles, and he propelled himself and Emma toward the edge of the ice, where he sank into a snowbank to rest his aching feet.

"Know what's cool?" he said, staring up at the night sky, grateful his snowpants were insulating him from his cold seat. They were in shadow, out of the floodlights, and he could see stars shining brightly above, Emma's shoulder brushing his.

"Hmm?" Emma's voice held a note of dreamy contentment.

"I like how you're embracing this place." She'd met with the child she was to mentor, unlike him, who'd put it off. She already had things planned for them to do together and was sucking the marrow from all the town had to offer. He'd yet to see the princess act he'd been worried about.

She leaned her head against his shoulder and he wondered briefly why it felt so right having her close. Was she just someone familiar to cling to in a new town? Or was it something more?

"I like hearing you laugh," she said.

"Speaking of laughing, you're not going to drag me out to something that will get me laughed at every weekend, are you?" A small part of him hoped she would say yes, even though the ribbing from the peanut gallery lining the ice had been a tad tough on his ego.

"Until the town views you as a regular guy, I think I will."

He groaned, but she lifted her head from his shoulder and

raised her hand for a high five. He slapped his mittened palm against hers.

Today had been fun. He'd probably regret it come morning, when he'd have more than enough work to deal with, but until then he'd pull an Emma and suck the marrow from the moment.

They leaned shoulder to shoulder, admiring the stars above. He bet if they walked away from the lights aimed at the rink the stars would be even more amazing.

"Is that the Big Dipper?" Emma asked.

"Yeah." He'd taken a weekend class on stargazing when he was a senior in high school, hoping to go out on his sailboat to look at the stars, and of course, impress a girl. His parents had kiboshed that plan, deeming it unsafe. He still remembered a few constellations, though, and pointed them out to Emma.

"Is there anything Luke Cohen doesn't know about?"

"Plenty." He watched her profile in the shadows, the way her expression softened while she looked at the stars, her lips tipped up in a satisfied smile. He wondered who she really was when nobody was around, watching her. Back home she was the proper socialite with a mischievous edge. Here she was…everything. The whole package, from businesswoman to lover.

Lover.

How were they going to handle that?

The way he felt right now, the three and a half months they had left in their marriage felt like barely enough time to solve the mystery of the intriguing and undeniably irresistible Emma Carrington.

"So when *are* you two getting married?" asked a woman, breaking Luke from his thoughts. He found himself scowling at the familiar intruder before catching himself.

"Mary Alice, how lovely to see you," Emma said to the large figure standing above them in a one-piece thermal suit meant for use on snow machines.

The woman placed her hands on her hips, the reflective

stripes on the thick garment flashing as they caught the light of the nearby floodlamps. "Don't change the subject, dear. I was asking when the two of you are getting married. Will it be August 28? Because it's not too late for me to change my bet, you know."

"Oh, Mary Alice," Mandy chided, coming up alongside the town's gossip. Luke hoped she'd distract the woman, seeing as he'd heard that Mary Alice and her sister, Liz, had an ability to spread information faster than a viral video on the internet, and the last thing he needed was the town watching and critiquing their "relationship."

"Don't mind her. She asks everyone when they're getting married," Mandy added.

"Who's getting married?" asked a woman with auburn curls.

"Hey, Ginger." Emma murmured to Luke, "She owns Veils and Vows here in town."

Where Olivia worked.

"Yes, I know," he said. Ginger was also Logan's wife.

"Do you need a dress?" Ginger asked. "Are you two tying the knot?" Her eyes gleamed in delight.

Luke stood. "I feel like there must be some men somewhere talking about things that require my immediate input."

Emma laughed and dragged him back into the snow beside her. "We're just friends," she said to Ginger, getting a skeptical look from Mary Alice.

"Yup," Luke added. Just friends who were married and slept together. He couldn't help but give Emma a small smile as he put an arm affectionately across her shoulders. "Best buds," he added.

They had the locals fooled, didn't they? Although, truthfully, they *were* just friends.

Emma met his eye and the two of them laughed like friends with history, secrets and private jokes. It felt good.

"I'm raising money for Beth's outreach program," Mandy said, rattling a coffee can. "The community bus that takes the seniors and her patients on outings is on its last legs."

"I'll say. Last time I drove that thing to the city so they could do their holiday shopping we had to tow it back," Mary Alice said with a harrumph.

"I'd love to buy a new bus for the outreach," Luke offered. All part of the Luke-is-a-human-and-part-of-the-community, right?

"I'm just selling raffle tickets and collecting donations..." Mandy said slowly.

"I wanted to win the TV," Mary Alice complained, hands on her hips again. "If you buy the bus there's no raffle and no prizes. I doubt you need a TV." She turned to Mandy. "Can I have it if he buys the bus?"

The group shared confused looks that Luke couldn't decipher.

"Maybe the raffle could be held for something other than the bus?" Emma suggested.

"Well, we had to get a license and fill out paperwork..." Mandy pulled a raffle booklet from her parka pocket, idly flipping through the stubs of the tickets she'd already sold.

Luke struggled for patience. He was giving them tens of thousands of dollars and they were worried about their raffle? "I'll write a check and you decide how best to use it. How about that?"

"I could use a new car," Mary Alice said with a wink, and the group of women relaxed.

"We could do that," Mandy admitted. "Thank you."

"That's a brilliant idea, Luke," Emma said. She was still pressed against him and the group quieted. The hush felt odd, significantly weighted. He realized the women were watching them.

"May," Mary Alice said quietly.

"Engagement or wedding?" Ginger replied in the same hushed tone.

"Engagement. August is the wedding. Fifty to get in on the bet."

"I'll take next month."

"That soon?" Mary Alice turned in surprise.

"There's something between these two." Ginger had her gaze trained on them, and Luke's attention perked. Her husband was shadowing him, and Logan might share intel, things he'd happened across… But there really wasn't much when it came to him and Emma. Well, other than the secret marriage, Aspen and last night. And that morning.

Man, they were racking up relationship frequent flyer miles, weren't they?

The women continued sharing dates.

"We can hear you," Emma said, her expression amused.

Luke wasn't exactly sure what was happening, but it wasn't good. Or maybe it was. The townsfolk betting on their relationship meant they cared enough to be curious, right? Disregard and disinterest were bad. Intrigue and gossip, good. Although a bit terrifying, seeing as they were dancing around the one secret he'd planned on keeping.

Then again, his father already knew about their marriage, so what did it matter if others did? Well, it would hurt Emma. And that couldn't happen.

A secret it would remain.

"Are you taking bets without me?" called a woman about Mary Alice's age. She hustled over. "Hi. I'm Liz Moss-Brady. Now what's this all about?" She glanced down at Luke and Emma. "Ohhh. I say July. No, August."

"I already have August 28 for the wedding. Luke agrees that's the date," Mary Alice said smugly. "You're not winning this one."

Her sister looked affronted. "Have you been cheating again?"

"I didn't cheat. I had good intel on Amber's wedding, and as for Nicola—*you* cheated."

"Did not."

Luke glanced at Emma, but she was trying to hide the fact that she was giggling.

"Married by May," Liz announced.

"March," Ginger corrected.

"August," stated Mary Alice.

"I'm not betting." Mandy held up her hands as she backed away.

"Oh, you never do." Liz raised her voice. "Fifty dollars to get in on the bet."

Luke began laughing, Emma, too.

"You think they'll win?" he asked Emma, as the group of women moved away to collect more bets.

"Not a chance," she giggled, leaning into him.

The women turned back to study them, and it was all Luke could do to refrain from telling them why everyone would lose their bets.

He said loudly, "Ladies, the two of us *won't* be getting married."

LUKE STRETCHED at the kitchen table and glanced over to where Emma was sitting on the couch with her laptop. Her head was resting on the stack of cushions she'd placed behind her and she'd dozed off.

She'd spent time with her sister that afternoon and had seemed drained of energy when she'd returned. He couldn't help but wonder if it was from the effort of putting on her happy and bubbly act for her family. Didn't she ever just want to tell someone to take a long hike off the side of a cliff? Even her own sister?

He padded over to her, lifting the computer from her lap. She stirred slightly, but continued to sleep. Emma was a surprisingly good partner, catching on to everything quickly, but he needed to remind himself that she wasn't used to working such long hours.

Word had come that afternoon that Cash needed him back at headquarters, so he'd be flying out for the weekend. He wondered how strong the culture shock would be for him. He'd gotten used to the routine of their days here in the mountains, and hated to break it even though reality was calling.

He draped a blanket over Emma, a homemade affair she'd bought at a church bazaar last weekend. He'd planned something simple for supper—tuna sandwiches, seeing as his second attempt at pizza had failed. So had his roast. And pretty much everything that was more in-depth than following the instructions found on a box or can.

Nevertheless, Emma didn't seem to mind, and serving her supper was pretty rewarding. It was a different form of pride than buying a woman an expensive trinket and he still hadn't quite figured out why.

Luke drained the can of tuna as outlined in the recipe he'd found on a cooking site, setting to work. Outside the window, the sky completed its phase into darkness. They'd been in Blueberry Springs for a month and he'd already noted the gradual shift into longer days as spring drew closer.

When they'd arrived in late January it had been easy to feel the satisfaction of an early day, up and working before the winter dawn. They'd check their preorders each morning, reply to emails and cross off a few more things on the lists lining the cabin walls. By noon, when they'd be ready for a break, the sun would be almost at its peak, the snow sparkling. More often than not, they'd take a short snowshoe hike through the woods before returning to work until supper. Afterward, they'd clear the table, and maybe finish up a tiny bit of work, or prepping for the next day, before watching a movie or playing a card game. Then they'd retire to Emma's room.

He knew it was rather domestic, but he enjoyed the routine of their days. The hard work, the scheduled downtime. Emma.

He set their sandwiches aside as he opened a bag of premade salad.

Emma was still sleeping. Should he wake her?

She seemed so delicate and vulnerable. When she slept, she wasn't at all like the fiery dynamo that made people change their mind about Carrington.

Her hair seemed oddly off somehow, and Luke slipped closer, peering at it. She *was* wearing a wig. Why hadn't she told him? He felt disappointed that she hadn't trusted him with that personal information. They were intimate, but she didn't trust him, hadn't let him in.

This wasn't a real relationship, though. It was just something to pass the time, loneliness and boredom of being in such a remote location.

And if that's what he wanted, why did it suddenly leave him feeling empty inside?

He opted to wait for Emma to wake up, and wrapped their meals, placing them in the small fridge.

He pulled his laptop toward him and began replying to emails that had come into his Cohen's account. Partway though his task, he stretched, listening to coyotes howling to each other out in the hills. Then the hooting of an owl. Things he never heard in the city.

He glanced over at Emma. Still asleep, her wig slightly off kilter.

Loudly, he cleared his throat. She barely stirred.

He added a few things to his calendar and paused. He hadn't heard a thing from his dad or the blackmailer in the past two weeks, nor anything from Zach. Luke was still paying Logan to shadow him. Had it all just been an idle threat?

He texted Zach, who replied almost immediately, saying there was no news. Luke told him Logan was no longer needed. Then he began his weekly email to Haddie, outlining the things he'd been up to in Blueberry Springs. What had he done that week? Bought a ridiculous number of raffle tickets to the ladies' auxiliary raffle, donated new nets for the soccer team.

He could just about hear Haddie's reply. *Throwing money around doesn't make you a worthy human.*

Didn't she understand? He wasn't the guy they needed building a fence around a community garden. He was the guy donating the lumber. There was a necessity for both, and just because his skill set didn't include using his hands, it didn't make his contribution any less valid.

Emma stirred on the couch, yawning loudly, her fingers expertly adjusting her wig with a subtlety that didn't let on to what she was actually doing. "I was supposed to call my sister back."

Olivia. Like he needed to think about her right now. He'd been lucky to have avoided her as much as he had, and he planned to keep it that way.

"The backhoe arrived while you were out earlier," he replied, changing the subject. "I had them leave it at the meadow, since we'll need it there in about four weeks."

"Great. Did you try driving it?"

He shook his head. He hadn't even seen it yet.

"Olivia wants us to go ice fishing with her on Saturday. I told her I'd ask you."

"I'm busy," Luke replied instinctively, before realizing he truly was.

"Yeah. Me, too."

He gave her a curious look.

"What?" she asked.

"Nothing."

"I know that look. What?"

He felt a hint of a smile. She'd tell him to take a long walk off a cliff, wouldn't she? He appreciated that more than he likely should. "How did lunch go?" He'd tell her about his scheduled trip later.

The twinkle that had grown in Emma's blue eyes faded. She gave a noncommittal shrug. "The usual."

"What does that mean?"

"She tried to tell me how to do everything." She added quickly, "I appreciate her trying to help, though."

"What does she think about me working with you?" It was a subject they'd danced around for weeks.

"I don't know. She gets this weird smile, but lately she's been even more..."

"Interfering?"

"And controlling. Possessive."

"Of...?"

Emma's face scrunched in thought. She sighed. "I don't know. Maybe I'm wrong. I think she's having trouble with all the big changes in her life. She'd always worked for Carrington and now she doesn't." She got up, pushing the blanket off, her curls a mess of tangles. Luke opened his mouth to ask about her wig, but decided against it.

"What do I smell?" she asked.

"I made tuna sandwiches and salad."

"My fav!"

"Really?"

"Anything you make is my favorite." She gently bumped her shoulder against his. It was going to feel weird returning to Charleston without her. Then again, he preferred the Blueberry Springs version of Emma to the South Carolina one, and appreciated knowing he could come back to her and this little life they'd carved out in the middle of nowhere.

She scratched her arms, then pushed up her sweater sleeves and made a face. "My skin is so dry here. Thank goodness I brought my Blissful Body Lotion."

"You use Cohen's?" He felt surprisingly pleased by the discovery. Their lotions weren't bad, but to know that a former model chose them as something she wanted to use...well, that was a nice shot in the arm.

"I love the pomegranate, but your coconut oil cream is the

best for the dry winter blechiness." She gave a sigh. "I'm out, though."

"I hear they carry it in town now."

She gave a small smile and patted his cheek. "Those deep pockets finally got us something worthwhile, didn't they?"

He raised a finger. "Hang on one sec." He dug through a box of samples he'd brought with him, finding the cream she'd been hoping for.

"Tell me you love me," he said. He quickly amended his statement. "Well, your skin loves me."

"Total lifesaver," Emma murmured, opening the jar, her cheeks bright pink. She slathered some on her arms and sighed happily. "Best cream out there."

He pulled her against him with a growl. "You should be in a commercial. I'd sell the cream by the caseload." No wonder Jack Carrington had placed her in so many ads for their cosmetics over the years. Although their target market of mostly females probably wouldn't react to Emma the way he was right now.

He lowered his lips to hers, drawing her attention from the cream to him.

"I'm going to miss this," he said when they came up for air. He'd scooped her into his arms, ready to take her to bed.

"What do you mean?" She slid out of his arms before he realized what he'd said.

"I have to zip home for the weekend. I leave Friday afternoon and return Monday night."

She gave him a look of disappointment. "I planned things for Saturday."

"What kind of plans?" He snugged her hips against his.

"Not that." She gave him a shy smile, her eyes lighting up. "Well, that." She bit back the smile. "But I meant other things. Now you'll just have to wait to see what I come up with later." She placed a finger against his lips, coyly lifting an eyebrow before slipping out of his embrace. His fingers trailed over her curves like a silent plea to linger.

"I made you supper," he said, trying to convince her to spill her plans.

"You spoil me."

He smiled, wishing that was true.

She'd slipped back into his arms, her smile soft and inviting. "I love that you cook for us." She placed a palm flat against his chest. "Thank you."

He gave a slight nod, trying to put a finger on the new sensation fluttering through him like a butterfly on a breeze. It was similar to the feeling when he donated money, but yet different. He didn't know what it was, only that he wanted it again and again, and the only way he knew how to make that happen was by making his wife happy.

***

EMMA ENTERED VEILS AND VOWS, looking for her sister. She felt shaky and nervous, but determined. Luke was supposed to leave for the airport in a little over an hour and Emma had just spent time after school with Keisha, the girl she was mentoring. They'd talked about honesty and secrets within Keisha's peer group, and Emma had come to the personal conclusion that she really needed to start coming clean with her sister about how she was having a little business relationship with benefits with Olivia's ex. But not about the marriage, because that was just a piece of paper that would get everyone wound up, expecting it to mean more than it really did or ever would.

Emma paused in the doorway. Was she really going to reveal it all to her sister?

While she was fairly confident Olivia hadn't experienced true love with Luke—the way she looked at Devon was entirely different than any of the cool, restrained ways she'd looked at

Luke. But that didn't change the fact that she would have the right to be upset if she discovered how involved Emma had become with Luke.

Working with him had given Emma a strength and resolve she'd never felt before. She didn't want to do anything that might impact that. But she also didn't want things to get weird or awkward between her and her sister.

Emma hovered in the doorway, frozen with indecision.

"Check this out." Ginger McGinty, the store's owner, came over, holding up a tablet. She snapped a photo of Emma, yanking her from her thoughts. "Great picture." Ginger tapped the screen and Emma jumped.

"I wasn't even smiling," she protested. She hadn't had time to pose or flash her practiced winning smile. In fact, she wasn't even wearing much makeup, not expecting to see anyone other than her sister and Keisha.

Ginger tapped her tablet a few times and the large screen on a wall near the cash register at the back of the salesroom showed a photo of Emma in a wedding dress.

Emma felt the urge to cover the screen. Not because she wasn't smiling or appeared a bit washed out, but because…well, how desperate did she look in a wedding dress? If Luke walked in to give her a ride home, it would not be cool. At all. She knew how guys reacted if you started behaving as if you wanted something forever, when you'd only just started sleeping together. And were a secret.

A secret that had the potential to send her pregnant sister into premature labor.

Emma should leave. Now.

Keep her mouth shut and hope for the best, because in three months she'd be divorced. In four months when All You was completely launched, Luke would be history.

"Take it down," she commanded.

Ginger blinked in surprise. "But look." She began swiping a

finger on her tablet, changing the dress on Emma's virtual form. The next gown was exquisite. Fitted with lace edging that crept up the bodice and over the capped sleeves, giving the whole garment a beautiful shape. "You like that one?"

Emma nodded as a lump of remorse formed in her throat. The dress was something she would choose for herself if she were to marry for real. But if she stayed with Luke, there'd be no need for a wedding. They were already married.

What was she even thinking?

When they were done, Luke would return home—just as he was today—and she'd continue on here to ensure things continued to run smoothly after the launch. They wouldn't even remain in the same time zone.

"Your sister designed it."

Emma looked at the dress again, trying unsuccessfully to breathe past the tightness in her chest.

Olivia had come a long way since cutting the lace off her childhood party dresses in hopes of disguising her "big boned" physique. These days she was rocking her figure with well-chosen garments.

The gowns she was designing echoed her new spirit. Verve. Moxie. They were powerfully sexy, and yet demure. Emma couldn't figure it out, but she wanted to wear one.

"Ethan Mattson designed the app. Isn't it amazing? Brides are going to get a kick out of this."

"You can download the app anywhere?"

"Yup. And we're working on a hairstyle update, but it's proving tricky."

"What about makeup?"

"I'd love that so much!"

"Could Carrington work with you?" Emma asked hesitantly, fidgeting with the zipper on her jacket. She should probably run the idea past Luke or her father or the board first, but she could see the ad potential, and Carrington had always fought for the wedding market.

"That would be so awesome!" Ginger bounded over and hugged her.

The bell on the door jingled behind them. Emma turned, spotting Luke, a feeling of warmth spreading through her. He was in a bulky coat, snow speckling his dark hair. He looked healthy and irresistibly handsome.

He lit up when he spotted Emma and she felt a rush of something—something that made her want to launch herself into his arms and never let go.

Ridiculous. It was simply the joy of making a deal with Ginger and the anticipation of a seldom heard "good job."

"Ready to head back to the cabin?" he asked.

She made sure she looked away so that happy frolicking her heart was doing in her chest wouldn't show on her face and give her away. "You were faster than I thought. I haven't actually chatted with Olivia yet. Did you get the greenhouse permits renewed?"

"Sure did."

"Do I hear Luke Cohen?" Olivia chirped, appearing from the fitting room that was attached to the salesroom. "Emma, too? What's up?" Her hand drifted to her lower back, causing her belly to push farther out as if she was trying to draw attention to her happy new life. Her light-colored hair was done up in a loose bun and she was wearing a high-belted dress that stretched over her baby bump. She looked like she had in the magazine, only more incredible.

Olivia caught sight of the screen by the register and her face lit up in delight. "Look at you! I designed that gown with you in mind. It's exquisite." Olivia's eyes danced, seeing her design imposed on her sister.

Luke, however, had a strange expression. "You're getting...married?"

"Yes," Emma said primly. "I have a secret lover and we're going to elope, because I'm nearing old maid status."

Luke's lips twisted into an amused smile at the joke. Beside him, Olivia's frown deepened.

"It should be you, by the way," Ginger said, elbowing Luke. "You two would make cute babies."

Emma gave Ginger an unimpressed look for the comment, even though she could totally envision offspring created by herself and Luke. Adorable in every way, and smart like he was.

Her sister's gaze was darting back and forth between the two of them as though she was trying to piece together something that didn't feel quite right.

Emma suppressed the urge to bolt.

"Ginger and I just made a possible deal with her app and the All You line," Emma said, by way of distraction.

"Really?" Olivia asked in surprise.

"Is that okay?" Emma asked, worried her sister would think she was overstepping somehow. It was silly to keep seeking her approval, as Emma now owned a majority share of the new line, but it was Olivia's brainchild.

"Of course it's okay," Luke said, coming to her side. "This is your project, Em. *You* didn't abandon it." Olivia's chin tipped up, as did his. "And you sunk everything you had into buying controlling rights, as well as making sure it gets the attention it deserves."

Olivia's eyes narrowed as she turned to her, to see if what Luke said was true. Emma swallowed and smiled feebly. She really thought Luke had missed that part when she'd accidentally blurted it out while he'd been sleeping on the cabin floor. Go figure that even half-asleep he absorbed everything.

"Is that true?" Olivia asked quietly.

"Okay then. This is fun," Ginger said, turning off her tablet and making Emma's image on the monitor fade to black. "Anyone want a coffee?"

"I own 61 percent. I had to buy it. Daddy didn't give it to me as a gift," Emma said.

"You sold your apartment?"

"It doesn't matter what she did. It's her product now. She bought you out," Luke said sharply.

Olivia inhaled, her shoulders rising. What was to come surely wouldn't be pleasant. Ginger, Olivia's old college roommate, quickly said, "Hey, Luke Moneybags Cohen, wanna buy me a car? Mine conked out last night. Logan says it needs a new battery, but I heard you bought the seniors a new bus, so why not help out a gal like me? I don't need anything fancy or big. Maybe just a little Lexus?" She batted her lashes, her green eyes alight with hope.

"If he's buying anyone a car," Emma snapped, feeling possessive, "it'll be me, so he doesn't have to drive me everywhere." She pushed him toward the door. "Let's go."

"I thought you came to chat," her sister said, her tone stern, and Emma stopped in her tracks. Olivia was going to make a good mother.

"I was just killing time while Luke got our permits renewed." She nudged him toward the door, but he was facing off against Olivia, who was coming closer.

"You look tired." Olivia dusted a thumb over the circles under Emma's eyes like a mother would, casting a suspicious glance at Luke, as if he was responsible for her lack of sleep.

Which in a lot of ways he was. Bedtime had become the favorite part of Emma's day lately. But it did push her to stay up late. Not that she'd ever complain. He was a patient and very thorough lover.

She really shouldn't be thinking about him like that with her sister right in front of her.

She lowered her gaze in shame. She should have kept her hands off him.

"Your hair looks flatter. Are you eating okay?"

"It's just the mountain water and dry air."

Emma felt Luke grip her arm through her thick winter coat. "Emma's been really busy, working hard to repair Carrington's image," he stated. "She's convinced a lot of bloggers to review the new products. She's also lined up interviews with critical scientists—"

"I still get company emails," Olivia said, interrupting him. She turned to Emma. "Are you sure this isn't too much? I know you don't have a lot of experience, and I feel like—"

"It has been too much since day one." Emma hated that her sister was worrying about her now that she was finally feeling as though she was close to succeeding. Where was the concern she'd needed months ago?

"I'm sorry," she added quickly when she saw her sister's hurt look. "I'm just tired."

"Luke," Olivia said, turning to him, "you take care of her."

"I am," he said firmly. "And she's got it under control. All she needs is a bit of guidance, since she's never done something like this before and it got dumped on her."

"Luke, it's okay," Emma said softly, not wanting the two to fight.

"No, it's not okay. You're doing an amazing job with this, and I'm tired of you and your family doubting your abilities." He looked so fierce and protective that for a moment she thought he was going to kiss her right there in front of her sister, among all those wedding gowns.

Instead, he clasped her hand possessively, sending a thrill through her. "Come on, EmmaLu. We have a job to do."

6

*L*uke got out of the plane and stretched, letting the humidity of the South Carolina evening leach into his bones. Home.

Did the air always feel this close, or was it simply the fact that he normally didn't wear jeans and a sweater here like he had back home in Blueberry Springs? There was that word again: *home*.

The four-hour flight had been unusually boring. He'd worked the whole time, but found he'd become accustomed to turning to Emma to run ideas past her. A lot.

Or maybe it was simply the effect of her not being at his side that made his subconscious always take note and remind him that he was alone.

She was just a business partner. A woman who didn't want anything more than what they had. He needed to twist his head on straight again and get it back in the game, because she'd surely call anything more than what they were enjoying "a mistake." Heck, their current affair could even be one, and she was just waiting to break it to him.

He walked through the terminal, stopping in the executive

lounge for a whiskey. It should really be a coffee, seeing how much work he had to do over the extended weekend. Cash had a mighty big list of things to go over with him while he was in town.

Luke knocked back his drink, inhaling to combat the burn of the aged liquor as it traveled south. A red dress in the lounge's shop window caught his eye and he found himself wondering what it might look like on Emma. Or puddled on the floor at her feet.

What size were those delicate feet of hers? Would she mind if he bought her a pair of do-me pumps?

Why did he want to buy her gifts all of a sudden? And what had she been about to say when they'd kissed goodbye, all sweet and tender, out under the snow-laden evergreens surrounding their private sanctuary up in those peaceful mountains? It had felt important, and he'd been disappointed when she'd quietly backed off, squelching the words before they'd been formed. Then, for good measure, had stuffed them under some internal rug and sat on it. That placid debutante look had replaced what had been warm, welcoming and personal just moments before.

Gifts. So why did he suddenly want to buy the world and lay it at her feet like a cat with a mouse for the human who lit up its life?

Emma liked pretty things and enjoyed being thought of, and he was a thoughtful guy. He'd noticed that her ex-boyfriend Vaughn had doused her in gifts, trinkets, dresses, spa days. All those things women liked. Pampering. Things that would make her even more beautiful, if that was possible.

She'd given up a lot to work in Blueberry Springs, and she deserved a treat. Credit, too.

He was still angry with the doubt Olivia had displayed so blatantly in Veils and Vows. She'd masked it as concern, but it had rankled him, erupting like a volcano of anger and outrage on Emma's behalf.

He'd wanted to draw a sword and slay all dragons in her path. Squash the spiders, behead the snakes. Trample the thorns. Lay his jacket across the puddles.

He knew it was likely nothing more than sibling rivalry between the women and, as Emma had said, Olivia feeling left out of a project she'd initiated that had her acting as she was. He should probably regret the way he'd claimed Emma, but she needed someone in her corner and she'd hired him to be that person.

He shook his head as he stalked through the terminal. She'd sold everything to make All You work, and her family barely believed in her.

A chauffeur holding a tablet with his name made eye contact at the arrivals gate. It was Zach Forrester.

Luke gave him a handshake and a shoulder clap, his briefcase and overnight bag slung over his other shoulder.

"You find out anything about that caller I mentioned a few weeks ago?"

"I'll tell you about it in the car."

"Lead the way."

Moments later they were in a Town Car, Luke in the back, his long legs stretched out. The air conditioner cooled him immediately, and he spotted various beverages and snacks at the ready in the minibar. He peered out the tinted windows, noting various businessmen arriving home, almost all of them in suits or sport coats. Luke looked down at his jeans and sweater. He smelled of wood smoke and was drastically underdressed for going in to the office even on a Saturday. Nobody went in wearing denim. Ever.

Blueberry Springs was rubbing off on him.

"Zach, on second thought, run me by my place before I go into Cohen's. I need a shower."

Zach nodded and made a right turn.

"About this new lead?" he asked, leaning back in the leather seat. The city felt foreign and busy, the luxury around him familiar, but not as comforting as he'd expected. The mountains and cabin already felt like light years away.

"It's someone who works for you."

Luke had suspected as much. "Who?"

"Not sure yet, but I placed a mole on the inside."

"My dad hasn't paid up yet?" He hated those words and what they implied.

"No. He wants to meet with you while you're in town."

Of course. To push him into doing what he wanted. To push him into giving up his quest for the inheritance. He wouldn't be having that conversation. Ever.

"Does anyone else know about this…issue?"

"No."

"Any more threats?" They were driving through a shopping district and Luke spied in a store window yet another red dress that made him think of Emma. "Stop the car."

Zach glanced at him in the mirror, but said nothing, pulling into the next available spot at the curb. The palm trees above swayed in a light breeze off the ocean.

"No threats that I've heard of," Zach said, when Luke didn't get out.

"What kind of risk do you think there actually is?" He reached for the door handle, wondering what size Emma was. The mannequin in the window looked about her shape.

"Hard to say at this point."

"Hard to say, or you won't say?" he asked sharply.

"Won't say," Zach admitted, giving him an easy smile through the rearview mirror.

Luke sighed. "Keep me informed if anything happens. I'll be right back."

He climbed out into the muggy air, wishing for the crispness of winter in the mountains. As he made his way to the boutique's door he looked at his phone's calendar, even though he knew what day it was. He had a feeling that being here wasn't going to be like Blueberry Springs, where he lost track of time. Quite the opposite, and he believed he'd soon be counting down the hours until he returned home to Emma.

"OH, COME ON!" Emma yelled at the truck as it slid backward on the final snow-packed hill heading up to the cabin. She was so close to home with her groceries and the week's mail. Luke had left not long ago, renting a car to take him to the airport so she could have the truck, and she'd felt inexplicably angry while out running errands.

Her mood made no sense. Of course he had to go home. He had a company to run. It was silly to be in a mood over the fact that he was back in the heat, living in the lap of luxury, not having to deal with snow, firewood or anything else.

And yet as much as she could go for the easy life right now, she knew it wasn't envy that had her upset. It was the fact that she'd almost told him she loved him. They'd been saying goodbye and the words had been right there on her lips, ready to be said.

She couldn't fall for him. They were getting divorced in three months. They had a business deal, not a true romance. Telling him she loved him would ruin absolutely everything.

The truck's wheels came to a stop at the edge of the snowy ditch and she lowered her head to the steering wheel.

Earlier, in Veils and Vows it had all felt so very real. Luke had been fiercely protective, jumping in to defend her against Olivia. She wanted to think it was because his feelings for her were deeply rooted, but she knew she was kidding herself. She only had to open her eyes to realize that his reaction had merely been thanks to the fact that he'd been duking it out with Olivia like a couple of divorcees, battling over a child who was caught in the middle. Only Emma wasn't sure if All You was the child or if she was.

She sighed and tried to get the truck to move forward. Nothing. She pushed the gas pedal down farther, sending the back end into the ditch, the front end threatening to follow suit. The driveway hadn't been this slippery before it was plowed after the big snowfall. Shouldn't it be better now?

Emma put the idling truck into Park with a sigh.

"I hate living out here."

No, that was a lie. She loved being holed up on the side of a mountain—when she was with Luke.

She'd spent what felt like hours listening to Vintra drone on about the key ingredients of their products and other stuff, trying to keep her mind on task. He didn't do that with Luke. He listened, then performed. Emma had lost patience, standing up and saying simply, "You're paid to take care of the science, Vintra. Make it so or I'll find someone else."

And then she'd walked out.

He was going to quit, she knew it. Good bosses didn't talk to their employees that way. Luke was going to come back to find that she'd messed up everything. He definitely wouldn't be talking up her skills after that.

Emma jumped as someone rapped on her window. She let down the glass, the cold mountain air slicing into her warm haven, bringing with it the scent of his overpowering cologne.

"You've got to commit to the hill," the older man said. He looked like a marine or something. He was big, broad, bald and near retirement age. How was his head not freezing in this cold?

"Pardon me?" She looked up the snowy trail. How was she supposed to commit to a hill?

"Don't let up." He was dragging some sort of long, wide belt, and he went around the front of the truck, disappearing for a moment before popping up again. He began walking up the hill, trailing the now-attached cord. He paused, looking over his shoulder. "You coming?"

"I'm from the South," she called to him as she opened the truck door, letting her voice take on the slight drawl that years of voice lessons had trained out of it. "Winter and vehicles aren't really my thing." She pushed her hands into her coat pockets and shivered.

"If you drive one, they should be." He seemed about to ask her something, but changed his mind. He toddled farther up the hill, and she hustled to catch up to him. He chuckled as her legs went out from under her when her leather ankle-high boots failed to maintain their grip. She landed hard on the snowy road and the man smiled down at her. "You ought to buy yourself some real boots there, little miss."

"These are real. Look at the fake fur." She pointed to her footwear with the cute trim around the top before standing up. If those didn't say winter, what did? "And you should be wearing a hat."

He smiled and ran a hand over his crown. "Touché."

"I'm Emma Carrington, by the way. I'm working on a cosmetics line here in town."

"I know who you are. My name's Leif. I'm a chef. Well, I was before some dolt burned down Benny's. That was the restaurant I worked in, on Main Street."

"I had the chocolate maven pie there once. Before the place burned down." Emma found her mouth watering just thinking of the creamy, rich pie. Dessert like that could solve all the world's problems.

"My recipe."

"Really? What does a girl have to do to get a slice?"

He chuckled. "The owner, Lily, is thinking of rebuilding. Convince her to go through with it and I'll give you free pie for life."

"You're serious?"

"You'll have to wait and see." He pointed to a stout tree in front of them. It was a ways up on the opposite side of the road from the truck and a good three feet beyond the cleared driveway. "Wrap this cable around the trunk."

Free pie. For life. That could be dangerous.

Emma put her mind back on the task, taking in what Leif expected of her.

"Shouldn't I call a tow truck?" Or maybe just leave the pickup where it was until Luke came back. She had enough food to keep her until his return, and at the rate her day was going, she'd wreck the truck.

"Don't give up on yourself just because it's difficult. Living out where cell service is sketchy you could freeze to death before anyone found you."

She shivered at the thought and adjusted her woolly hat. She longed to be back in the cabin, where she could rest her scalp by taking off Cousin Itt, and do nothing but toss logs on the fire and relax.

Sighing, Emma waded through the snow, following Leif's instructions.

"Pull the slack." He gestured with his hands. "Now come here and start winching." She made a production of climbing out of the ditch and brushing the snow from her leggings.

He passed her the handheld winch. She began shaking her head. "I'm not strong enough and I just got my nails done."

Which was true. She'd ditched the gel nails and had a nice, simple manicure. She'd planned on having decent nails for at least a week. Not a mere two hours.

"Cut the helpless act and believe in yourself."

Emma felt shamed by his words and snatched the winch from him. She flung the handle back and forth a few times, to no avail. She was cold, cranky and didn't need more examples of how she couldn't take care of things. She needed Luke back in

Blueberry Springs. "See? It's still in the ditch. I'm calling a tow truck."

"Come on," he coaxed gently. "Put your back into it and win my respect."

She blinked back tears.

"Trust me," he said kindly.

She glared at him and began furiously working the device in her hands, ready to prove he'd given her an impossible job. The belt connecting the truck and tree tightened. Then it got harder to move.

"See? Too hard."

"Push this button. It'll help."

"Please, just do it for me."

"There's a raging blizzard. It's dark. Nobody around for miles." He crossed his arms, refusing to help, and she shivered, imagining his scenario much too vividly when a coyote howled nearby. Her attention on the woods, she pushed the button and cranked the winch, worried about which animals might be out looking for a tasty snack.

"That's it… Now, would you look at that."

Emma glanced behind her and her jaw dropped. The pickup was out of the ditch. How had that happened?

The man grinned. "Now get into that truck and commit to the hill. Eat it one tire rotation at a time. It's just like life. When it gets tough, you take it slow and easy and keep pushing."

As she got in the driver's seat, she glanced down the driveway to where his truck was parked at the bottom. Like in her nightmares, she could imagine her vehicle slipping backward, out of control. Only this time she'd hit his truck instead of going over an embankment.

"You're self-sufficient and resourceful. Determined," Leif called through her open window as he coiled up the cable.

Determined. She could do determined.

She listened to his instructions on how to finesse the truck up the hill, and cheered when it crested the top. She could see the cabin up ahead in the waning twilight. The windows glowed with warmth and wood smoke still billowed gently from the river-stone chimney.

She'd done it.

Leif had believed in her. Luke believed in her.

She was silly to think Vintra would quit just because she'd been firm with him. After all, she was EmmaLu. The woman who'd convinced bloggers to try the All You products. She'd wooed scientists into analyzing their new line and giving it an honest shakedown. She had hundreds of thousands of followers on her beauty blog.

It was time to put the doubt where it belonged—in her past.

LUKE PARKED the rental car with its nearly empty gas tank in front of the cabin. The place looked cozy and welcoming and he was eager to see the woman who was waiting inside.

He grabbed his bags, as well as the gift he'd bought for Emma, and skipped up the steps, noting an extra set of snowshoes on the porch. His gal had been shopping again.

He swung open the door with a "Honey, I'm home!"

The sweet scent of apple pie assaulted his nostrils and he grinned. Emma turned from her spot at the counter where she'd been eating a slice. She was smiling and his heart lifted.

"You've got to try this pie. It's amazing."

Luke's steps to Emma slowed as he spotted a young man sitting on the couch. Luke's visions of her launching herself into his arms, dragging him off to bed to create more X-rated memories for him to fall back on when they were apart, quickly faded.

Company.

He didn't want to entertain company. He wanted to bring reunion fantasies to life with the woman he'd been thinking about all weekend. He'd spent hours upon hours in his old office poring over documents with Cash, trying to ignore the way his cousin flirted with his assistant, Alexa, causing distractions. Add in an awkward lunch with his parents where his father had quietly urged Luke to allow him take care of the inheritance when his mother had slipped to the ladies' room, and Luke was more than done with Charleston. He was happy to be back in Blueberry Springs with Emma.

Only she wasn't alone.

"Hello," he said politely as he leaned his bags against the counter. The man looked to be in his early twenties and not the type of guy Luke thought Emma was usually attracted to. He was wearing thickly insulated, camouflage-print work pants and a flannel shirt, his hair slightly scruffy and flat, as if he'd kept it under a hat all day. Which he likely had. Definitely not Emma's type. Then again, this was Blueberry Springs and pretty much everything Luke had once thought true had been gradually shifting.

What was he thinking? Just because she had a man over didn't mean she was looking to date him. She was involved with Luke, *married* to him. That, at the end of the day, still counted as something.

"This is Pete Lunn. Pete, this is Luke." Emma was speaking clearly, but ever-so-slightly slower than usual, and Luke wondered if Pete had a hearing issue.

"Nice to meet you." He went to the couch and shook the man's hand. It was firm and he gave a polite nod.

"Pete doesn't talk," Emma said. "He was injured by a horse a few years ago." She scooped up some pie on her fork, one hand cradled below it to catch anything that might fall off. "Come here. You have to try this."

"Maybe later."

"No, seriously. Pete's been cooking for me all weekend and I told him we'd discuss hiring him as our personal chef."

Luke glanced at Pete again. He didn't look like a baker, but the flaky crust and scented cabin seemed to disprove that image. Luke couldn't help but wonder if the old saying about the way to a man's heart being through his stomach was true for women as well. If so, he might have a little competition.

Emma waved her fork again and Luke sidled up beside her, inhaling her aroma. He wanted to kiss her, but not with an audience. How long would Pete be hanging around?

Feeling self-conscious, Luke took a bite of the offered dessert, his eyes drifting closed as the perfect blend of sweet and tart hit him. "Wow. This is amazing." He slid Emma's plate closer and took another bite.

"No way. This is my slice." She laughed and stole back her fork. "So? Can we hire him?"

Luke nodded. He'd been enjoying experimenting with cooking, but he wasn't getting anywhere fast. Plus the next few weeks were going to get insane as they moved toward launch.

But having Pete around all the time? Well, that would take some getting used to.

It was good though. It would help keep Luke focused on work and not Emma.

Probably.

"You're hired, Pete," she called.

The man grinned. He stood up and came over, all limbs and awkward smiles. If Luke didn't know better, the man had a crush on his wife.

Luke crossed his arms and let out a long, unimpressed sigh.

"See you tomorrow then?" Emma asked Pete. He nodded. "Thanks for keeping me company. And making pie."

She walked him to the door, and when he was gone, she said in a quiet voice, "Apparently he's a fan of my work. Modeling stuff. He asked me to sign an ad from a magazine."

Luke's hackles rose. "Are you sure it's okay having him here when I'm gone?" Concern was escalating inside Luke. "How well do you know this guy? You're in the middle of nowhere, Emma."

"He's totally harmless!"

"How do you know?"

"Luke."

He knew that tone.

"I am *not* being unreasonable." He no longer had Logan shadowing either of them, and anything could have happened in his absence, a thought that nearly downed him.

"I'm a grown woman. How about you try trusting me and my judgment?" There was a stern edge to her glare and Luke found himself backing off.

They were quiet for a moment, things settling out between them as they took stock of each other.

"I talked to the real estate agent," Emma said quietly, her hands on the counter, her gaze lowered. "There might be a four-bedroom home coming on the market. She said she can get us in to look at it ahead of time."

"Okay." Luke felt as though he was being kicked out, and he swallowed the flash of hurt and anger. "I got you something." He moved to the other side of the counter, retrieving the gift he'd picked up for her in South Carolina. The tissue paper poking out the top crinkled as the bag exchanged hands.

He couldn't read her expression. She looked pleased, wary and mad all at the same time.

She unwrapped the gift and smiled politely. "A dress. Thank you." She set it aside.

"I hope it fits. And there's more in there."

She peeked in the bag, pulling out the pumps, her expression faltering.

"You don't like them?"

She gave him a sweet smile. Placid Debutante Shut Down mode had been initiated, telling him he'd somehow missed the mark. "They're lovely. Thank you, Luke." She placed a dry, chaste kiss on his cheek.

He was starting to think that instead of hurrying from the airport, coasting up the driveway on gas fumes, he could have taken the time to fill up, even return the rental, because Emma hadn't missed him nearly as much as he'd missed her.

"I hired a new assistant for Vintra."

"You did?"

"He was being weird and I snapped at him. When I went to check in with him this morning and make sure we were still okay, we got to talking. He needs more help. So I hired someone he knew back in college. She arrives on Wednesday."

Luke moved closer to Emma, curious whether her nervous avoidance was simply from not knowing where she stood with him, or if it was something more. Instead of turning to him, she began bustling around, tidying and talking quickly.

What had happened while he'd been away? While he'd realized how much he cared for her, had she realized how little she returned those feelings?

"I made an appointment with a woman named Jill Armstrong to talk to you about her natural products. Soaps and lotions. It's similar to the All You line and it sounds like a possible expansion project for Cohen's. I found her medicinal lotions helped my radiation rash better than the prescription stuff my doctor gave me." Emma was talking quickly, babbling almost. "There's definitely potential there—especially with the Canadian market. I read online that one in two Canadians are expected to have cancer in their lifetime."

"That's a scary stat."

"There's a market, Luke."

"Okay." He leaned against the kitchen counter, watching her. She was moving with a purpose and edgy confidence he hadn't noticed when he'd left. Was it new? Or was he seeing everything with fresh eyes due to his time away?

"I've also been thinking about a few things in regards to us and the town."

No doubt. How to get rid of him by the feel of things.

"Me, too. Can I go first?" Luke felt a bout of sudden nerves, as though he was about to propose, which was silly.

"Fine. Go first." She sat at the table, folding a leg under her, hands clasped on the tabletop. He focused on them instead of how her V-neck sweater was giving him a glimpse of pale flesh he longed to feel against his chest as they moved together.

"I propose that on Monday mornings we go out for breakfast and have a power meeting where we set up the schedule for our week and brainstorm. We get out of the house, set aside time to strategize…"

"Sounds good. I'm in."

He had way more to his sales pitch.

"I'm not done." He tried to hide his anger at her interruption. "I think this will really help the town see us as fixtures and—"

"Luke, I said I'm game." She had gotten up to take an empty cup to the sink. His heart sped as she passed, and he hooked his fingers into hers, stopping her.

"Maybe we could also go out one night a week. On top of our weekend adventures."

"Like…" her eyes narrowed "…a date?"

Yes.

His heart felt like it was going to explode from its sudden forced speed as he lied to her. "No," he said casually. "Just two friends hanging out, having supper. Combating cabin fever. Letting the town get to know us better. I can do this town relationship thing if it's important to you."

"So you're placating me?"

He coughed, feeling awkward. His date offer had sounded lame even to his own ears, but admitting he thought of it as a date felt wrong due to her current mood. So much for Mr. Smooth winning his wife over again.

"I'm trying to show I trust you, Emma. I believe in you." He pushed back from the table. "Maybe we could go out tonight. Get dressed up—see if the dress fits—and catch up with each other."

Her cheeks grew pink. "Thanks, but I have work to do." With that, she took the remaining pie, her fork, and went into her bedroom, closing the door behind her, effectively shutting him out.

7

*E*mma loved open-mic night. The attention, the laughter, the excitement. Brew Babies, the local pub, was full of warm bodies, and it was another perfect opportunity for her and Luke to become members of the community.

Last week she'd been nervous about seeing him after his time back home. Would he be the same man she'd come to adore in Blueberry Springs, or would he have reverted back to the Luke she'd grown up with? Entitled and throwing his money around instead of being real?

Then he'd breezed in, right on schedule, that intense look in his eyes as though he was ready to devour her. The urge to throw herself into his arms and lose herself had been tremendous. And then she'd seen the bag from the high-end boutique and her heart had nearly stopped in disappointment.

Inside had been a slinky red dress. Sexy shoes.

She couldn't help but think that Luke saw her as a mistress to dress up and keep happy. Someone he needed to ply with gifts instead of true affection. She didn't want to be the pretty show-piece. She wanted to be the friend, the lover, the partner and confidante, the woman he found beautiful even without makeup, or wearing the right things.

So she'd kept their reunion about business and politely put on the dress and heels for open-mic night.

"Be nice, approachable, real, friendly," Luke said, repeating her earlier instructions. "Don't throw my money around. Win over the town. Be one of them."

Emma nodded. He'd dressed down in jeans and a button-up shirt, the sleeves rolled up to showcase his muscular forearms, and he was simply irresistible. She wanted to drag him into the hallway that led past the washrooms and into the alley behind the pub, and kiss him senseless.

"Emma?" he prompted.

"Yes?" She felt teary-eyed.

"Are you all right?"

"I'm fine. I think we should…" She turned to him, the words dying as he gave her a smoldering gaze that trailed down her dress. It fit her form beautifully and he'd even brought the right shoes to make her legs look extra sexy. But he was dressing her, and it felt like a controlling move. If this was the start, where would it end? She'd already been through the heartache of this kind of relationship with Vaughn. She didn't have it in her to do it again with Luke.

She smoothed his shirt, her hand lingering. "Just…be good tonight."

He gave her a crooked smile, oozing sex appeal and hunger. She met his eyes, that helpless feeling she got around him taking over. It would be so easy to lose herself in the fire that burned between them.

She dropped her hand and turned toward the stage at the back of the bar.

She needed to stay focused. She'd seen what the environmental protesters had done last summer when they'd decided they didn't like Carrington being in town. In the end, it had actually been a rival of Devon's stirring everything up for them, but the lesson was there. Be a part of the community.

She hooked her arm through Luke's, pulling him up to the low stage as it became vacant again.

"I don't know…" His glass of beer sloshed as he paused at the steps while she took her place under the bright lights. She waved him forward.

"Come on."

She batted her eyes at the audience as she stepped up to the microphone. "My business partner and friend, Luke Cohen!" People clapped politely. "He's shy." She gave a pout.

She walked over to her husband. "I tell a joke, you tell a joke. It's easy. Whoever gets the best response wins."

"Wins what?"

She shrugged. "Bragging rights."

"You know I don't tell jokes."

"You tell them with me." He'd lost some of that tight edge he used to have. If he could tell a joke up on stage it would help them out, laughter being a shortcut to the doors they needed unlocked. Especially since Luke's purchase of a backhoe had insulted the construction foreman they'd hired to take care of their meadow snow clearing, and Luke had definitely had to do it himself.

She gave him a bright smile and returned to the microphone. "Hi! I'm Emma Carrington. Luke and I are new to town and we each have a joke for you."

"Hi, Emma!" someone from the back called.

She squinted against the stage lights, shielding her eyes. "Oh! Hey, Jill! Have you guys tried Jill's oatmeal lotion? It's *amazing*. Best all-natural moisturizer ever." She turned to Luke, who had come up on stage and was dutifully standing beside her, his jaw looking extra strong and delicious in the shadows created but the stage lights. Although maybe it was just the way he had it clenched, like he was trying to crack walnuts.

She smiled at him appeasingly. "Your lotions are pretty good, too, Luke. He's a hand lotion expert."

Someone cackled and Emma bit her cheek to stop from grinning at the inadvertent innuendo.

"What?" she asked innocently. The laughter grew and she released a giggle before turning serious again. "Okay. Here's my joke. Knock, knock." She looked to Luke, waiting for him to reply so she could say her next line.

To her surprise the audience, happy to participate, called, "Who's there?"

"Little Red Riding Hood."

"Little Red Riding Hood who?"

Luke was shaking his head, staring at the ceiling, amused but patient. Such a good man.

She echoed the audience, making "Little Red Riding Hood who" sound like a yodeling call. She gave a sassy flick of her hips. "I didn't know y'all could yodel!"

She received a few peals of laughter.

"Think you can do better?" She handed Luke the microphone.

He had that serious look, his eyes boring into hers.

"Please?" she pleaded breathlessly.

Luke took the mic. Cleared his throat. "Why isn't..." He paused. "Uh, why isn't a bear qualified to be a real koala bear? No. A real bear."

The pub was quiet.

"You mean why isn't a koala a real bear?" Emma asked, leaning in to speak into the microphone. He always fell back on this joke when he was nervous, and he got it wrong every time.

"Yeah, that."

She smiled and waited a beat. "Why, Luke?"

"It doesn't have the right koala-fications."

He got a few chuckles and groans, but overall...painful.

Luke lifted his glass of beer with a grimace. "Next round is on me!"

The pub erupted in applause.

"Looks like I won, sweetie." He gave her a satisfied wink, his smile sly and utterly, intoxicatingly sexy. He slid offstage to hand the bartender, Moe, his credit card, with Emma hot on his heels.

LUKE STEPPED into the law office, figuring the local lawyer, John Abcott, was probably ready with divorce papers for him and Emma despite the two of them having fulfilled only six of the required sixteen weeks of their wedding plan. There was nobody at the reception desk, it still being quite early in the morning. When he'd left the cabin, having received an email from John saying he could see him at seven, Emma had been in her nightie, looking sexy and rumpled with sleep. She'd asked where he was going and he'd blurted out a lie about having a meeting with Haddie in the city, and then had hightailed it out of there before he did something stupid like try and take Emma to bed.

He'd embarrassed himself onstage last week and he didn't think he'd won over a single soul like Emma had hoped he would. He wasn't sure why he always tried the koala joke, since he never got it right.

But he'd tried to win over the town and had even pulled out his wallet to buy a round for everyone in the pub when he'd failed to do it Emma's way. She'd said something about money not creating relationships, and then had shut him out of her room again that night. And all nights ever since.

They hadn't been intimate since his Charleston trip, and he didn't know what was going on, but something had definitely changed for her while he'd been away. When he'd left he'd thought they'd had a good thing going, but now they were back to being business partners and nothing more. He had been trying to be patient, but maybe he'd failed, since she now wanted a divorce.

Although maybe this meeting wasn't about Emma. Maybe someone back at headquarters had discovered that Luke had approved Zach's cameras and phone taps to try and flush out the mole, and were looking to sue him for an invasion of privacy. He was starting to think Zach was never going to find the blackmailer, and that the threat of whoever it was coming forward at the wrong time with Cohen's secrets was going to be hanging over him forever.

The good news was that his father's phone was also tapped, which would provide Luke a heads-up if anything looked ready to happen. He'd also told his mom she could take over his emergency account and leave Franklin. He'd seen the hope in her gaze, but she hadn't said anything other than thank you.

Thank you. Two small words that could feel so big. Last week, while he'd been getting a coffee in Mandy's café, he'd ended up talking to a kid about to drop out of high school. The youth, Trey, had scoffed at Luke's expensive shoes, but Luke had seen the need in his eyes. The kid was skinny and his own shoes were splitting, the tops peeling off the sole, exposing his toes. Luke understood it was hard to look toward your future when today seemed so bleak. The teen had been held back a year or two because he'd spent more time working part-time jobs to keep his siblings fed than in school. He needed a break, someone to look out for him and Luke had handed him his business card and promised him that if he graduated, he'd pay his way through any college of his choice. Then he'd opened a tab at Mandy's so Trey could get enough to eat without having to take on a third job.

The kid had looked shocked, stunned into silence. As Luke had taken his coffee, Mandy, who'd been behind the cash register with a baby in a swing thing, had silently mouthed *"Thank you,"* while looking immensely relieved.

"Is that Axel?" Luke had asked, pointing to the little one, who was gurgling to himself while trying to fit his fist in his mouth. "He's cute."

Mandy had smiled warmly.

Luke shook off the memories and the flood of other kangaroo thoughts jumping around in his mind, stepping toward the inner law office when a voice called, "Come on in. I'm back here."

Luke joined John, shaking the older man's hand as he stood to greet him.

"I have a letter," the lawyer said, pushing an envelope across his desk.

"A letter?"

"From your late maternal grandparents."

No divorce?

Luke felt relieved, hopeful.

He stared at the envelope, not reaching for it. But what was going on? Was this his father's doing?

"It came from your company lawyer, Stewart, with the utmost confidentiality."

John got up, moving toward the door that led to the reception area. "I'll give you a minute or two to read it over. I'll be just outside if you have questions or need anything."

"Have you read this?" Luke asked, holding up the sealed envelope.

"I have no clue as to its contents." He gave a small nod and exited the office.

Luke took a moment to focus his thoughts, his attention drifting to the pastel seascape hanging on the wall beside him. Finally, he flipped over the envelope, which had his name written on it in his grandfather's familiar bold hand, and slit the top edge using John's jade letter opener. Luke sucked in a deep breath as he pulled out and unfolded a two-page letter, a flash of unexpected grief hitting him low in the gut. He wiped his eyes when they dampened.

DEAR LUKE,

Know that if you receive this letter, your grandmother and I are quite pleased for you. We have always had the utmost faith in you and we only wish that we could see you as you are today as a man, a husband. Possibly even a father-to-be as well as CEO of Cohen's.

You are now over one quarter of the way to claiming the inheritance we have left for either you or your mother. We hope that you use this money wisely and remember that the lives of others are not always what they appear from the outside. Take care of your family, Luke, and know that however you use this money, we will approve if it comes from a place of love and caring.

As for your marriage, trust us when we tell you that the honeymoon will soon wear off, but that true love is patient and kind, and only strengthens over time. Trust your partner and show her you care. Every day.

We believe there is a strength and power in working with the person you love, and we hope that you and your new wife are experiencing it in its full glory. We also hope that you will continue to allow your wife to help lead you and your life. We feel that Cohen's has bankrupted itself on some levels by shutting out your mother's voice. When you bring a smart woman to the board table it always expands the thinking and vision of a company. We hope you don't feel we are backwards or close-minded in saying that women are different. They deserve to be treated equally, and you should always demand that they receive the same pay and respect, Luke. But also know that they deal with different expectations from family, friends and society. They don't have that same instinct to kill and destroy like most men you'll find in the boardroom. They have a softer, more caring and nurturing side that can save a company from itself. They can also see things most men can't, or won't. Women know markets in a different way; they know how to communicate and reach others. They also carry a greater burden than men, and your expectations should be different when it comes to how they approach things. We expect them to be caregivers and always have it together, even for us sometimes. They have to be strong, but gentle, not overbearing or overpowering. Many carry this burden with a grace we men will rarely find. Be there for your wife as she travels this road.

With Cohen's primary market being women, we are proud that you have chosen to work with the woman you love at your side, and we hope and pray that you're listening to her as an equal. From a partnership borne of mutual respect, caring and consideration, the two of you will go far. Not just monetarily, but spiritually as well.

We hope that each of you holds everything the other needs.

We are confident you are well on your way to becoming the man we always saw in you. Be kind, resourceful, protective, strong, compassionate, patient, respectful, and to borrow from the Jewish language, every bit a mensch—a man of integrity and honor.

With love and respect,

Your grandparents

LUKE FOLDED UP THE LETTER, a mix of grief, hope and disappointment in himself whirling inside.

He was not a mensch. He was a lying, scheming, deceptive schmuck and not the man his grandmother had hoped he would become. He hadn't even made time for the kid he was supposed to be mentoring.

As for having Emma at the boardroom table—the kitchen table in their case—she did bring a different perspective, but so far he hadn't listened to it. She'd hired him to make the calls and he had been doing so. But since his return from South Carolina she'd been pushing back, arguing her beliefs with more conviction. Was that a sign he wasn't listening with respect and patience, like his grandparents suggested in their letter?

If so, what had he missed while not listening?

She kept telling him his new video ideas weren't giving her the interactions she used to enjoy with her viewers. But of course not; they were changing the focus to marketing.

She kept telling him to win over the town. But he didn't have time to become best friends with everyone.

Luke tucked the letter inside his winter jacket.

If he failed, both he and Emma would lose everything. Emma was trusting his expertise and that's what they had to lean on at the end of the day.

And yet he couldn't help but wonder if there was something in that letter that might serve as a clue as to why things didn't seem as easy with Emma since he'd been away.

EMMA DRANK a big glass of water and threw another log on the fire and rubbed a hand through her short, dark hair. It felt liberating to be free of her wig for the day, since Luke had slipped out at dawn for a meeting a few hours away in the city of Dakota with Haddie. Always Haddie. That woman was up to something, Emma could feel it.

She needed to keep focusing on her work, not the way things between her and Luke had fizzled despite the current that still surged between them. Emma knew she was being foolish holding him at bay, and yet the courage she needed to talk to him and sort out their relationship kept dancing out of reach. It was like a deep-rooted sense of self-preservation was trying to save her and the project from a big meltdown fight, because she couldn't test the larger mass-production system he'd set up in the old warehouse down by the river on her own. She needed him.

But was there something going on between him and Haddie?

There were late-night texts and emails. And then this morning he'd looked freaked out, as if he was hiding something, before bolting to go see Haddie.

Knowing she wasn't ever going to figure it out, at least not today, Emma yawned and pulled a throw blanket around her shoulders. She poured herself a cup of coffee and sat in front of the fireplace, mindlessly watching the flames, enjoying the peaceful silence.

As soon as Luke's truck had vanished down the driveway, she'd gently washed Cousin Itt, setting him on a form to dry. Then she'd washed her real hair, enjoying the feeling of having her fingers massaging her scalp without the wig in the way. By the time Luke returned, it would be dry and pinned back in place. But in the meantime…freedom.

Freedom from her hair. Freedom from the tension that had settled between her and Luke, neither of them willing to make a move.

Emma finished her coffee, then checked on her still damp wig before inspecting her real hair in the mirror. It was so much darker, thinner. It was getting better, thicker, and she experimented with twirling a few short pieces, trying to make it look spiky and cool, then flattened them with a palm before giving up. When it got longer and thicker she'd go to a salon, but right now it was hopeless. And she had a video blog to save.

After pulling out her brainstorming notepad she rolled her pen between her hands and began writing down various possible dialogue bits, as well as shots. It all felt trite. Fake. Boring.

She ripped out the page, tossed it into the fire, then started jotting down ideas of things that would be fun to watch. Before long she was engrossed, barely noticing when the front door opened.

Without looking up, she said, "What if we did some videos showing our customers where the valerian and other ingredients are grown? Not like the one I tried to shoot back in January about the location, but something more professional. A mini documentary almost that shows them the meadows, greenhouses, and people hand-crushing the leaves. You know, prove it's real and grown in a real place. No additives."

She didn't hear the door shut or a reply, and she looked up, expecting it to be the silent Pete Lunn and not her business partner. But it was Luke. He was standing a foot inside the cabin, staring at her in shock. His eyes flew around the room.

"What happened?" he asked breathlessly. "Are you okay?"

"What?" She stood, alarm rocketing through her. "What's wrong?"

He was at her side in a flash, his coat bringing cold with it from the outdoors, his freezing hands framing her face. Emma realized with gut-wrenching despair that Cousin Itt was still on his form. Luke was staring at her real hair. Her ugly, useless, limp strands that wouldn't hold a style for the life of her.

She reached for her head, trying to cover it with her hands as she backed away. He pursued her, not releasing her, not allowing her to get more than a step away from him.

"Em...Em..." He was using a gentle voice one would use to quiet a caged animal.

"Don't look at me." Her own voice was trembling and all she could think of was his shocked expression. Vaughn's disgust. "Please."

She was begging him, tears streaking down her face. She struggled to escape, but Luke's arms wrapped around her, hauling her against his body. He was still using that soft tone and it was scaring her.

She didn't want his pity; it was worse than disgust.

"Look at me." He turned her in his arms and she complied reluctantly.

He tenderly tipped her head up, crouching slightly so they were eye to eye. He was studying her, but not her hair. Her face.

His expression wasn't what she expected. It was understanding, kind.

"Em. You're beautiful."

Her chest felt like someone was slowly winching the pickup truck over it.

"Look at me," he repeated, when she cast her eyes downward, not wanting to believe there was any truth to his words. She wasn't even wearing makeup today. She was still in her pajamas and looked horrific. She'd seen herself in the mirror and knew he was lying. A man like Luke could have any woman and there was no reason to choose her, not when he could now see the truth of who she was.

She felt a heartbroken sob bubble up in her chest, too big for the space, expanding her lungs in a way that seared her soul.

"Emma, to me, you are the most beautiful thing."

She couldn't figure out his game, but knew he had to be lying. She just couldn't grasp why.

LAST NIGHT LUKE had felt as though he was finally getting it right. He'd taken his wife to bed, this time making love. It wasn't just sex, but so much more. A certain something that caused a lump to form in his throat whenever he thought about it and the way he'd felt moving with her. Connected. Vulnerable.

It had been scary, and yet he'd felt safe. He trusted her, she trusted him, and their moment together was something he knew would never be repeated. The emotion, the trust. Everything. It was unlike anything else he'd ever experienced.

He rubbed his eyes and sifted through the mail Emma had stacked on the counter. They'd been up until the wee hours of the morning, hashing out everything from their relationship to their launch and staff, to her videos, which would revert back to their original, casual format.

They were a team.

A really good one.

And maybe closer to the kind his grandparents had wished for on his behalf.

Knowing Emma was in their once-again-shared bed, warm and welcoming…he was tempted to join her. Although then they wouldn't be sleeping.

He found himself smiling. There was something special about being out in a remote cabin with a beautiful woman all winter, wasn't there?

He was feeling sappy. Was that love? If so, he'd never experienced anything like it before.

He wanted to take care of Emma. He wanted to solve her problems and make her feel every bit as beautiful as he thought she was. He knew her hair was a confidence blocker and an identity issue, so he figured why not throw some money at the situation and see what happened?

After propping his laptop on the kitchen counter, he began making an oven omelet while researching endocrinologists, dermatologists and oncologists who focused on helping patients overcome hair loss. As he waited for the stove to reach temperature, he scanned an online article, while ripping the end off a large brown envelope with his name on it. No postage. No return address.

He put the omelet in the oven when it beeped, tapped his touch screen to make sure his laptop didn't go to sleep, then pulled a stack of papers out of the opened envelope, which he dropped on the chipped kitchen counter—into a puddle of spilled coffee. Luke pushed the envelope out of the liquid and sighed. More documents. It seemed all he did these days was read, amend, reread, then sign them.

His gaze drifted toward the closed bedroom door. Maybe Emma would like a cup of coffee delivered to her in bed. And then maybe need someone to help her stay warm. They could take the morning off...continue to catch up on a few more *personal* matters.

The documents in his hand slipped, due to glossy photos clipped between the pages. He glanced at the covering letter as he adjusted his grip to fan through the attached photo sheets, instantly recognizing who the package was from. The blackmailer.

His blood ran cold.

Zach was supposed to be on top of this.

"What's that?" Emma asked sleepily as she entered the room. She was wearing her wig again, acting as if he hadn't told her she was beautiful without it. What was it going to take to have her believe him?

"Luke?"

He was inexplicably angry. At her. At the blackmailer. Even at the oven, which was still cooking his breakfast.

Luke felt as if he'd stopped breathing, words caught in his throat by the anger. He stuffed the papers back in the envelope. "I made coffee. You look like you could use some."

"What are you reading?" She turned the laptop to see the screen better.

"I was looking into stuff for you."

"I've already seen an oncologist." Her voice was thick with something he couldn't identify.

"I know, but sometimes if you throw some money at a problem it helps. I was thinking I'd call this guy, and next time I head home you could come along and see him. He's only an hour from my penthouse."

Her face was flushed.

"What?" he asked.

"Nothing," she said tightly.

"I know this bugs you and I want to fix it for you." He pulled her into his arms and she complied, but didn't soften, didn't curl into him like she normally did. "Is that okay?"

He glanced at her expression. Apparently it wasn't.

"You said it doesn't matter," he murmured.

"It doesn't. Not to me."

She gave him a dark look and he dropped his arms, freeing her from his embrace.

"It's obviously a big deal to you. You came out here wearing The Addams Family or whatever you call it."

Her expression turned darker at his mention of her wig's pet name.

Women were confusing.

"Just know that I think you're gorgeous bald, short-haired or whatever." He kissed the top of her head, feeling like he wasn't actually kissing *her*.

"Sorry. I'm just…" She gave her head a shake, then poured herself a coffee. "Sorry. Anything good in the mail?" She turned to the stack.

Before she could touch the envelope from the blackmailer, Luke scooped it up and headed for the front door. "I need to make a call."

"To a reporter?"

He heard the tone in her voice. He knew she thought he was calling Haddie, and that there was a sense of rivalry there or something similar.

"Possible investment." He hated lying and felt like a heel for it, but he needed to protect her from that part of his life. She'd revealed so much, been brave and trusted him.

And he wasn't man enough to return the favor.

Not a mensch, that was for certain.

"Luke?"

He turned slowly, feeling like a kid busted with chocolate all over his face, but professing his innocence on a chocolate bar's disappearance. She waved his phone. "If you're making a call…" She gave him a laughing smile.

"Right. Thanks." He took the phone, barely able to meet

her eyes.

"Luke?"

He hesitated, making sure his expression was calm before facing her again.

"It's freezing out there. You might want a coat."

He pulled his parka off the hook near the door and threw it on, stepped out, then closed the door behind him as he stared up at the jagged mountains surrounding the cabin. The air was crisp, fresh. Punishing. And exactly what he deserved.

Knowing Emma might be watching, he lifted his phone to his ear, talking nonsense into it. In his other hand the envelope felt heavy. He'd seen the amount listed on the letter. It was what was in his emergency fund and more.

He lowered his phone and pulled the documents from the envelope, his hands aching with the cold.

Luke slowly let out a breath, hoping the photos were of something as innocent as he and Emma pausing to kiss while snowshoeing. That would be easy. He'd reveal the marriage and not pay up. Yes, he'd married her, fallen in love with her. And to make his mother happy, they would be holding a reception at the Portia House in August. Simple.

The only downside would be that Cohen's stock would fall if anything else bad happened to Carrington.

Luke flipped to the stack of eight-by-eleven photos, nearly dropping them along with his forgotten phone.

The enlarged snapshots were of a slightly younger Emma, and he was most certainly not in any of them.

They were seductive, the lighting dusky and sensual, as was the look in her heavy gaze. Her makeup was smoky and thick, unlike anything pure and innocent Carrington carried. The photos weren't indecent. Not quite. She was covered in all of them either by a hand or a flimsy bit of lace. They were erotic and with a sole intent to stimulate a man, to awaken him.

They were working.

But they were of his wife. Photos that should be for his eyes only, and he hadn't even known about them.

His Emma.

He wanted to shout, demand an answer from her.

He read the letter. Pay up or the images would be splashed across the world, tainting the sweet Carrington Cares marketing campaign Emma had started with a focus on healthy, innocent tweens.

But these photos? If he was a parent he wouldn't want his daughter emulating Emma. Not the one photographed here.

He flipped through the stack again, unsure what to do. The last picture, which he'd missed the first time, was of him and Emma, shoulder to shoulder, laughing. It wasn't professionally taken and it was grainy, as though taken from a great distance. He wasn't sure where or when the photo had been snapped, but it showed how close the two of them had become. There was also a date handwritten on the bottom. The date of their wedding.

Just like in skating, if one fell, they fell together, but this time neither of them would be laughing.

Luke stared out at the woods, his breath causing clouds of condensation in front of him.

Letting the world know they were married? Not a big deal. He'd say with pride that she was his wife.

But Emma wouldn't want these photos out in the world. In one swoop they could decimate the Carrington image the company had spent years cultivating.

Luke picked up the stack of prints again, pausing at a shot of Emma that had been taken upside down. His wife was on her back, her teddy dipping low, her eyes meeting the camera, a wide expanse of her chest and neck exposed. He knew that look in her eyes and it was inviting.

A look he didn't want anyone but himself to receive.

He flipped the picture over, slowed his breathing. Why had she allowed these to be taken? They had to be private. Personal.

Luke picked up his phone and texted Zach, sending him on Vaughn's tail.

Emma wouldn't want these out there. *He* didn't want them out there. And he sure didn't want other men reacting the way he was.

He stuffed the photos back in the envelope, knowing he couldn't take them to her, as the letter made it obvious this wasn't the only thing Luke was being blackmailed for.

He would take care of this for her. He could protect her. She'd been through enough, first with her illness and the backlash against the company, then fighting for this product line. Add in dealing with her hair and her jealous sister... Emma didn't need the humiliation of these photos on top of it all.

She was his wife, and, if he had to, he would pay these jerks off if it took every last dime he owned.

***

EMMA CLUTCHED her cup of coffee and watched Luke through the kitchen window, which overlooked the front porch. He was out there freezing his butt off, moving like an agitated tiger, his head surrounded by a fog of warm air streaming from his mouth.

Why had he taken the call outside if it was for an investor? What was in the large envelope? And why was he still out there now that he was off the phone?

In other words, what was he hiding?

She wanted to trust him, but he kept giving her reasons not to. For example, last night he'd seemed so sincere when he'd told her he thought she was pretty with her short hair. But when she'd come into the kitchen this morning he'd practically already made her an appointment with a specialist—even though she'd already told him the doctors said her body just needed time. That didn't show he was fine with it. Her lungs had shut down faster than if she'd walked out in subarctic temperatures and taken a deep breath.

She sipped her coffee, trying to clear her mind while struggling not to obsess about Luke. It was what it was right now, and she would bend herself into a pretzel if she kept it up.

He came in, the door banging shut behind him, sending a chunk of snow off the roof. Through the window she saw it fall, landing with a soft thump on the growing pile just beyond the porch railing.

Luke, moving with purpose, brushed past the table.

"Good call?" she asked mildly.

"What?" He was clutching the envelope like a lifeline.

Emma took another sip of her cooling coffee, eyeing him carefully. He closed himself in the bathroom, reemerging moments later, his hair combed, face washed. "I'm heading to the city. Are you okay if I take the truck?"

"Of course." *The city.* Haddie. Cymbals crashed in Emma's brain and a piano played some deep, ominous notes. Stupid brain, assuming the worst. "What's up?"

"Just something I have to take care of."

Something he obviously didn't plan on sharing with her.

"Maybe I can help?"

"It's complicated."

She felt the sting of his rejection, the slice of the knife and the squeeze of lemon in the wound. She pasted a fake smile in place to hide her feelings, knowing she was likely overreacting.

"I can handle complicated." The one thing about Luke was that he usually made her feel like a real partner. Not someone he couldn't explain complicated things to.

He continued getting ready. Wallet. Coat. Keys. All the while avoiding eye contact.

"You ever wonder if something you once thought was a good idea..." He clamped his mouth shut, his expression softening slightly as he regarded her. "It doesn't matter. What's done is done. I'm going to take care of things."

"Of what?"

"Don't worry your pretty little head over it."

Another squeeze of lemon in that wound.

"I thought we were partners." She was stumbling over her words, her heart racing. "I thought we shared everything."

He looked up, watching her closely. "Do we?"

Emma hesitated, toying with her gold bracelet. "I trust you." She hated the way that came out like a question.

"I'll be back by suppertime. Hold down the fort for me."

He gave her a quick peck on the lips.

"Hey, before I forget," Emma said quickly, wanting him to leave on an upbeat note instead of in a stressed-out state. "Jen Kulak, the local guide, said the frozen lakes are perfect for a little skiing, and I thought I'd buy us some cross-country skis. Maybe mix up our outdoor breaks a bit."

"We need to focus on work, not play," Luke said curtly.

"Right, but I thought…"

"Emma, it can't all be playtime. There's a lot at stake and we really need to stay on top of this image change for your company."

He closed the door behind him without a goodbye.

Emma breathed out slowly, trying not to take his mood personally. He was under a lot of stress. It wasn't about her. She knew that.

But it felt like it was.

She quickly brushed her tears away as the front door opened again a few minutes later.

"Luke, I'm sorry. I—"

It was her sister, who looked back through the open door before she closed it. "He barely even said hi before he ran off, muttering something about investments. Was there a market crash I didn't hear about or are you two fighting?"

"We're working together and living under a tiny roof, so of course we're fighting." Emma felt the front of her wig, making sure it was properly hiding her real hair, and cleared away her empty cup, wishing there was more for her to clean up to keep her busy.

"I'm sorry," Olivia said, catching sight of her expression.

"Well, you should be."

"I was going to invite you both out to go ice fishing with us, as I heard Luke was pretty handy at it and I know he likes fishing."

"He's not yours any longer," Emma snapped.

"I didn't say he was…" Olivia was watching her carefully. "I'm sorry if I've been acting weird lately. It's…never mind. I don't want to fight."

"I just…I just want a beach somewhere with someone bringing me drinks. Not…not *this!*"

"I thought everything was going well," her sister said cautiously. "That you two were a good team?"

"What if Carrington's image doesn't improve, Ovvy? What if…" She caught herself reaching for her wig again and stopped herself. "What if Luke is just here for the money and there isn't any?" What if she failed? What if they both lost everything?

What if he was mad because she'd screwed up something big last week, and now he had to go fix it, rescue her, but didn't want to worry her about it, didn't trust her with it?

Man, her brain had out its biggest boxing gloves and was ready to defeat every bit of mental fortitude and confidence she had today.

"I'm stuck out here trying to make this stupid dream of yours come true," Emma muttered defensively.

Olivia blinked as though startled. "I thought you wanted this?"

"Just leave me alone so I can forget this whole reality exists." Emma strode to her bedroom and crashed under the covers, which smelled like Luke's delicious cologne.

She felt the edge of the bed sag as her pregnant sister sat

beside her. Emma had no doubt she was noticing Luke's clothing and personal effects in the shared bedroom. Items that had once been in the living room, but had gradually moved in over the weeks.

"Are you okay?"

"No," Emma snapped, tossing the cover down so she could see her sister. She looked beautiful with her light hair swept up in a bun, her cheeks flushed from her pregnancy. Not like Emma. She looked pale and her wig was itchy.

Plus she wanted to have a pity party and her sister was interfering.

"You know why I went back to school? Why I'm trying dressmaking?"

Who cared? She'd left Emma with a mess that nobody thought she could handle. Not even Luke.

"Because I know you're the one woman who can really make this product what it needs to be."

"Liar."

"You're smart and tenacious. People like you. If anyone's going to get the world to forgive the company, it's you."

Emma was tempted to yank off her wig and show her the exact reason nobody should forgive Carrington.

"You can do this," Olivia coaxed gently.

"No, actually, I can't," she replied primly. "But thanks for the vote."

They were quiet for a moment and Emma felt herself forgiving her sister. As always. She wanted to stay mad this time, though. All the way mad. Like up to her eyeballs. Not drift away from anger and act like all was okay and forgiven, but still have a ball of it stewing inside. Growing and growing. Ready to explode.

"Are you and Luke okay? As friends," Olivia added awkwardly.

"Yeah, we're *friends*," she said, surprised by the bitterness in her voice.

"I know you've always had a crush on him. That you stepped

aside when…you know." She broke off awkwardly, both sisters knowing she was referring to the day she'd informed Emma that there was a Plan with a capital P in place for her and Luke, and that Emma and her fancies could take a hike. Well, she'd been nicer about it, but that had been the essence of the conversation.

"Olivia…" Emma warned. She didn't want to talk about her feelings. If she did she might learn just how deep their taproot went and how far out the rest of the root system had spread.

She ducked her head back under the blankets.

"I'm just saying," Olivia said softly, her voice slightly thick, "that if you're worried about me…don't be."

"Why would I worry about you and your perfect life?" Emma said, purposefully misinterpreting what her sister was saying about Luke being fair game. She peeked out from under the covers when Olivia remained silent.

The sisters shared a look, the tension between them slowly easing.

"Want to feel the baby move?"

Emma nodded silently. Olivia directed her hand on her shifting belly. Movement was everywhere.

"Is it a girl?" Emma asked.

"It's a secret."

She groaned. "I hate secrets."

Olivia laughed and the baby moved again. Emma withdrew her hand.

"Luke is a wonderful man," Olivia said quietly.

"I *know* that."

"And he's different around you. Even better."

"That's because his pretense doesn't go very far in Blueberry Springs."

"Don't discount his actions. You guys are good together." Olivia swung her legs up onto the bed so she could lie down beside Emma. She groaned, one hand on her very pregnant belly. Only a month to go.

She inhaled deeply, her expression suggesting she was putting two and two together as she cast a glance around the room, her gaze flitting like a butterfly from item to item—all of which belonged to Luke.

"Don't," Emma said, knowing her sister would understand what she was asking her not to say. They'd never been super close like some sisters, but they'd been through enough to read each fairly well.

"I wasn't going to say a thing," Olivia said with a growing smile.

"Good."

Her sister's voice was soft, full of delight and humor as she added, "Especially about the fact that the bed smells like Luke's cologne."

Emma sighed heavily.

"If this is what I think it is, hold on to him."

The connection she'd had with Luke had once felt close to something real, something precious, but now she wasn't so sure. Still, she found herself wishing that their relationship was exactly what her sister thought it might be.

LUKE HAD MESSED UP. He'd been condescending to Emma, but what was he supposed to do? Tell her it was all going to be okay and that her past actions weren't going to ruin their launch? She'd hired him to take care of things, and if anyone released those pictures they'd defeat the pure and innocent image of Carrington at a time when they needed it most.

After leaving the cabin, he'd sped all the way to Dakota, parking the truck abruptly in front of the first bank he'd seen. He'd strode to the first available teller and cashed in every investment in his emergency account, and when the bank couldn't fulfill the entire cash order, he'd moved to the next branch, on and on through the city until his duffle bag was full, the banks depleted of cash, a new loan for the remaining balance secured.

It had hurt. A lot. But his emergency fund was the only account he could access such an amount from at short notice. There was no other choice. He had to protect himself. He had to protect Emma.

Now, as he sat in his truck watching the noon traffic roll by, it was all he could do to shut out the memory of the late night sounds of homeless shelters. The insecurity of not knowing whether you'd have a bed that night.

He was an adult and there was no safety net besides one of his own making.

Luke made sure his doors were locked, and he checked his side mirrors. Having a few million in cash waiting in the backseat was making him nervous.

He tapped the steering wheel with a finger. Now what?

He flipped down his shades as the sun came out from behind a low, gray cloud, giving the snowy city a blinding brightness. Luke squeezed the steering wheel, then started the engine.

Knuckles rapped the window at his side and he jumped, banging his knees. He got himself under control again and pushed back in the seat, letting the window down for Logan.

"Hey," the bodyguard said casually, resting an arm on the sill. He scratched at the edge of his black skullcap with his other thumb, looking like a bouncer in the puffy black ski jacket and cap. Either that or a thug.

"What's up?" Logan asked.

"Nothing."

"Yeah?" The man's voice lifted in obvious disbelief.

"Yeah," Luke said softly.

"Not sure I would recommend that line of action, mate," Logan said offhandedly, his Australian accent thick.

"Which one is that?"

Logan leveled a stare. "This won't make them go away."

"We'll see, won't we?" He put the truck in gear.

"The people who sent the photos mean business."

"The photos?"

"The contents of the envelope you were clutching on your porch earlier this morning."

"You were spying on me?"

"You pay me to, pal."

"I told Zach I don't need a shadow any longer."

Logan studied him for a long minute. "Huh." He removed his arm from the truck's window. "I never received that message."

Luke dragged a hand down his face and rubbed his chin, considering his options. He carefully put the engine back in Park. "Well, maybe it's good you're here. I'm being blackmailed."

"Different from earlier?"

"Same guy. Different problem."

"Got this morning's envelope with you?"

Luke reached for it, then thought better of it. He didn't want to share the photos of his wife with another man. He didn't think he could handle the reaction, nor exposing her that way.

"Let's just say they're private."

Logan's lips curved into a sly smile. "Sent some skin pics to a sheila and now she wants a piece of the ol' pie since you're looking like you might hit pay dirt, eh?"

"They're of Emma."

Logan's expression became stern, hard. A little bit scary, quite frankly.

"How much do they want? Are there any negatives? Digital? How can you guarantee there aren't copies? It doesn't matter," he added, with a slice of his black-gloved hand. "I'll put Zach on it 24/7 until we hit a homer."

Logan pushed away from the truck. "Go home, stay close to her. I'll have something by tonight."

Luke just hoped that was soon enough.

8

*E*mma kept pace with her animated protégée, Keisha, who was skipping along beside her in the snow as she described her school day. Her pink mittens were a blur as she illustrated the story of how she'd won a game against one of the toughest boys in gym class.

"Wow," Emma said, directing her down the sidewalk. There was a brisk wind rolling off the mountains and she feared the small girl would have frostbite by the time they reached their destination—Mandy's café for a hot chocolate and a chat, before hitting the library to choose some new books to sign out for the week. So far the girl was kicking Emma's butt on their reading challenge.

"It felt so good," Keisha said, her eyes gleaming as she mentally relived her moment of phys ed glory.

Along the sidewalk vehicles were idling to keep their interiors warm, and Emma tried to hustle the girl out of the clouds of exhaust, directing her to where they could cross the street. A truck pulled up as they neared the crosswalk, blocking it. Keisha stepped off the curb to squeeze between the vehicles.

"No," Emma said, drawing her back onto the curb. "It's not

safe to go between the cars. Drivers can't see you and the roads are icy."

The man in the truck had his window down despite the cold, and Emma told him, "You can't park here. You're blocking the crosswalk."

"Your husband pays bribes."

"Please move your truck. Someone's going to get run over."

"Your husband pays well, too."

The man's tone sent a chill down Emma's spine despite the warmth of her parka.

Luke's earlier mood.

His secrecy.

His sudden need to leave town for a meeting.

It all led to this, didn't it? To the message this man was delivering—a message she didn't like, because there was no denying he knew who Emma and Luke were.

She gave the girl beside her a quick glance, worried about where this conversation might wind up.

"You must have my *business* partner mixed up with someone else," she said firmly.

"Tell your husband to pay," the man replied just as firmly, "or I'll get creative."

"I don't understand."

He gave her and the girl a meaningful look that made Emma panic inside and draw Keisha behind her.

"I see we speak the same language," he said, pulling away. He called out as his window began to slide up, "I have to move along. This isn't a good place to park."

"I don't like him," said the small girl.

Emma clutched Keisha's hand the best she could despite their bulky mittens. "Me neither. Always listen to your gut when it comes to people, okay, Keisha?"

Emma hadn't when it came to the way Vaughn treated her and had spent way too much of her life trailing after him, trying to stay on his radar. She knew now that a man who truly loved her would have kept her at his side without her needing to constantly beg and preen.

"Always, Keisha."

She dropped the girl's hand as she realized the truck was getting away. She fumbled through her large coat pockets for her phone. She needed to take a photo of the license plate, but she was already too late. The truck turned a corner, out of sight.

"Do you know who that was?" Emma asked.

Keisha shook her head.

"Recognize the truck?"

The girl gave a thoughtful pause, then asked, "You're married?"

Emma sighed. "Let's go to Mandy's and get some hot chocolate and a brownie."

Luke was going to have to provide her with some serious answers when he got home.

"What do you mean, some guy threatened you?" Luke knew his voice was too loud, his reaction too stressed. He could tell by the way Emma cringed and stepped back.

He pinched the bridge of his nose, inhaling slowly, struggling for control over his fear. He felt like he was on the brink of losing everything.

Every. Thing.

"I'm sorry," he said carefully. "There's a lot going on right now. Are you sure that's what he said?"

Tell him to pay, or I'll get creative.

There was no positive way to interpret that.

They'd found Emma, were closing in and making threats. His father was not taking care of this, and his problem was now officially Luke's. He couldn't go to the police about the photos without it coming to light that Cohen's had paid what could definitely be interpreted as a bribe to get around packaging laws.

There was only one thing to do, because waiting for more intel was no longer an option.

"I have to go."

"Luke…"

He closed the cabin door behind him, then thought better of it and opened it again. "Don't go anywhere. Don't let anyone in. I'm going to ask Logan to put a patrol car outside."

"Ginger's husband?"

But what if he needed Logan as backup?

"Okay, the police. Someone. Anyone."

Out in his truck, Luke sped down the slick hill, connecting his phone through Bluetooth to Logan.

"Nothing yet," the bodyguard said as soon as he picked up.

"I need to make a deposit. And I need you there watching my back."

Luke heard him inhale. "Let's take things slow and think—"

"They threatened Emma today. She was with Keisha."

Logan cursed quietly.

"It's time to shut this down."

"You're the boss, but I advise you to speak with Zach first. Come up with a plan that will keep everyone safe."

"This will keep everyone I care about safe." Luke disconnected the call and immediately dialed Scott Malone, the local police officer. "Scott, I need a patrol car up at the cabin."

"What's wrong?" He was immediately alert.

"A man threatened Emma outside the elementary school today. I need someone watching her."

"Where are you?"

"I have a meeting."

"A meeting?"

"It's important."

"More important than being with your wife and keeping her safe?"

"*My wife?*"

"I might be small-town, but I know things, Luke."

"Logan?"

"What about him?"

"Did he tell you?"

"It's called a database. I run all out-of-towners through it, and from what I've seen, you like to try and talk your way out of traffic infringements."

"Right. Sorry." Luke rubbed his chin. "Can you send a car? I'm trying to get to the bottom of this."

"Why not let me?" Scott said quietly.

"I'm sorry, I can't." Luke hung up, then pulled out the phone number on the letter in the big brown envelope as he maneuvered the steep mountain road. "I'm ready to pay. Tell me where to meet you."

EMMA COULDN'T HELP but feel as though she'd done something wrong. She didn't know how else to explain the sudden change in Luke.

And the threat. What had that been about?

She shivered and hugged herself. Luke had been gone for a half an hour and all she'd done was pace and try to sort things out in her head.

She needed to do something productive beyond what she'd done already, which was lock the door and tell Keisha's parents about the threat in case something came of it all.

Sitting down at the old desk Emma used as a makeshift vanity, she propped her phone on a stack of paperbacks and hit Record. She stared at the screen for a moment, tempted to rip her wig off and reveal everything. Which was ridiculous, and certain to be utterly defeating.

She took a deep breath and began talking about fashion and makeup. She explained how to make a simple outfit look dressed up or down, using her own dark jeans and fitted sweater as an example.

She chatted about which Carrington eye shadow she preferred for which looks, and ended the video with a bit on accessories. It had run long and she thought she might edit it into a three-part series. But then she wouldn't be talking about the makeup in each segment. And while she had the go-ahead from Luke to skip the product placements, she understood where he'd been coming from.

Luke. What was going on with him? Was he even safe?

Emma dropped her head in her hands and, for the first time since arriving in Blueberry Springs, wished the entire project was done and over so she could go home and back to her old life.

The sound of a vehicle coming up the driveway distracted her and she hurried to the door, pulling it open before remembering Luke's warning not to answer it.

The vehicle was a police truck.

"Hi, Miss Carrington. Just making sure things are okay up here."

It was Officer Malone, looking uncomfortable.

"Fine, thanks."

"Luke asked me to watch the place, so I'll be sitting out here tonight."

"That sounds cold. Do you know what's going on?" she asked.

"I heard you were threatened, and there's concern that it might be… Would you like to make a statement?"

"I don't have a lot of info…but sure. In case." She thought of Keisha, so young and trusting, and what the man in the truck had said about Luke. It was deep, whatever it was, but it seemed that whenever she looked for answers, all she found was more questions.

LUKE FOLLOWED his GPS directions to the drop location in the city of Dakota, a few hours from Blueberry Springs. He weaved through the late afternoon traffic, slowly drawing closer.

His phone rang, going through to the truck's speakers thanks to Bluetooth.

"Hello, Luke here."

"Luke, honey."

"Mom. Nice to hear from you." Just not right now.

"I left your father."

The truck swerved as Luke processed the unexpected news, and he corrected before he hit a lamppost.

"Luke?"

"Mom, are you sure?" Despite his years of prompting, he hadn't seen this coming.

"You said anytime I wanted out..." Her voice was quiet from shame, but there was a hint of something else there, too. Something that sounded like anger—anger at Luke.

"I promised to set you up. I know, Mom. I haven't forgotten." He pushed a hand through his hair. He was thousands of miles away, and the money he'd promised her was about to be handed over in exchange for silence. "What do you need?"

"I signed the papers on a penthouse in the building a block from yours and used the card to withdraw the first installment— that card you gave me during your visit. The transaction bounced."

That card took money from an account he'd just drained.

"Mom? Why didn't you warn me first?"

"You said there was enough, and that I could count on it

because you would never touch it." Her voice was getting louder. She wasn't one to shout, but she was nearly there.

"I was shifting investments today." Not a complete lie, but it burned his gut just the same.

"You don't know how humiliating it was." Her voice was trembling with emotion. He could just imagine. His mother had finally found the courage to leave, and went through all the work and effort of finding a place, proving to the world and herself that she could do this, and there was no money in the account.

"I am so sorry, Mom. I'll fix it. You can stay with Cash at my penthouse tonight."

"I have twenty-four hours or it goes back on the market and I lose my deposit."

"You had a deposit?"

"I took it out last week."

Luke scowled. That made no sense. The amount he'd withdrawn was the same amount he'd expected to be in there.

"Where did the deposit come from?"

"I made a quick turnaround investment that paid off handsomely, so I repaid your account and used the profit for my down payment."

"You invest?"

"I have nowhere to live. I was so embarrassed, Luke."

"I know, Mom. I'm sorry."

"I need you here."

"Maybe I can…" What? Fly out there? He had to fix things with Emma first or there would be nothing to return to. "Maybe I can fly home tonight. I'll take the red-eye," he said, making up his mind.

His mom let out a sob and Luke had to pull over as visions of the homeless shelter flashed through his mind. The only time he'd ever seen her cry was when men had tried to sidle up to her, making offers that even he'd understood at the innocent age of nine.

"I'm so tired of it all, Luke," she said, her voice tight with tears. "I told your father and I just…"

"I'll wire you money as soon as I'm out of this meeting I'm about to go into, okay? Enough for your down payment." He'd go into overdraft, arrange for another loan. He couldn't leave his mom destitute. Not when she'd taken such a big risk in leaving.

Charlotte's voice was thick with relief as she ended the call and Luke took a moment to collect himself. Then he slammed the steering wheel and pulled away from the curb, trying to deal with one problem at a time so he didn't do something stupid like steer his truck into a concrete divider.

The streets were quiet in this part of the city, discount liquidators boarded up, distribution centers with broken windows, everything reeking of decay.

He was pretty sure he'd seen Logan tailing him earlier, but he wasn't sure how the man was going to follow him here and act as backup without being noticed. It was like an eerie, empty scene from a post-apocalyptic movie.

Luke drove the truck through the opening in a sagging chain-link fence and up to building 681.

He couldn't believe his life had brought him here. He was going to hand over his safety net to some creep who wanted to tarnish Emma's reputation, her world, her business. Money his mother had been counting on. Cash he was now going to have to borrow in order to fulfill his promises.

His mom hadn't been able to save up because his dad controlled everything.

This was why Luke wasn't married. It was this kind of crap that messed up lives.

He let out a choked laugh.

He *was* married. To a very nice woman.

A woman who'd kept numerous secrets from him and had him currently preparing to pay off the scum of the earth with a bagful of cash.

He was a fool, Luke thought with a shake of his head. At least they'd signed a prenuptial agreement, so she couldn't take everything when she left him at the end of their agreement. Or sooner, at the rate things were going.

He parked the truck. Today sucked.

Really, really sucked.

He got out of the vehicle and looked around, keeping a grip on the door handle. He didn't see Logan and the area was quiet, with just dried leaves skittering over the dirty snow that had drifted here and there, leaving most of the pavement clear. The wind was brisk and Luke's eyes teared up at the sudden change from warm truck to unforgiving winter.

A man stepped out of a metal shed. Luke didn't recognize him, and he tried to think of something remarkable about his appearance that he could use later to describe him to the police in case Logan didn't get a chance to snag him.

"You got the money?" the guy asked, his voice rough and deep.

Luke went to the back door of the truck, and found the man was quick. A second later he was at Luke's side, a gun muzzle pressed against his temple.

Luke sure could use Logan right about now.

He froze for a long moment, waiting for Logan to do something.

Nothing.

"Just getting the bag," Luke said, careful not to move too quickly.

The fellow was shifty, his eyes darting. He reeked of alcohol and desperation. This guy was going to blow through Luke's hard-earned money. He was going to live the life, enjoy the cash Luke had put away for his retirement, his mom and his future kids' trust funds.

It wasn't right. It wasn't fair.

This money should go to the people who mattered to him, not some thug who was likely to use it on hookers and blow.

"You're the blackmailer?" Luke asked.

"I run errands." The gun twitched against Luke's cheek. "For a nice fee, 'cause I don't mind getting my hands dirty." He winked in Luke's direction, his eyes never settling anywhere for longer than a split second.

There was no way.

This was not how Luke Cohen was going to go down.

"Tell your puppy trainer next time you see him that I—"

The man punched him solidly in the gut.

Luke coughed and hung on to the side of the truck. He didn't know whether to breathe or throw up.

Where was Logan? He'd paid the man good money to have him protect him today. What good was the bodyguard if he couldn't show up before Luke got taken by a brute who wasn't above sucker punches?

It was time to take charge.

"Money's in there," Luke wheezed, pointing toward the backseat.

The man opened the cab door and leaned in to grab the bag. Luke threw his weight against the door, knocking him against the frame before he could react. Luke moved on pure adrenaline and anger, hauling him backward, then serving him a right cross that had his head lolling back. Out cold.

Luke didn't pause to celebrate, but dropped the man on the freezing asphalt and slammed the door before hopping in the driver's side and peeling out of the lot.

He sped past a black car that looked a lot like Logan's. The bodyguard wasn't inside.

Luke wasn't paying that slacker one dime, that was for sure.

As he sped away with his emergency fund, he realized he'd likely just caused himself more grief. The kind that could unravel everything he'd spent the past few months working toward.

"Man, that was not smart."

Luke scowled at Logan. They were in the middle of nowhere, halfway between Dakota and Blueberry Springs, the mountains rising up nearby. Logan had come up behind him about fifteen minutes ago, eventually signaling for him to pull over on a dirt road.

Luke had finally stopped shaking from taking on an armed man, and had spent the past half hour mulling over all the ways things could have gone to hell, as well as all the ways they still could.

"What's your plan?" Logan asked, his Australian accent thick. The man was large enough that he made his sedan look small.

"Where were you?" Luke demanded, striding closer.

"Providing cover. Trying to figure out who your blackmailer was. He wasn't the guy you bashed, that was for sure."

"I figured that out on my own, thanks."

"I was expecting you to give me more time to set up my equipment. Did he say anything helpful?"

"Yeah, he said you suck."

Logan smirked at Luke's snippy remark, not at all put off by his anger. "No, he didn't."

"Sorry, I guess that was me," Luke said dryly.

Logan gave him a discerning size-up. "Think they'll release the photos of Emma, since you roughed up his assistant and made a run with the cash?"

Luke dragged a hand down his face and let out a sigh. He was exhausted. How did men like Logan deal with this sort of stuff every day? Then again, crooks probably weren't trying to mess with his livelihood, nor his wife.

Wife.

He didn't have time to think about how that word made him feel right now. She was working so hard, pushing beyond her comfort zone, trying to do good... Emma was the woman he was trying to prove himself to. She had integrity, grit and resiliency, and he was still paying blackmailers. And what had he done? Put her and everything she was counting on at risk.

No wonder she was pushing him aside. She'd realized she'd be better off without him.

But he still couldn't let this project fail. No matter what. He needed it now more than ever.

His phone rang and he checked caller ID. It was his mother. Right. She was waiting for money. How about he overnighted her a duffle of unmarked bills? That ought to keep her off his back for a bit.

"I need a drink," he announced, silencing his phone. His mother could wait until Luke was back in Blueberry Springs. Then he'd wire her a few hundred thousand.

"Okay." Logan popped his trunk and rifled through various bags until he came up with two bottles of ale. "This do?"

When Luke nodded, he cracked one for him and passed it over. It was a local Blueberry Springs brew. Lucky it hadn't gone skunky from being in the cold trunk for who knew how long. They leaned against the front bumper of the truck and drank the crisp, cold beer.

"Why can't Zach find anything on this blackmailer?" *In other words, you guys aren't worth the money and are about to get pink slips.*

Logan was silent for a long time, not acknowledging Luke's comment. Finally, he said, "I think there's something going on with him."

"What does that mean?"

"He's dealing with stuff. It's common when you come out of the field and try to reenter civilian life. You're my client now." Logan stood, placing his bottle on the hood of the truck. The cold didn't seem to bother him the way it was nipping at Luke.

"So I hired a dud?"

"No, he's one of the best field agents, but I'll take care of things from here on out."

Luke hoped so, seeing as he still had the unresolved threat of

Emma being exposed, thanks to his anger taking over back there. The rage he had felt flooded through him again. The man had thought it funny to take money from Luke as though he'd never miss it, as if he didn't deserve it, hadn't sacrificed or worked for it. Luke had felt helpless and angry, just like he had when the men in the homeless shelter had pushed him aside so they could talk to his mom without her kid trying to protect her. One had held him against the wall while another had talked softly to Charlotte, trying to coax her into sexual favors, barely backing off when she swatted his hand away from her arm. It had filled Luke with helpless rage, a feeling akin to the emotion that had filled him in that abandoned parking lot.

"What does Emma think about the photos?" Logan asked.

"I didn't tell her." Luke swirled the last of his beer around in the bottom of the bottle.

"But you two are married?"

He looked up in surprise.

"He's sharing private information about me?"

"The best way to find out who's hassling someone is to find their secrets and follow the trail."

"Great. I'm paying you guys to investigate me." Luke took another sip of his beer, the taste somehow flatter than it had been moments ago.

"He knows everything."

"I doubt that."

"Your parents split up for a week when you were nine."

"Nobody knows that," Luke snapped, eyes narrowed.

"Zach does," Logan said easily. "If he dug that up, so could someone else. Although he is one of the best."

"So what do I do? How do I shut them up for good?" He felt as shaky as his voice. "I'm running out of cash."

"Why are these secrets such a big deal to you?"

"They're *secrets*," Luke retorted.

"Worth being bled dry over?"

He let out a long breath. He didn't know what he thought any longer.

"What if your family's secrets get leaked?" Logan asked quietly.

Man, his father sure had messed up with Cohen's.

"What will happen?" the bodyguard prodded.

"Are you threatening me or are you saying I'm wasting my money because you can't protect me?"

"Nobody can hide from their secrets forever. Nobody." Logan stood up, collecting the bottles and tossing them in his trunk, which Luke figured was large enough to hold several bodies. "I recommend you and your wife have a nice long, honest talk. You'll know where to go from there."

"You're quitting?" Luke had enough money in the back of his truck to make sure Logan would to stay on the job. He hoped.

"You may discover you don't need me. Oh, and talk to your mom."

"I'll pay you well. New house? No problem. Pool out back?"

The man turned to give him an amused smile.

"What?" Every man had a price.

Now Luke was thinking like his father. Why? Because Franklin's actions had put him in this position. But so had Emma's. So had his own, by him not having a backbone at some important juncture in his past that would have sent him down a different path, where the actions of others wouldn't be the end of him.

Logan simply started up his car and drove away, rolling down his window despite the cold to give him a friendly wave goodbye.

Frustrated, Luke got into the truck and sped back to Blueberry Springs, not bothering to slow down as he entered the residential streets. Before long, red and blue lights were flashing behind him.

Great.

Best day ever.

Luke pulled over, realizing he still had a bag of cash in the back.

Even better.

"Hey," he said, letting down his window as the officer came up alongside him, ticket book at the ready.

"Blueberry Springs has speed limits. You were double the one on this street."

"Aren't you supposed to be watching Emma?"

"License and registration, please."

"I was working with Logan today. Logan Stone. I'm Luke Cohen." What was this, *The Twilight Zone*? Could Scott Malone not remember him? "I donated the new roof to the seniors' complex, or whatever it's called." He offered his hand for a shake. The officer ignored it. "Do you have a policemen's ball each year? I'd like to support the local—"

"Don't bother finishing that sentence, unless you want to be charged with bribing a police officer. Step out of the vehicle, please. Hands above your head."

"What?" Luke smiled. The guy had to be kidding. "Wait. Aren't you supposed to be sitting outside the cabin and keeping watch on Emma?"

"We had a call from a bank in the city."

"Is she okay?"

"We need to talk about you, Mr. Cohen."

"Scott, I'm sure we can work something out here tonight. I'm tired and just want to get home and make sure Emma's all right."

The officer's hand went to his Taser.

Luke sighed and stepped out of the vehicle.

Scott ran his info through the computer as Luke tried not to act humiliated. He'd talked his way out of a lot of speeding tickets before, but could see it wasn't going to happen this time.

"So? Emma? Is she somewhere safe?" he ventured to ask.

"Can I see the backseat of your truck?"

Shoot.

"Not without a search warrant."

"Pardon me?"

"Be my guest, but I'm guessing you're not going to like it." Luke opened the back door, knowing his day was about to get a whole lot worse.

EMMA BRUSHED out her wig and made sure it was pinned in place. Jill Armstrong had given her a few lessons that afternoon on how to handle the cabin's shotgun, as her father owned the local gun range and was a bit of a pro. Within an hour, Emma had numb fingers from the cold and the ability to hit a tin can from seventy paces. Scott Malone, assured that she was fine on her own at the cabin, went back to his regular rounds, as he was the only officer on duty for not only Blueberry Springs, but the entire surrounding area.

He'd offered to take her to Olivia's so she wouldn't be alone, but Emma was hesitant to drag her sister into anything, especially if there was actually something to worry about. Plus Pete Lunn had come by to keep her company, his big black dog with the ginormous bark acting as a deterrent to anyone who ventured near the cabin. Which had been interesting, seeing as there had been a semiconstant parade of locals popping by to check on her after hearing news of the threat.

There was a knock at the door and Pete answered it for her, his dog going into a barking frenzy. There was a patrol car in the driveway and Emma took Pete's place at the door in order to talk to Scott who was taking up most of the doorway with his large frame.

Pete tipped his head toward the darkening woods, asking if he was okay to go home and Emma nodded. He strapped on his snowshoes and took his path through the forest toward town, his dog bounding through the drifts alongside him.

"What's up?" Emma asked Scott, hugging her arms around herself as a breeze swept down the mountain. "Would you like to come in?"

Scott shook his head. "Do you know who Luke was meeting with today in Dakota?"

"No."

"Do you know why he was traveling with several million in cash?"

"What?" Emma's mind was racing as she tried to connect the dots of Luke's rash behavior.

"Do you know who threatened you outside the school?"

"No. What's going on?"

"That's what I'm trying to find out. How long has Luke been acting strangely?"

"He's stressed about things."

"Emma, I need your cooperation. I know he's your husband—"

"We're not... We..." Emma couldn't meet Scott's eyes.

"He's concerned about your safety, as am I. And while I know you're not required by law to give up your husband's confidence, if there's anything you can tell me it might help me keep you both safe."

Emma swallowed hard. "I wish I could help."

Scott sighed. "Fine. Want to come bail him out? He's asking for you."

"He's been arrested!"

"I caught him speeding with several million dollars in the back of his truck and beer on his breath. He wasn't over the legal limit, but he was acting edgy. I brought him under custody."

Emma grabbed her coat and followed Scott to the patrol truck, feeling uncertain. What was going on? Did Luke know more than he was saying? Was he putting her at risk with his secrets?

Numbly she rode into town with Scott as he hinted at various scenarios that would have Luke speeding through town with an unreasonable sum of cash. She remained silent, her mind a hum of frantic thoughts, as she walked into the log building that served as police headquarters.

When Luke saw her outside his cell, he rushed to her, reaching through the bars. "Emma! Get me out of here."

"With what, Luke? I don't have the fifty thousand for bail, and Scott's holding your *duffle bag* until you've seen a judge."

"Em, you have to understand. It's not how it looks."

She'd never seen Luke so worried or stressed, and his disheveled appearance left her at a loss.

"So it's not money laundering. Bank robbery?" She listed the few things Scott had suspected. "What was that phone call about? The one on the porch a few weeks ago?"

"I need to transfer money to my mom tonight. She left my dad." He wasn't meeting her gaze. He was hiding something. He pressed the heels of his hands against his eyelids.

"Your mom?" she asked warily, feeling as though the topic was a diversion from what she really wanted to know about.

"I told her I'd send her the money for the first installment on a penthouse."

"Were you planning to drive it to her? There's this invention called wiring money, Luke. Some people call them e-Transfers."

He dragged a hand down his face, momentarily stretching his features.

"Tell me what's going on," she whispered, fearful of his answer.

"I can't."

"I'm really tempted to leave you here to rot, you know," Emma said, turning on her heel.

"EmmaLu, *please.*"

The note of panic in his voice made her steps falter.

"Fine," she said, not looking back. "But don't expect me to keep covering for you."

At the front desk she flirted with Scott, trying to find a way around posting bail. There wasn't one, and after he grumpily threatened to throw her in a cell for obstructing justice, she ended up going to the bank and opening a line of credit against her percentage of the company.

Luke was released late that night. He went straight to bed, and in the morning, when Emma awoke, he was gone. By the time she got a ride down to the courthouse to see how his meeting with the judge was going, he'd been cleared and was already halfway to South Carolina. It turned out he knew a guy who knew a guy who was married to the judge's daughter, and had called in a favor, granting Luke a 6:00 a.m. meeting with Judge Radcliff instead of the one scheduled at 9:30.

Emma wrapped her arms around herself as she stood in the early March sunshine on the front steps of the Blueberry Springs courthouse.

"Where did he go?" she asked Logan Stone, letting out a shiver as he came up the stairs to greet her. She knew he'd been helping Luke with private security stuff, and she had a feeling he had a decent idea what was going on—likely better than she did, not that it was difficult to surpass her current level of knowledge on all things Luke related.

"Said his mom needed him." Logan had his hands stuffed in the pockets of his puffy black jacket. "Want to grab some breakfast? I'll fill you in on a few things."

She wasn't really hungry, due to the worry zipping through her system, but she nodded. Coffee and company would be good right about now. Especially since her husband wasn't answering her text messages.

Only a few days ago Luke had felt like the perfect man for her. Like he was *her* man. Now she felt as if she was spinning in the dark and about to fall.

He was supposed to go to a trade show with her tomorrow. Apparently, it had once been part of a Valentine's Day event, but had been moved to March to stand on its own as it continued to grow over the years, drawing people from hours away. She'd planned to take the opportunity to make arrangements with local vendors for their official launch party, as well as have Jill run a booth for them. She knew so much about their products already that Emma had been trying to convince her to come work for her after selling her natural creams to Cohen's for big money. But Luke had missed his meeting with Jill. Although Emma got the feeling Jill wasn't ready to sell her formulas anyway.

She was quickly becoming a good friend, and might understand the fact that Emma, who had been looking forward the trade show, now just wanted to stay home, eat chocolate and get lost in a book. Not play the sparkling debutante. She was going to have to layer on makeup and get dressed up. But having had so little sleep lately, she honestly didn't think she'd be able to make herself look any better than the magazine photo she'd burned in the fireplace weeks ago.

She used to live for getting all dressed up, and now it just felt like work.

At Mandy's café, Logan ordered them huge platters of food, as well as extra large coffees. She'd be lucky to get through a quarter of it, but thanked him nevertheless.

"Logan?"

He raised his eyebrows to show he was listening as he took their plates to a table near the window.

"Can we sit farther back?" She had a feeling that the news of Luke's arrest was going to be the gossip of the week, taking the place of last week's—when Devon's grandfather had streaked through the retirement home sans pants, causing quite a stir with the ladies. Sitting at the window, on display, wasn't Emma's current idea of fun.

Logan moved with her toward the back of the restaurant, and as they sat down, she said, "Tell me what's really going on."

"How much do you know?"

"Just spit it out," she snapped, immediately feeling bad for being rude.

Logan, however, seemingly unaffected by her outburst, said in a lowered voice, "Luke's mom is in financial trouble. His father has been trying to keep it covered up for years. I'm pretty confident she'll gamble away anything Luke gives her."

"But he just sent her money and he plans to give her his inheritance. The one we're—" Emma caught herself in time. "Does Luke know?"

Logan shook his head. "They've worked hard to keep it a secret from everyone, as well as protect him."

"He's trying to protect her, because Franklin is super controlling. Are you *sure* she'll gamble it?" It would kill Luke to find out that it had always been his mother and not his father at the root of the couple's financial conflicts.

Gambling just didn't seem like Charlotte's style. It wasn't completely beyond the realm of belief, but it was still a bit of a shock. She and Franklin had done a good job of hiding it from everyone.

"If the past is any indicator, it'll be gone within a week."

Emma sat back, mentally running through the implications of Luke's plan. "I have to stop him."

"His parents don't want him to know. It'll change the way he thinks of her if he finds out she's an addict," Logan said gently.

"He's believed his father is a controlling jerk who's been unfair to his wife for all these years. That's not right."

Logan's large hand clasped Emma's as she pushed away from the table. "And it's been his choice not to correct Luke. Both of theirs. It's not your place to tell him."

"The inheritance was his grandparents' legacy. I can't help him ensure she loses it."

"Luke's dad was hoping Luke wouldn't claim the money, so he could lock it away in a trust when she inherits. But Luke encouraged her to leave."

"And she did," Emma said with a groan. She leaned forward, propping herself against the table. "But now if Luke gets the money, he'll give it to her and it'll be gone."

"There's only one way you can help."

Emma met Logan's solid gaze as her stomach dropped. "Don't let Luke claim his inheritance," she whispered.

And to do that, she'd have to ask for a divorce.

$\mathcal{L}$uke straightened his cuffs and scanned the crowds for Emma as he checked his coat at the Blueberry Springs trade show. His quick trip home to help his mom had only made him realize how liberated he felt while in the small mountain town. He despised the weight that came with the responsibility of running Cohen's Blissful Body Care. He was tired of worrying about his mother. He used to feel powerful and righteous, having her count on him.

So instead of babying her, he'd handed her wads of bills and taken the first flight back home to Emma.

Emma, who had secrets that could ruin everything. Just like he did.

He hadn't heard a peep from the blackmailer since whacking his lackey with his truck door. Had the man died from head injuries? Was Luke a murderer? Had the blackmailer thought he'd been double-crossed? There were too many unknowns, and Luke was starting to feel the paranoia settle in.

He turned, scanning the crowd once again. He spotted Logan watching from afar. That meant Emma had to be nearby. The two men shared a nod, and some of the tension riding in Luke's shoulders eased. Logan said he'd narrowed down who the black-mailer was, and that he was awaiting some final intel before pursuing things further. Bringing in the authorities, in other words.

Luke should feel relieved, but instead felt even more ill at ease. He suspected he wouldn't completely relax until the black-mailer was behind bars and the All You line was fully launched.

He felt the air stir beside him, his body responding in a way that told him Emma was near. He turned to find her beside him. The first thing he noted, other than his relief, was that she looked unhappy.

"EmmaLu." He took a half step toward her, prepared to hug her, hold her close. Her expression warned him off making that mistake.

She was wearing too much makeup. It was expertly applied and similar to what other women of the country club wore back home, but after seeing Emma barefaced for so long, Luke felt it looked unnatural, masking her genuine beauty.

"You look nice."

She gave him a dark glance. "You left without telling me."

"I'm sorry. My mom needed me."

There was something in Emma's shrewd gaze that made him hesitate.

A woman in jeans and a frumpy sweater came up to her and started chatting. She brought a friend over and the volume of chatter increased, Emma working her magic, smiling, giving hugs, asking them about their lives in a way that was both genuine and, he thought, entirely exhausting.

It was like she'd reverted back to her old self from Charleston. All glitz and pretense. And as she smoothly and expertly removed herself from the group to glad-hand members of the local town council, he found himself wishing she'd change back.

Then again, this was what she lived for. This was her life. She'd been raised to be a part of events, dressing up, being pretty.

This, here, was the Emma he'd always known, but not the one his heart rate picked up its pace for.

"It must feel good to be back," he said, as she made promises of joining the women's auxiliary in a few weeks for their monthly tea and fund-raiser.

Emma gave him a confused look, her bottom lip gleaming under the lights. If he kissed her, his lips wouldn't taste like her, but like gloss.

"You know," he said, "being the popular socialite." His words hadn't come out right and they'd sounded more like an insult than a conversation starter.

He felt he was losing her, that she was becoming cooler toward him with every passing moment. It wouldn't be long before she repeated, "This is a mistake. We're a mistake. Things got out of hand and I think it would be best if we acted as though none of this ever happened."

She was toying with her bracelet, a thin gold chain he'd noticed she often wore. It had been a gift from someone, if he recalled correctly.

Maybe that's what she was waiting for—a gift, so she'd know she mattered to him. Something a bit more personal and romantic than the dress and shoes, which she'd merely been polite about. He'd stashed over two million dollars in a safety deposit box in the Blueberry Springs bank, when it looked as though the teller would faint if he handed her more than a few hundred thousand in bills to reinvest. He could withdraw a few stacks of hundreds and buy Emma something nice to help start putting this whole awkward mess behind them.

Realizing she was on the move, Luke hustled to catch up, nearly bumping into her when she stopped.

"Luke? We should hire Lily Harper-Mattson to cater for our launch party." She was pointing to a booth that had food samples laid out on silver trays. "Instead of it being a private affair like we first agreed, I think we should invite the whole town as thanks."

"Yeah, okay. I'll wear a tux and we'll go all out. Show this town who we are. Linens. Champagne. Flowers." She could dress up and be herself. The hostess with the mostest.

"I was thinking something more casual and comfortable for our guests."

"Nah. Everyone loves getting dressed up." That's what she liked, right? And he didn't mind wearing a tux. They made a fine couple. "We'll rent tents. String a ton of lights. It'll be like a… wedding reception," he said. Maybe he could propose to her for real that night. Show her he was still part of the world she adored and wanted. "Ice sculptures. The works."

She was looking uncertain.

"I'll pay for it all."

Still no response.

She moved toward the booth and started talking to Lily about what she could do for them, as well as something about getting a restaurant rebuilt so Emma could have some guy named Leif's chocolate maven pie.

Why did chocolate come up with women so often? Maybe chocolate was what breasts were to men. Magical. Irresistible. Distracting.

Luke bounced his leg. He needed to fix things with Emma, but didn't know how. He needed to show her she'd been the one on his mind when he'd been putting out fires back home.

Back home. He didn't want to return to that life, but he would if Emma wanted him to. He needed to show her that, too.

"Emma?" He touched her elbow lightly, interrupting her conversation. "I have to slip out for a moment. Be right back."

Luke reclaimed his coat at the checkout and stepped into the air, surprised at how soft and warm the breeze coming over the mountains felt. He had become accustomed to the brisk winter wind, and the hint of spring caught him off guard.

The sidewalk was covered with grit that had been used on Main Street throughout the winter to combat the ice, and the snowbanks in front of the town's jewelry store were dirty, the windows as well. He stepped inside and found himself coasting toward engagement rings before he knew it.

"Can I help with anything?" asked a salesclerk standing behind the counter, hands clasped behind his broad back. Luke caught a glimmer in the man's eyes as though anticipating him dropping a large amount of money. The clerk was not incorrect.

"I'm looking for a necklace. Earrings. Something classic. Yellow gold." Emma could pull off just about anything, but Luke had planned to complement her bracelet by creating a set.

He was certain there was a story behind the piece, and he realized there was a lot about his wife that he didn't know. For a moment he wondered if taking her on an actual date might make more sense. Sit down, chat. Maybe spend a week on a beach—have a real vacation, no work.

No, jewelry could be passed off as a simple gift that meant nothing, if he was barking up the wrong tree. A date or vacation implied a whole lot more, and Luke wasn't sure he could handle being shot down. Not at the moment, anyway.

His gift would be a promise of times to come.

The clerk brought out the selected necklace. It didn't quite match her bracelet, but was delicate, and similar in style.

"That one."

"We also have earrings that match." The clerk placed the necklace on top of the glass case, moved down several displays and pulled out a pair of earrings. They were simple, classic and of good enough quality that Luke wouldn't be embarrassed to have his name associated with them.

"Fine. I'll take them, as well."

The clerk flipped over the price tags, eyebrows raised in question. Luke gave a nod and passed over his credit card.

"Wrap them. They're a gift."

The door to the shop opened and Luke glanced over to see who it was. He did a double take. It was Haddie Goodchild.

"What are you doing here?" he asked, before he could catch himself.

"Good to see you, too, Luke." She quickly took in the scene. "Bribing someone?"

"It's a gift."

"Always is," she said with a knowing smile. "I was hoping to get a few quotes from you."

Luke sized her up. "And you couldn't do it over the phone?"

"I also wanted to interview a few people around town. Find out more about your recent arrest and the staggering amount of cash you were speeding around with. It's an odd thing to do."

"I have nothing to say. I'm a good man." He swallowed hard, taking his purchases and card from the clerk. "If you can't see that then it's your loss."

In a moment he was out the door, trying to keep from breaking into a run.

EMMA SMILED and chatted with everyone, feeling like a fraud. She wasn't sure if it was the compliments on her hair or the fact that she felt as though she was intentionally working people over, trying to get them to like her.

She'd rather be back in the cabin, watching snow fall through the trees, playing cards with the old Luke from a few weeks ago and sipping tea.

But those times were over, and she didn't know how she was going to broach the subject of divorce. It would be easy for him to drag his feet until they passed the four month mark, being nearly halfway there already. Plus she'd been counting on that extra marketing cash from her cut. However, she knew she couldn't face herself if she allowed Charlotte to get her hands on the money, only to blow it all. Luke would be so crushed.

Jill was taking a break and Emma had been manning the

booth, talking up their new products. In the booth beside her, Oz Reiter, a local craftsman, had a display of handmade china cabinets, rocking chairs, pine bed frames and a cedar sweater box that smelled amazing.

Emma felt Luke's presence before she saw him as she straightened the products at their table.

"I have something for you," he said, his voice low and full of promise.

She found herself shivering in anticipation as she turned.

He was holding a bag from the jewelry store and her hope faded.

"I'm sorry I've been so busy lately."

Emma felt a lump rise in her throat that felt a lot like anger. He was trying to buy her affection and forgiveness instead of giving her what she really wanted—into his world. She wanted him to trust her, let her help him.

He handed her the bag.

"Thank you."

"You're not going to open it?"

She fingered the corded straps of the bag. "Here?"

"Yes."

There were two boxes inside. Things were that bad. Two gifts, she knew, meant major suck up. Major forgiveness required. What had he done?

A smile at the ready, she set down the bag and opened the first box, a narrow, long one made for necklaces, then blinked at the fine gold chain. It was very similar to the bracelet around her wrist.

She stared at it for a long moment, trying to make sense of it.

This was a thoughtful gift.

But it was still a bribe intended to soften her, help her overlook the way he'd shut her out when he was obviously dealing with some sizable problems.

He pulled the necklace from its box. "Let me put it on you."

She blinked away the emotion brimming in her eyes, and held her hair out of the way as he clipped it around her neck, his fingers brushing the fine hairs along her nape and causing her to shiver. His hand hesitated, hovering over her shoulder, its heat radiating into her flesh before he dropped it, not touching her.

She placed her fingertips against the chilly gold chain. It was perfect. He couldn't possibly know what the bracelet meant to her, but somehow he'd picked up on it. And yet…he was still so clueless about her.

Maybe his obliviousness was intentional. A way to keep her at bay, from expecting more than she should.

"And this." He handed her the smaller, square box, which could hold either earrings or a ring. She wasn't sure which she hoped for at the moment.

She opened the navy box and her breath caught in her throat. Earrings.

She was relieved, but her eyes filled again.

"You don't like them." He was watching her expression carefully.

"Oh, Luke. Don't be silly. They're perfect." She gave him a hug so he'd couldn't keep studying her.

"Pretty things for a pretty woman. Now let's see if I can win you a teddy bear."

At his fake joviality, Emma glanced up, only to find his gaze was fixed on someone in the crowd behind her. Emma turned, certain she caught a flash of Haddie's black curls and her graceful walk that gave her hips a sexy sway.

Luke steered them in the opposite direction, toward the small carnival set up in a corner of the large building.

"I have to man the booth," Emma said, stopping.

Just then Jill came bounding over with a big smile. "Hey, don't worry about the booth. I've got it." She headed to the table where an older lady was inspecting the various lipsticks. Jill swung around to add, "Oh, and thanks for the tip."

"Did it work?"

"Burke Carver says he's going to be at the conference and has approved a meeting with me!"

"That's so great." Emma gave her a double thumbs-up. She had a feeling Jill and Burke would hit it off, and if they arranged things right, their businesses could sell a lot of products cooperatively.

Emma followed Luke, the jewelry bag dangling from her wrist feeling as conspicuous as a public fight between lovers.

Over at the mini carnival, dads were trying to win toys for their kids. Luke stopped in front of a baseball game and handed a five dollar bill to the man behind the counter. Then he whipped a ball at a stack of milk bottles, knocking every one of them off the pedestal.

"Pick your prize, Ms. Carrington," Luke said proudly.

She pointed absently to a stuffed toy.

"This is for any needy kids who want to play," Luke said, setting a wad of bills on the counter. "Next round is on me, kids!" he called.

He was acting like a shopaholic who'd just had his accounts unfrozen and had been let loose in a mall full of bargains. Emma couldn't help but wonder if his strange mood and spending were related to his recent arrest.

"Luke?" she said, trying to pull him aside as uncertain children came up to the counter. He kept trying to push a pink elephant into her arms. "What's wrong?"

"I'm just a nice guy, doing nice things for others, with no promise of personal gain," he said loudly, his head held high as though he wanted his voice to carry. "And I know how you feel about needy kids. They deserve a little fun, too."

"All right. We need to talk." Emma hauled him by the arm, plunking him in a fold-up chair in front of an empty stage at the back of the trade show where a few people were waiting expectantly.

"Let's buy you a hat or something," he said, his eyes jumping around as though he was on the lookout. "Something to complement those pretty eyes of yours."

"Luke. Stop."

"I'm having fun. This trade show is great."

Emma didn't know what to say, how to figure out this abrupt change in him. "Are you on drugs?"

He laughed silently.

She turned away, her body tense. Something was really wrong and she didn't know how to get Luke to trust her enough to confide in her. But did it even matter? She needed to let Franklin take care of that inheritance, and that meant divorcing Luke. But that would put a wedge between them that would not only ensure he didn't share his problems with her, but would likely send him out of her life forever.

She needed more time to think it all through.

Five ballerinas dressed in pink tottered onto the stage as someone began playing on an upright piano. The girls were barely past the diaper stage, and they looked slightly stunned at being in the spotlight. Seeing their parents sitting in the front row, the girls smiled and waved.

"I'm a nice guy," Luke said out of the blue. He sounded sullen, morose.

"Just watch the dancers, Luke." Emma clutched the jewelry bag, perched on the edge of her chair.

"They're out of sync with the music."

The little ones were bending and moving, pausing to wave at people they knew.

"Do you remember feeling like that?" she asked.

"Like what?"

"Like the whole world was a stage where you could be your true self, share what you felt in the moment. Be honest and free with your joy. Nothing was complicated."

Luke looked at the girls again.

"This is what's important," Emma said, gesturing to the dancers. "Not stuff or money. People. Spending time with them, sharing important moments."

"I know."

"Do you?"

He met her eyes. She saw fear.

"The lovely couple!" It was Mary Alice in a bright floral blouse.

"We're *not* a couple," Emma said, too sharply.

The woman dragged her eyes from the jewelry bag to Emma's new necklace, then to the teddy bear under her arm. "Is that so?"

"Yes."

"I heard you've hired Pete to cook for you. That's wonderful of you to give him a job."

"We're not much for cooking, so he's really saving us by helping out," Emma said.

"But surely you know a few Southern recipes? We were hoping you'd bring some grits or fried chicken to our church potluck next Sunday."

Emma shook her head. The idea of going to a potluck felt exhausting right now. "I'm sorry. I don't—"

"We'll bring something delicious, Mary Alice," Luke said, leaning across Emma. "What time should we be there?"

She frowned. "Luke, dear, I heard you robbed a bank."

He laughed loudly. "We'll bring enough pie for everyone, how's that sound?" He smiled. It was forced.

Mary Alice gave an uncertain nod and backed away.

"Luke," Emma muttered once the woman was gone. "What's gotten into you?"

"Want a rose?" He jumped up, moving to a nearby booth selling roses in support of the local soccer team.

"Luke?"

"Two dozen." Luke stuffed money in their donation jar. Moments later, he pushed the flowers into Emma's hands. She looked like a date. A wife. She had jewelry, a teddy bear and flowers. She shoved them all back into his arms.

"Would you quit trying to buy me!"

Luke blinked.

"You're throwing money around like a big pompous you-know-what." Her eyes brimmed with tears and she wanted to run, but knew everyone would see her and the rumors would start. She quickly dabbed at her eyes, promising herself that if she got out of here she could have a good cry later.

"What's the point of having money if you can't use it? Someone will just find a way to take it. I may as well win some people over with it before it's gone." Looking angry and as though he wanted to swing at something, he stalked off, his arms laden with her gifts.

As Emma watched him leave she felt as though their world was slowly imploding, their hard work unraveling.

She wanted the old Luke back. The one who didn't have anything to prove and just was who he was. Sweet, wonderful and kind. The one who'd never given her hope because he'd never given more than a hint of reciprocating her crush, and therefore could never truly break her heart.

LUKE SAT at the bar in Brew Babies and nursed a beer. Emma was still at the trade show and he'd given up on impressing her when she'd basically accused him of acting like every man she'd ever dated.

He got it. He really did. She'd liked them and their gifts. Not him and his.

Luke flicked one of the roses resting on the bar beside him. They smelled like love. They looked like love.

They were rejection.

He took a swallow of beer. He knew he hadn't been around in

the past few days while he'd been putting out fires, but didn't she know him? Trust him? Know that whatever it was they felt between them was strong?

"Women, huh?" The bartender, Moe, nodded to the cliché gifts that surrounded Luke. Teddy bear, jewelry bag and flowers. At least she'd accepted the necklace.

"Yeah," he muttered. Luke didn't want to talk about it. He wanted answers. Answers as to why his gut hurt and he felt more confused than he'd ever been in his life.

He'd finish his beer and move on with his life. That's what he'd do.

The man two stools down said, "You're that guy who donated some money to the continuing care unit."

He was nearly bald, his remaining hair creating what looked like a half-formed crop circle. Emma would know who he was. Luke just smiled politely.

"Yeah. That's who you are." He pointed a finger at Luke. "I fixed the indents on the soccer pitch after your helicopter landed there last summer. Then you came right back and put them back in again not long after."

"Sorry." Luke contemplated abandoning his beer. Dirty looks from Emma might not be so bad, after all. "I didn't come in the helicopter the second time," he added weakly.

"Aw, Jim, don't give him a tough time," the man beside him said. He was looking at Luke as though the two of them had unspoken business, but Luke wasn't sure what it was. Again, Emma would likely know. "He was just looking out for his girl."

"How is that woman of yours?" the first guy, Jim, asked. "That smart one."

"Olivia?" Luke asked. "She's married. Moved on." He took a swallow of beer, feeling a twinge of sorrow. Or was it regret? Feeling sorry for himself?

Envy. That's what it was.

But why? She was in a small town, in a small house, married

to a small-town mayor who drove a rust bucket and called it a car. And she was about to have a baby while changing careers. Hardly a situation to envy.

The unfinished-business guy was giving Luke an odd look.

"No, no," Jim corrected, smoothing the hair at the back of his head. "That one left you." He nudged his neighbor. "Olivia married your boy instead."

The man gave Luke an apologetic smile. Luke knew who he was now: Cory Mattson, Devon Mattson's father. And Devon would be the unfinished business. While Luke had seen Devon as "the other man," Cory had no doubt seen Luke in the same vein.

"Sorry for how things worked out for you and Olivia," he said.

"She's happy now," Luke said uncomfortably. That was what he was supposed to say, right? He added, "Water under the bridge."

"I was talking about the one who figured out how to get valerian to grow in those sheds," Jim interjected.

"Greenhouses?"

"Yeah, them things."

"That was Vintra," Luke said.

"Nope, *her*. The pretty bit of a thing."

"Emma?" Luke asked in surprise. It wasn't often that men saw her brains beyond her beauty.

"There was a water problem and I was putting things together, and then before I knew it, she was getting her hands dirty, smiling like it was the funnest thing in her day. A smart woman who is willing to rub shoulders and get dirty is a find."

Luke agreed.

"I didn't expect a woman with money to act like that." The man gave a chuckle before contemplating his beer. He laughed again. "Man, I was so broke growing up we had one chair and it was reserved for my dad. I wore bread bags over my feet in my winter boots so I wouldn't get my socks wet. They leaked, you see."

"Remember that car I had when the kids were little?" Cory asked Jim.

"That one you had to park on a hill so you could let it roll to jump-start it?"

Cory smiled as if the memory of his old clunker was a fond one. "When you don't have much, everything seems simpler," he explained to Luke.

"But it's hard," Luke insisted. He thought of the few uncertain and frightening days he'd had with his mom in Arizona. He never wanted to be in that position again, and with every passing moment he felt as though he was drifting closer to it.

"Sure, it's tricky if you have a family," Cory agreed finally. "Never could afford all the things the kids wanted."

The men were quiet for a long moment.

"I still wake up in sweats worrying about buying shoes for the kids, even though they're all grown up and I've turned that financial corner. Still," he said, with a reminiscent shake of his head, "I wouldn't trade those times and the hardship for the world."

"Why?" Luke asked.

Cory turned, taking him in. "Because it made me who I am."

"You wouldn't have that wife of yours, Trish, if you were a rich man," his pal pointed out.

"That's right. We met trying to start my car. That woman puts her back into everything and gives it her all even when she's struggling. But you'd never know by looking at her." Cory smiled wistfully, like a man in love.

Luke found himself thinking of Emma and her willingness to do the hard work, even on days when she obviously hadn't been feeling like it. Similar to Cory's wife, she was one of a kind.

"You know, I have all of our family photos in the trunk of my car," Cory was saying. "Everything from back when my grandfather homesteaded just up the valley, right on up to photos from Devon's wedding."

Luke tuned the man out for a moment to let the reminder of

Olivia and Devon's wedding sink in. It didn't bother him in the way he'd expected. It still stung a bit, but not in the same way it had not that long ago.

"Some of those photos are part of the town's history," Cory was saying. "Blueberry Springs turns a hundred-and-twenty-five in a few weeks and we're donating some of the oldies to the historical society. Town's pretty excited. I've got them in the trunk of my car so I can get them preserved on that acid-free paper stuff. Doing all the photos from the museum, too. Got rare pictures of the old wooden sidewalks, the founder and his horse on the dirt main street, the little miner camps set up along the river. The girls are going to make a scrapbook for Trish, too—our anniversary is coming up."

"Congratulations," Luke said. He wondered if Emma was done sulking yet. He also wondered if she'd keep him past their four-month, "inheritance-earning" anniversary at the end of next month.

A week ago he'd have bet on them making it beyond that date. Now, he doubted they'd even make the week.

He rubbed the spot where his ribs met as though able to rub the pain away.

"You should marry her," Jim said to Luke.

"Marry who?"

"Emma."

Luke sobered up. "Why?"

"She makes you smile." He nudged Cory. "You see that dopey grin he gets? He's got it bad."

"We're business partners," Luke said, after clearing his throat.

"That's not what I heard," the first man said slyly.

"Don't believe everything you hear," he said, thinking of Haddie and her upcoming article as he stood.

"If she makes you happy, spend time with her. That's how you'll know." The older man eyed the gifts littering the bar. "Those can help, but they're not what women truly want."

"They want your heart on a platter!" exclaimed a man from the end of the bar who'd obviously been eavesdropping the entire time. "Just like my Mabel. I told her no." He thumped his chest. "It's staying right where it is, thank you very much."

"That's why you make a pledge to marry your friend when she turns thirty." Moe, the bartender, chuckled, wiping his way up the long bar. "And for the record," he called down to the man, "you're cut off."

The customer grumbled in reply.

"Marry her," Cory said quietly. The other two men nodded.

"Thanks for the advice." Luke collected the earrings, but left the rest. He pushed the flowers down the bar. "Take those to your wives. Nice talking."

"Good job scaring him off," Jim muttered into his glass of beer.

In many ways Emma had become the partner Luke's grandparents had wanted him to have. He relied on her, enjoyed spending time with her whether it was work or play. But somehow, after all they'd been through, spending time with her didn't seem like enough when it came to convincing her to trust him with her heart.

It was time to open up, tell her everything and see what happened—even if it meant losing everything.

"I'M sorry I've been acting odd," Luke said quietly to Emma when he caught up to her in the trade show.

She flicked him a long glance, sizing him up as he fell into step beside her.

"Can we talk?"

She turned to him, hands on her hips. "Haddie just asked me a lot of in-depth questions about your arrest and hinted at a few business practices that felt a little shady. You want to talk about those?"

Luke rubbed the back of his neck, anxiety bubbling inside him, making his limbs itch with a need to run or fight. "I'm worried she's going to pull apart everything we'd done."

"How can *one* reporter do that, Luke? What does she know that I don't?" Emma stared into his face, her bright eyes flashing. He wanted to press his body to hers, tell her everything. But he was afraid that would be the end for them.

He still wanted to buy out Cohen's. Still needed that positive publicity for the company. He also needed to make sure his mom continued to have her new life covered financially. He couldn't risk losing his deal with Emma.

But he'd never forgive himself if he lost her.

"I...I probably have a few things I should explain," Luke said softly, avoiding eye contact with Olivia, who'd spotted them and looked as though she wanted to join them. "Can we go somewhere more private?"

Emma studied him for a long moment and he thought she was going to refuse. "Fine. I'll text Jill and tell her we'll be back to help with the takedown in an hour."

"This is going to take a bit longer than that."

Again, that deep, studious look. "Fine." She texted Jill, waited for a reply, then said, "All set. But you can't miss the next meeting with her about her products."

"Pick a date and time and I'll be there." He didn't recall missing the first meeting, but his mind hadn't exactly been on the ball for minor things like product acquisition meetings.

"Good, because I'm pretty sure when Burke Carver hears about them at the Metro Conference he's going to snag her line, and it would be dumb of you to miss out on first dibs."

"Duly noted," Luke said as he claimed their coats from the checkroom. He helped Emma into hers, then held the outside door for her. "Shall we?"

She said nothing, but marched onto the sidewalk just as a speeding SUV jumped the curb, tires squealing.

Luke felt the glass door twist and shatter as it was ripped from his grip, the blurring vehicle sending Emma against him as she tumbled from the hit. He couldn't catch her in time, her bulky coat slipping from his hands as he grabbed for her.

"Emma!" He was at her side in a flash as the black SUV fled the scene. She was on her back, staring at the sky, her wig peeled back, revealing the cap that went over her short hair. "Emma!" He knelt in the debris from the door, brushing tiny squares of safety glass from her face as he gently tried to hold her wig in place. "Are you hurt? Please, say something." He scanned her body, fearing he was going to discover she was too broken to continue breathing.

"Ow!" She winced and shifted slowly.

"Are you okay?"

"No," she said faintly.

Olivia had pushed through the gathering crowd and was trying to kneel, her large belly in the way.

"Get the license plate!" someone kept yelling. Luke realized it was him. "A five-thousand-dollar reward for the license number or identity of the driver."

He gently stroked Emma's cheek. "This is all my fault. I'm so sorry, Emma. I'm so sorry."

He'd done this to her. He should have done better. He should have paid the blackmailer. He could have prevented this.

He was shaking uncontrollably, apologies falling from his mouth as he gently checked her over, his old first aid training from his days as a teenaged lifeguard kicking in like a habit. Emma tried to sit up.

"No. No, stay where you are. Someone call 9-1-1. Don't move."

Olivia was talking quietly to her sister, her gaze drifting up to the wig, which had fallen back again. She reached forward, tenderly pinning it in place, while Emma softly replied to her questions.

Luke resented Olivia's calmness. This was an emergency.

Olivia was trying to get Emma to sit up, glass tumbling from her hair.

"Don't touch her!" he shouted.

"I think the door saved her," her sister said.

"My leg really hurts," Emma whimpered.

"Don't move!"

She was sitting up now, wincing again. She moved stiffly, one hand going to her crown, patting her wig to ensure it was in place.

People had gathered, and a siren sounded in the distance.

Devon had come along at some point and was trying to help Emma stand. Luke didn't know what to do. They couldn't just let her walk away. She'd been hit by a speeding vehicle. The door had been broken right there in his hand. Surely she couldn't be okay.

He had to bend over, hands on his knees, to allow the nausea to pass, as he wondered what would have happened if she'd been out the door a second sooner. Or if the door hadn't been there?

"Em." He went to her side. They were walking her back into the building. He elbowed Devon out of the way. "You need medical care."

"My car is just around the corner," Devon said.

"No. An ambulance is coming. She was just a victim of a hit-and-run. She needs urgent care."

"I know. But there's no need to pay for an ambulance. The hospital—"

Luke wanted to slug him. He really did. "She's riding in an ambulance," he said through gritted teeth. "And call Scott Malone." The local officer needed to run some plates, check security footage, traffic cameras. Everything.

It was time to shut this down once and for all. No more

waiting for intel or the perfect moment. It had to be now or it might be too late.

"And get Logan Stone on the phone."

People were looking at each other, confused by his orders.

"Do it!"

Someone scrambled for a cell phone, dialed Logan and handing the phone to him.

"Logan? It's Luke. Meet me at the hospital. Things just got real." He repeated the message to Scott when the next person had him on the line. Luke handed back the phones and picked up his wife, carrying her to the ambulance as it pulled up at the curb.

Within minutes he had her secured in the hospital and in a private ER room—not one that was merely curtained off from the other patients. She was sitting on a gurney and looking depleted of everything he identified as solely her.

The doctor entered the room, looking crisp and professional. No-nonsense. Just the way Luke liked his doctors.

"I'm Dr. Nash Leham."

"I'm Luke Cohen and this—"

"Luke! What a pleasure." The man's handshake turned into a two-handed affair. "Thank you so much for the donation so we could put a new roof on the seniors' wing. I wasn't sure that roof was going to last another winter. You really helped us out. We truly didn't know what we were going to do."

"My pleasure. This is Emma Carrington. She just got hit by a car." He clamped his jaw shut, locking down the emotion that threatened to boil out.

"I'm here!" Olivia came bursting in, belly first.

"Ovvy!" Emma said, a nickname for her sister that Luke knew she used only when she was emotional.

"We've got this," he said tightly, steering Olivia toward the door she'd just come through.

"I'm her sister," Olivia said, digging in her heels. "You're her business partner."

Nash frowned at the intake form. Luke had written "husband" under Relationship. Why not? This was an emergency and technically he was her next of kin. He saw now that he probably shouldn't have. Emma was going to be okay, according to the EMTs who had brought them over, and there was no honest emergency except that his life was currently falling apart and crashing in on his wife instead of himself.

"Well," Nash began hesitantly, taking in each of them as though deciding the best way to proceed. "I think it's up to Emma which next of kin stays in the room. *If* she wants company."

"*I'm* her next of kin," Olivia said, jabbing a thumb against her chest. "I'm *family*." She froze for a split second, then whipped around to face Emma, who gave a sheepish smile.

"I'm her husband," Luke said. For a moment he thought the doctor might have to deliver a baby for Olivia, but she shook off her shock without even requesting a chair. Then her mood began to morph into betrayal, then anger.

Every reason for keeping their marriage a secret flooded through Luke's mind as his ex faced him. She was shaking her head furiously. "No. You're not married."

"We are," Luke said.

She held one hand protectively over her stomach, the other palm out as though that could stop his words from seeping into her mind.

"I'll come back in a moment," the doctor said, slipping from the room.

Olivia turned to Emma. "This is just for the inheritance. Luke doesn't love you."

There had been a time when he'd thought he and Olivia would vie for the money together, but he never pictured this scene.

"Nobody said he does," Emma said in a small voice.

"You deserve love." Olivia eyed Luke. "And I thought…"

"Olivia…" Emma pleaded. "Please. Not here. Not now."

Luke didn't need to hear whatever the two felt they had to hash out. He really didn't. Emma had enough doubts on her own without her big sister marching in and illustrating them in bright sweeping colors.

He knew Olivia was just looking out for her, but he and Emma still had a lot to discover about each other and their relationship without interference. He didn't need Olivia trying to point out that it wasn't real.

Because for the first time, Luke realized what it truly was.

It was love.

Real love.

Not the fake stuff he and Olivia had been playing at, trying to formulate a picture-perfect life that would somehow make them happy. This was the nitty-gritty kind of love that had you throwing stuff one minute, then feeling as though your heart and soul were tethered to a hot air balloon the next.

Luke was glad Devon had come along last summer, because he knew what real happiness and love was now. It was what he and Emma had in that little snowy cabin, and he would fight to keep it.

"I'm the one who's been here for her," he stated.

"Well, I'm here now so you can go," Olivia replied.

A stab of anger ripped through Luke. He knew all that Emma had been sacrificing for Olivia and their family, working herself to the bone. Had Olivia even looked at her sister recently? She was pale, bags under her eyes, her fingernail polish frequently chipped.

"I choose Emma," Luke said, standing beside her gurney. "I'll be there for her and have been since we slept together in Aspen." He felt the weight lift off his chest with the confession.

Olivia's mouth dropped open. "Aspen?" she whispered.

"When you were with Devon. After you hurt Emma by telling the press she was sick."

"I didn't tell them," Olivia said firmly.

"You kept secrets from her and shut me out of your life. You and I were supposed to be partners. We were supposed to work together."

"So you turned around as soon as you thought I was gone and slept with my sister, then married her as revenge?" Olivia's voice was growing louder. "I thought you two would be cute together, but you're just using her."

"I *like* Emma."

"And you never liked me? Is that why you two are in cahoots? Is that why you were always so reserved with me? Reserved in ways you aren't with her?"

"We didn't cheat," Emma stated, her voice thick with tears. "It was all an accident. A mistake, and we're getting a divorce."

"In a few months," Luke added, hoping that's what she'd meant, because he couldn't imagine her not in his life, at his side. "The point, Olivia, is that you aren't Emma's confidante. You didn't know about her wig. She needs people who will stand by her and make her feel smart and strong. Not like she's in over her head. Now if you'll excuse us, I'm going to get my wife the best medical care money can buy."

Luke turned to Emma, but she refused to meet his eye as she pointed to the door.

"Get out." She finally met his gaze with a glare. "Both of you."

EMMA WATCHED the door to the ER room close before she let out the sob that had been threatening to rip through her chest.

Luke had acted like a possessive jerk who was in charge of her life. And he had told Olivia everything—things she doubted her sister could overlook. Emma had overstepped, secretly marrying her sister's ex and then falling in love with him. And for what? A man who'd just tried to create a divide between her and her sister.

The doctor returned, pausing in the doorway. "Want a minute?"

Emma shook her head. The sooner she was out of here with her throbbing leg, the better.

"That was something," he stated, after going through the chart the EMTs had created on the ride over. "Are you doing okay?"

She nodded, not daring to speak.

"I guess Mary Alice is going to lose her bet about you two getting married in June. Or was it August? I can never remember the bets." His ice-blue eyes twinkled.

Emma tried for a smile.

If the doctor had heard the fight outside the room, who else had? Surely everyone had seen her wig flip back. That was going to hit the press right along with Luke's arrest. How long before their recent actions destroyed all their hard work?

She had no hair. Thanks to their products.

She'd married a man in secret to swindle their way through a clause so Luke could claim a dead couple's life savings. Savings his mother planned to gamble away. So now Emma had to divorce him—something that would surely hit all the gossip rags and make them look flaky.

Her husband was her sister's ex.

Luke had been arrested while doubling the speed limit, with several million in cash.

It wasn't good.

None of it was.

"So? A hit-and-run?" Dr. Leham rolled his stool away from the gurney, watching her.

She nodded. Luke's comment about someone taking all his money came to mind and she wondered if the car had been meant for him. Was it the same guy who'd threatened her and Keisha, but in a different vehicle?

"Want to talk about it?"

Emma shook her head. She was still in shock and was afraid

talking would allow her to fully process it. And then what? She didn't think she could handle it all, quite honestly.

"These types of things don't happen in Blueberry Springs. Any suspicions? Enemies?" Dr. Leham looked up from his clipboard.

He was making it quite difficult not to think. She attempted to distract him with a flirty, perky question, but found she couldn't muster the mental strength.

"Well, Officer Malone will want to talk to you, but know that I'm here if you need me," Dr. Leham said as he stood up, his medical coat a perfect, crisp white. He began checking out her leg, pressing in places, flexing the joints. It hurt. That's all she knew. Everything did, from her heart right down to her toes.

*L*uke continued to pace outside Emma's ER room. He wanted data. He wanted a prognosis. But most of all, he wanted to know she was going to be all right.

His gut rolled.

What he had done? Who was after him, and how could he stop them?

"Do you need anything?" a nurse asked, pausing in front of him.

"Is Officer Malone here yet?" Logan had come and gone already, getting the full story in less than a minute before disappearing again, his face a reassuring mask of serious determination. He would make someone pay by nightfall. Guaranteed. It had felt as sure as a stock crash after a bout of bad publicity.

The nurse shook her head and Luke resumed his pacing as she hurried off.

Luke looked over as footsteps came rushing his way. It was Olivia, looking composed now despite the redness of her eyes. She placed her hands against his chest and gave him an angry shove.

Devon hustled up behind her, placing an arm around her shoulders, glaring as though he wanted to sock Luke in the jaw.

"She married you," Olivia stated.

Luke straightened his back. "Yes."

"To free your inheritance. You know your mom is just going to lose it all."

"You don't know what you're talking about." A cool anger came over Luke.

"Luke, open your eyes. How is Emma going to feel when your mom gambles it away? After going through all the humiliation of being found out with your fake marriage."

"Nobody needs to tell anybody anything. And my mother is not a—"

"She told me, Luke. She told me everything. And why didn't Emma tell me about her wig?"

Luke hushed her, glancing around for eavesdroppers, even though he figured the word about Emma's hair was likely already being spread around town.

"I don't know what my mom told you, but Emma's got an image to maintain so if you don't mind lowering your voice—"

"Did you convince Emmy not to tell me?"

Luke stepped closer, his voice low. "Do you have any idea of how badly this could impact her products if this story gets out? Any idea how torn up she was over the mess in the press the first time?"

"Oh? And you know?" Olivia spit back at him.

"Yeah, because she came to me."

"For sex."

"For comfort. We're good at being there for each other, in case you haven't noticed. Especially when you rip apart our lives."

"I had *nothing* to do with this. This is *your* fault. First you get arrested with a bag of cash, then my sister gets run over. Did you put a hit out on her?"

"No!" He was shocked Olivia would even suggest such a thing.

"Then what's going on, Luke?"

"Things are…complicated right now."

"Complicated? And so you convinced her to sink every dime she has into this…this risk." Olivia was sucking air, crying. "She could lose everything." Devon tried to shush her but she waved him off.

"She's not going to fail." Emma had known all along what worked with her beauty videos. Not him. She had good instincts and knew what other women wanted.

"She trusts you, Luke." Olivia's anger had vanished like a storm on the ocean. Her voice was quiet again. "She liked you as a teenager, but she gave you up—for me. She'd do *any*thing for you."

"No, she'd do anything for *you*," Luke corrected.

"I'm sorry." She reached out and squeezed his arm—hard. "Don't break her heart."

Luke tried to keep up with Olivia's sudden topic switches. "What are you saying?"

"You protect her," Devon snapped, pointing a finger. "Get security—"

"Don't tell me what to do," Luke said coldly. "Ever."

The two men glared at each other.

"You've got to look out for her," Olivia urged.

"Mr. Cohen?" It was a nurse, looking unimpressed by the men's showdown. "Your wife would like to see you now."

Luke gave Olivia and Devon a look. That's right. His *wife*.

He stepped into the ER room, where Emma was sitting up, a cold pack against her leg. No cast. The vise in his chest that had been pressing on his lungs, making it impossible to breathe properly, eased its grip.

He dropped into the chair by the door, suddenly exhausted.

"Luke?"

He looked up.

"I need my family."

Luke stood. She wanted Olivia?

"You can't take charge of my life. Can't tell me and everyone else what's best."

He sat again, realizing she was scolding him, not kicking him out.

"I don't like secrets," he said softly, thinking of the photos.

"Neither do I." She looked small, vulnerable, afraid.

"What do you mean?"

"Who ran me over and why?" Her voice was shaking.

"Why didn't you tell your family about your hair and the photos?"

And what had Olivia meant about his mother gambling away the inheritance? Surely she was grasping at straws to make her argument seem stronger.

"What photos?" Emma was on high alert now.

"The sexy ones of you that I'm being blackmailed over." His earlier anger was back, misdirected at Emma, but with his life feeling so out of control he couldn't stop himself.

"What?"

He described one or two of them vaguely. Her. Lingerie.

He felt a stir just thinking about a few of them.

"They go against your brand. I went to pay off the guy so he wouldn't use them before our launch and ruin everything, but things didn't work out." Luke stood, feeling the need to move. "Say goodbye to Carrington's pure image, because I'm pretty sure this was just a warning shot." He gestured to her leg.

Top that with the way her wig had folded off her head earlier and they were going to need some serious damage control. Damage control that was well beyond his means and abilities.

Was this how his father felt? If so, he might have to cut the man a little slack.

Not much, but a tiny bit.

"Luke." Emma closed her eyes. "Between the money and your arrest, you've made a bigger mess."

"Me?" he exclaimed.

"Did it ever occur to you to trust me for a minute?"

"Did it ever occur to you to own up to your life? How is it going to look if the spokesperson has no hair—hair that fell out while being treated for a disease given to her by the very products she's trying to convince others to buy? Your job is to look beautiful and make others want to be like you."

Her eyes filled with tears.

"Emma, I'm sorry." He pinched the bridge of his nose. He was being an insensitive, hurtful, mean-spirited, first-class jerk. "We just need a game plan."

"Those photos were part of a pitch I made a few years ago," she said quietly. "A sexy line to flesh out Carrington's offerings. I can't believe you were going to pay someone to keep those quiet."

"You hired me to take care of this stuff."

"Maybe I was wrong," she said quietly, her head tipped to the side in thought.

"Please, Emma. Don't do this." This was the moment he'd feared. The one where she discovered the truth about everything he'd tried to cover up and shut him out of everything they'd worked so hard to obtain.

"Maybe it's time for me to come clean to the public." She looked suddenly lighter.

"Emma," Luke said, his hands in prayer position as he enunciated his words with care. "You will sink us. You've been through a lot today. Don't make any big decisions right now."

"I won't be ashamed of those photos. I won't hide who I am or my illness any longer. I want to handle this my way even if it means I could lose everything."

"No." He was struggling to cling to the life raft. She couldn't take it away, couldn't kick him out, couldn't slash a hole in its side.

"I'm sorry, Luke."

"I need this."

"No, *women* need this."

"People will demand answers. Are you ready for that?"

Her expression hardened and she pointed toward the door.

"Fine." He stood. "Flush it down the toilet. I won't sit around and watch."

"Maybe I'd rather have integrity than a big bank account."

"Integrity is a great gimmick for the poor and righteous. It doesn't talk the way money does."

"I'd rather be broke than without integrity."

"Would you, Emma?" he asked quietly. "Because from what I've experienced, neither of them gave me what I truly needed."

EMMA WAS ALONE in the cabin. Luke had silently dropped her off at home before vanishing into the late afternoon dusk. Just like she'd wanted him to.

She'd had a good cry, hobbling to the door on her sore leg—just badly bruised, not broken—with puffy eyes to collect the key for the rental Jeep he'd had delivered from the local dealership.

Then it was just her.

It wouldn't be long before the week's myriad of disasters hit the news and the negative publicity started. Why hadn't Luke told her about the photos? Why had he believed she should be ashamed of them? Brands were constantly evolving and changing, and she was a model. Those photos were art.

Unless…unless Vaughn hadn't deleted the more risqué ones. He wouldn't have kept them, shared them with someone else… would he have?

What if he was the one blackmailing Luke?

She began frantically riffling through Luke's stacks of papers, looking for the photos. When she couldn't find them, she sat in front of the fireplace, inhaling slowly, trying to center herself, calm some of the anger building inside her.

It didn't matter. What was done was done. Even the more risqué ones weren't indecent. She could handle people finding her too sexy.

She let out a chuckle, shaking her head.

Luke had been so certain that things were going to fall apart that he'd pulled back all his faith and trust in her. She knew he hadn't earned millions in the past by taking insane risks, but it still hurt.

Emma got up, knowing she needed to follow her gut even if it went against everyone's advice. Feeling calmer, she began videoing herself on her phone at her little table in the bedroom.

Without thought, she began talking. It was time to be herself. Because in all this mess it was the one thing she'd found that she truly couldn't bear losing.

Besides Luke, but he was already gone.

"Beauty is more than cosmetics," she said into the camera. "More than applying mascara and smiling at the camera from the right angle. Being smart is beautiful. It's also about owning up to yourself, being true and genuine."

She pulled out her makeup removal kit and began swabbing damp cotton balls across her face, removing every bit of the cosmetics she'd applied for the trade show.

"Don't hide behind too many products. Own up to who you really are. Beauty is real when we are real."

When her face was bare she found herself removing the pins that held her wig to the cap and her scalp.

"I thought my outer beauty was what drew people to me, and maybe it helps, but it's not the whole picture. The place where I live now, people want to be my friend for reasons other than what I look like."

She set down the pins she'd removed, thinking about Luke, about his words.

You're beautiful without makeup.

That moment had felt real. Empowering. She stole the emotion from that moment to use in her video.

"Today I want to be honest with you. I make these videos because I enjoy them and I think of you as friends. I'm sorry if I've ever failed you or have taken advantage of our relationship with blatant product placement. That isn't who I want to be.

"I hope you still trust me, and know that I care about you. To feel worthy of your trust, I have to be true to myself and own up to who I really am. Because it's difficult to trust someone who doesn't know who she is."

She took a deep breath.

"So today I'm owning up." She gave what felt like a nervous, feeble smile and removed her wig, then the cap that went underneath. She ruffled her inch-and-a-half-long, patchy hair, making sure she looked right into the lens of her phone's camera.

"This is me, Emma Carrington. The real me. You might find me less beautiful like this, but I know there are thousands of other women out there facing the same problems I am. Being treated for cancer meant increasing my chance at living, but also losing my hair." She gave a small smile. "A small price to pay, really, but I felt the need to hide the truth. I felt ugly." She tossed the wig aside. "And today I'm done hiding."

She smiled. For real.

"This is how I'm approaching my life from today forward, because its mine, and mine alone. Mine to live."

She paused. "I think there are many ways to be beautiful and so I ask you, my loyal friends, how are you beautiful today? Is it real? Will you be beautiful in the same way tomorrow or will it grow and evolve along with you?"

She titled the video Real Beauty and left it unedited as she uploaded it online. Next she began recording tips on how to deal with the side effects of the treatments she'd undergone last year. But mostly, how to feel beautiful when you felt ugly, bloated and puffy, bald, pale and covered in horrible rashes. The works. The best creams, the best wigs. She left nothing out. It was raw, honest and real.

Before she could doubt herself or let Luke's beliefs about what she was doing stop her, she uploaded the rest of the videos and crawled into bed for a cleansing, ugly cry, her wig still on the bedroom floor.

***

LUKE SAT on a bench near the river that weaved its way around the outskirts of town, turning the key to his safety deposit box over in his hands. The river had been frozen most of the winter, with an opening appearing here and there occasionally as fast water kept the ice from covering it completely. Right now its level seemed strangely low.

He'd come here to try and come up with a game plan, as well as understand how quickly things had gone south between him and Emma. He should reclaim his safety deposit box of cash so he didn't ever have to come back.

He didn't move. All he could focus on was the river.

He was avoiding the truth, his life, and he knew it.

He didn't want to go back to Cohen's as CEO. He'd enjoyed being more involved on a ground level and feeling as though he was making an actual difference, not just pushing papers.

The company would need him, though, when the full news of everything came to light over the next day or so. All You would take a hit, as would Cohen's.

He rubbed his eyes, then focused on the frigid water tumbling over exposed rocks. A jogger came by on the paved river path, Luke recognizing him as John Abcott, a local lawyer.

"Is this normal? The river level?" Luke called to him.

The older man paused, taking in the reduced flow, his expression turning to one of concern. "Upstream there must be an ice jam blocking this week's runoff." He was breathing lightly, hands on his hips. "Stay away from the edge in case the ice dam breaks. I'll ask Scott to investigate—I've never seen it this low before."

Scott Malone. The officer who'd found Luke suspicious enough to bring him into the station for carrying around more cash than the average man. The officer likely assuming that Luke was the prime suspect in Emma's earlier hit-and-run due to the way things in his life hadn't lined up like the officer felt they should. Luke had kind of blown it around town, hadn't he? He'd come off like a pompous, arrogant, self-serving, egotistical, spoiled rich man who believed money should solve all of his problems.

And now he was here instead of up at the cabin, making sure his wife stayed safe.

"I'll warn Devon, too," John said, "in case we need to implement the town's emergency plan."

Right. Devon, the mayor.

"Is there anything I can do?" Luke realized he was asking, not to compete with Devon, but because he cared. There were a lot of houses and businesses that could possibly be flooded or damaged if the river suddenly rose above its banks—and people who should be warned to move to higher ground.

"Money's not going to help this one."

"I meant warning people. I could knock on doors. Or I have a backhoe we could use to..." He glanced around the landscape, trying to figure out how he could quickly engineer something with his machine to ensure the river stayed within its banks. "Create a berm?"

"Start with knocking on doors and maybe get that backhoe down here, as I'm sure it could come in handy." John gave him a reassessing look and Luke felt as though he'd moved up a notch in the man's estimation. It felt good.

The lawyer gave him a small salute and jogged off.

Luke crossed the narrow grassy strip that separated the riverside pathway from the town, and climbed into his truck.

Where to start? The few businesses along the river were beginning to close already, as it was a little after four and their winter hours tended to be shorter, but that meant the houses farther upstream were filling up as people came home from their day.

He'd planned to spend a bit more time feeling bad over Emma, but he could do that for the rest of his life. He could also empty his safety deposit box tomorrow. Right now he needed to warn people. Quickly.

John rapped on Luke's closed window and he let it down. "Any chance you could give me a ride up to city hall? Save me some time."

"Sure." Luke unlocked the passenger side and pulled away once John was buckled in.

"How's Emma?"

"Okay. Her leg is just bruised."

"Did they find out who did it?" The man's expression was grim.

Luke shook his head. "Not yet."

"Well, put me first in line to have a go at him when they do."

"I think I might be first," Luke grumbled.

John let out a soft chuckle. "I don't blame you. She's an amazing woman." He got a wistful smile. "Reminds me of my girlfriend, Gloria." He waved away the topic. "Anyway, tell Emma I said hi and that I think she is one brave woman."

Luke gave him a curious look.

"Her latest beauty video," John said.

"Oh?" Luke tried to think which had been the latest. Likely one of the product placement pieces that hadn't really connected with her audience, thanks to him.

It made him think of the letter from his grandparents and how much he could use their sage, levelheaded advice right now.

"It's got all the women talking. I heard it from my secretary, Liz, who said all the women at Betty's salon were chatting about it. Taking off her wig like that. She's got courage." John pointed to a spot just up the way. "You can let me off there."

Wait. She'd taken off her wig in a video? Was she trying to torpedo the entire project?

Luke pulled over, his heart pounding with fear for Emma and her future.

John climbed out just as Devon was coming down the front steps of the town hall, jauntily swinging his briefcase in his hand like a man without a care in the world. Luke watched him for a moment, wondering if he'd ever had a chance to be like that. Devon had waited a decade for Olivia and found a way to get past their hurt and misunderstandings. Now look at him. Happy. Content.

"Have a good night," Luke said to John absently, long after the truck's door had closed. He drove a ways down the street before his curiosity became too much to bear. He pulled over and opened the web browser on his phone, pulling up Emma's video channel.

There were four new videos from today and one of them was already nearing a hundred thousand hits.

Oh, boy.

Good thing he'd gotten out when he had. She was obviously a loose cannon.

Hopefully she hadn't named his company in any of her clips.

Knowing he should be warning homeowners along the riverbank, he tapped the arrow and the video began playing, Emma's voice soft. He set the phone on the dash so he could hear her as he drove. She was talking about beauty. Hokey stuff, but when he glanced at her image, he could see her expression was so honest and compelling, it lent a power to her words he couldn't have predicted.

And then she pulled off her wig. He covered his mouth, despite knowing it was coming.

Emma was indeed one brave woman. Or crazy as hell.

Luke watched the road, swiping at his damp eyes. He cursed under his breath.

Man, but she *was* beautiful. Not solely in a traditional sense, but because of the strength with which she carried herself. It made her shine.

In the video she owned up to everything—even the photos. That was one woman who wasn't going to be cowed by fear or let anyone threaten her into a corner.

She was braver than he was. And quite likely smarter, too.

Thinking about Emma, he drove to the north end of town, where a flash flood would hit first. Trying to suppress the photos hadn't truly protected her, it had only given the enemy more power, because hiding didn't make them go away. Facing it all and owning it did. It took the power and shame out of her secrets. And *that* was protection.

Luke's only job had been to stand by her so she could withstand the slings and arrows, and he'd blown it. He'd spent his time chasing enemies instead of giving Emma the armor to defeat them once and for all.

The next video played as he drove and he could hear her chatting about the side effects of her earlier illness. Her approach was fresh, honest, brilliant. Sensitive and real.

It was still a risk, though. A really big one. But if anyone could sell viewers the new line, it was Emma.

Luke parked his truck and called the man who'd been building the new greenhouses for them, letting him know Blueberry Springs might need Luke's backhoe and to bring it to town and use it in whatever capacity was required. He'd pay for the gas and driver.

Then he got out of his truck. He'd warn the people living near the river's edge, then empty his safety deposit box into Emma's account and leave town.

He would put all of his financial support behind her even if it was the scariest thing he'd ever have to do in his life. She might not accept it and she might cut him out of the contract, but even if he lost every dime it wouldn't be poverty—because he knew now what true poverty was. It was living without Emma.

EMMA COULDN'T SLEEP. Even though it wasn't quite suppertime, she'd tried. She wanted nothing more than to shut out the day, the heartache, and the pain in her leg. Instead, she was reading through the comments on her videos with shaking hands. Real Beauty was trending on several social media channels and the outpouring of sympathy, empathy and sisterhood was overwhelming. Emma brushed the tears from her cheeks, still unsure whether she'd done the right thing.

It *felt* right, though. And that was what mattered. Even though Luke would tell her she was sinking her own ship.

And then she saw what he'd warned her about—the photos of her acting demure and sexy in lingerie. Vaughn hadn't deleted the racier photos and they had been leaked to the press, published under a derisive headline that suggested that Carrington wasn't as innocent and pure as they claimed to be. It went on, exposing her ill health and hair loss. No longer beautiful. No longer innocent. On and on.

Just like Luke had said would happen.

She flipped back to the videos to soothe her panic, scrolling through the endless comments—both good and bad—and mindlessly answered her phone when it rang.

It was Olivia.

"Emma, you've got to get down here. Luke's trying to save the town from the rising river, but he's going to get himself hurt."

*L*uke struggled against the freezing water swirling around his calves. The current was strong as the river spread across the roads and yards, swelling higher and higher by the minute. Men and women were stacking sandbags to create a protective barrier around a home in the darkening night, but Luke could see they needed more time, more sandbags.

"We need more by the bank," Devon Mattson commanded. He was still in a shirt and tie, John having thrust him into action right there on the town hall steps two hours prior.

"Jump in," Luke said, climbing into his truck, which was now empty of sandbags once again. The man had already hoisted himself into the box, banging the roof to indicate Luke could pull away. Right now their differences had been set aside. It was the thing Luke admired most about a good man—they were able to set aside their disagreements and misgivings to work together when it mattered the most.

It made him feeler lighter to know Olivia had chosen well.

The ground under the truck was swampy and his tires spun on the sodden lawn as he made his way back to the street in front of the house. There had been a few times when he'd steered too close to the moving floodwaters and felt the power of the current push against his truck. It had caused his hands to grow damp on the wheel and his heart to thud hard in his chest.

He drove back to the pile of sandbags outside the town's maintenance department to get a new load. They were almost out and a helpless feeling rose inside him. There simply wasn't enough time to save everything.

Mandy's husband, Frankie, was currently using Luke's backhoe to try and redirect the flow with a few boulders, but the river knew where it wanted to go and with so much of the shoreline already flooded, their efforts were becoming a case of too little, too late.

Luke and Devon heaved the last of the heavy sacks into the truck, Luke's arms and shoulders feeling the strain from the nonstop work. The two men were both breathing hard as stopped and stared at each other.

"Now what?" Luke asked. There weren't enough sandbags to save the rest of the businesses and homes that were in danger.

"We do what we can," Devon replied, with a hard look of determination.

Luke gave a nod and drove back to the half wall they'd left minutes before. The water was already deeper, swirling past the barriers the men and women had created, large chunks of ice flowing freely across lawns.

It seemed like half the town had turned out to help and Luke nodded at faces he recognized. Looking downriver he could see sheering ice grinding against the side of the building where his money was held. The lights were on in the bank and his safety deposit key was in his pocket. He could slip over there for just a minute.

But a minute over here might save someone's home.

"We're out of sandbags," a desperate voice called.

Choice made. There was nothing else he could do here. Helping Emma was more important than moving his truck to higher ground, and Luke headed toward the bank, the current nearly sweeping him off his feet as the earth under his boot shifted. He shivered as the freezing water sliced through his clothing.

A wall of sandbags had been started near the bank, the river curving around the partial barrier, its power redirected with more force against the building's foundations.

"My car!"

Luke turned to see Cory Mattson standing in the frigid waters, his face white in the headlights of another vehicle. Behind Luke and closer to the old riverbank was a late model family car with water up to its doors and rising fast. Every once in a while the car would shift slightly as though trying to decide whether to get pushed downriver. The waterway wasn't playing by the rules and was greedily taking everything that wasn't driven into the ground. And even then it was taking, sucking at foundations as if they were made of sand.

Luke closed his eyes, realizing why Cory looked so stricken. The photos. The ones of his wife, who had loved him through raising teenagers and near poverty. The rare town photos that had been entrusted into his care.

"Photos still in the trunk?" Luke called.

Cory gave a ghost of a nod. Luke could see him debating whether to go into the deeper water to save the pictures. "They're in plastic bins, but the lids aren't watertight."

Luke opened the back door of his truck and grabbed the tow cable Leif had insisted Emma continue to borrow after she'd used it to winch the truck from the ditch a few weeks prior. The thick nylon cable might be long enough to reach the car.

Cory was wading out into the thigh-deep water, struggling to stay upright. "Dad!" Devon was trying to organize a human chain to help his father reach the car without being swept away.

"Stay back!" Cory called. "It's not safe for you."

It wasn't safe for anyone. And especially not the man who was going to be a grandfather to Olivia and Devon's baby in a few weeks.

"Pull him back," Luke commanded. He held up the cable, which he'd tied to the back of the truck, the other end wrapped around his waist.

Devon nodded, snagging his father's hand and yanking him hard, tugging him back toward solid ground.

Luke took a deep breath, surveying the men standing in the twilight. This could be it.

Goodbye, Blueberry Springs.

"Keys are in my truck," Luke said to Devon as he waded deeper, heading upstream among the thick chunks of ice, hoping he had enough cable to reach the car and that the current wouldn't swing him past it, a few feet short.

"It's not safe," Devon called.

"Nothing worthwhile is," Luke replied, as he reached the end of the cable and let the current carry him along, his footing lost, then regained, then lost again. The freezing water stole the air from his lungs and an ache settled deep in his bones. He hit the side of Cory's car with a smack, sending the vehicle drifting and bobbing before it snagged on something under the water. One false move and the vehicle, which was now closer to the raging current, would be gone.

A chunk of ice floating in the water hit Luke in the back. He arched in pain, his legs growing weak.

"Tell Emma I love her," he said, knowing his words would be lost under the roar of the river and the cracking of ice, just before he went under.

EMMA STOPPED at the bridge that linked the road to the cabin to town.

A man in a reflective vest was putting up a barricade and a Road Closed sign as night settled in.

"What's going on?" she called out the Jeep's window. She was riding the brake and the pressure was killing her bruised leg.

"Best you come along unless you want to be stuck on that side of the mountain for a few days."

Emma put the vehicle in gear and rolled across the bridge before stopping again, this time putting it in Park.

"I didn't hear about construction," she called, over the crushing, grinding noise of ice forcing its way under the bridge. Now that she was on the other side, where was she going to spend the next few days?

"We've got an ice jam upstream that's breaking up. From time to time we get some strange weather that forms big ice, and then a warm spell that unlocks it all. Now it's on the move and threatening to take out bridges."

"Really?"

"Yup. Happens every few springs." He had leaned against her Jeep, but pushed off. "I'd better get moving. I have two more bridges to close."

"Good luck."

"Thanks." He paused, his expression softening. "That was really brave, what you did in your video." His gaze traveled to her wig, which she'd put on at the last minute, feeling uncertain about showing up in public without it. Revealing her own hair in a video was one thing, in real life another.

She adjusted the wig, feeling self-conscious. "Thanks."

"My wife had cancer and the beauty part of it was the hardest for her. Wish you'd been around then. Your going public about it all would have made her feel less alone."

Emma blinked back tears of gratitude. Impulsively, she reached out and squeezed his hand. He felt warm despite the snap in the air, and his eyes teared up along with hers.

"Thank you," she whispered.

He gave a brief nod and turned. Then he paused and said over his shoulder, "If you're looking for that man of yours, he's hauling sandbags."

"Sandbags?"

The man pointed north, toward a part of town Emma hadn't been to yet. "Hauling them from maintenance to the river's edge to protect the buildings along the shore. But my guess is they've run out by now and are sitting in the bar warming up with one of Moe's hot toddies."

She hoped that was true, but judging from Olivia's panicked phone call, Emma had a feeling he wasn't taking it easy in a pub.

LUKE MANAGED to pull himself onto the hood of the car, his entire body feeling like an unresponsive block of ice. Now what? How could he attach the strap when his hands were barely functional, his entire body screaming from the cold? Devon was hollering something over the roar of the raging river, ice chunks scraping past the car's frame, spinning it every so often. At any moment, Luke could be swept downstream. Well, actually not him, as he was still attached to his truck, which meant things could get interesting.

The undercarriage, the best place to attach the hook, was underwater, but there was no way he was going back in. He might not come out again.

It was becoming harder to think and Luke knew he had to move fast, faster than the hypothermia that was closing in.

Carefully, he knelt on the hood and threw his weight against the windshield. Nothing. He needed to break the glass so he could hook on to the frame of the car. He'd buy Cory a new windshield later—it was replaceable; the photos were not.

He sat and fumbled with the cable tied around his waist. He loosened the knot just as the car spun as it was hit by a large slab of ice, tossing Luke onto his side. He began to slip off the hood and he dropped the cable, nearly losing it into the water.

He scrambled, catching himself, then the cable. Using the windshield wipers, he hauled himself back onto the hood, pulling himself into an unsteady kneeling position.

He raised the metal hook on the end of the cable, lifting it high like a scepter before crashing it down, cracking the glass. Once. Twice. Again and again until his chest was heaving from the effort and a hole had been made for him to reach through, hooking the cable onto the first thing he could reach—the steering wheel. Good enough.

The cable tightened and the car spun as Devon began to tow it toward shore. Luke could see his truck struggling, its taillights bright in the darkness that had settled in. Cory's car was like an oversize fish, refusing to be pulled in as it hunkered down in Park, making the truck work doubly hard.

A floodlight was aimed in Luke's direction and he squinted against the brightness. The water was rising faster than he could calculate, and Devon kept adjusting the truck's angle and speed, its tires almost clear of the water.

Then an ice floe snagged the cable that joined them, a chunk of white in the dark waters, pulling the truck deeper with a determination found only in nature. The truck tires spun as the car began to drift. Devon gunned the engine, water spraying out from behind him, arcing in the lights before disappearing into the darkness. They were both going to be dragged downriver at this rate.

"Cut me loose!" Luke hollered.

Someone in a reflective coat ventured farther into the water, hand crooked around his ear. Another chunk of ice hit the side of Cory's car with a loud thump.

"Cut. Me. Loose!" Luke repeated. He fumbled with the hook attached to the steering wheel, but the tension was too great.

He could hear someone yell, "Don't!"

"We h-h-have to!" he shouted, beginning to stutter from the chill. The last thing he wanted was to drag Devon into this mess, and for Olivia's baby to be born fatherless.

Suddenly, the truck had traction and Devon revved the engine like an expert racer, yanking the cable tight, weaving and pulling, causing the car to jerk free of the ice.

Luke didn't allow himself to feel relief until his ride was fully on dry land and then some. Cory was there in a second, unhooking the cable as another man helped Luke down from his perch.

"Thank you, Luke. Thank you," Cory kept repeating.

Luke was so cold he could barely move, his jaw chattering. He'd never experienced anything like it and was grateful for the hands that propped him up, guiding him along the uneven ground. Even if they were Devon's.

"You d-d-did g-good," Luke stuttered.

"Not bad yourself, you crazy city slicker," Devon replied. He looked as though he wasn't sure whether to hug him or deck him for endangering himself.

Honestly, Luke would take either one. Instead, he held out his hand in truce, not sure whether he'd be able to bend his fingers, they felt so frozen. "B-b-brother."

Their eyes locked as Devon shook his numb hand, clapping him on the back and dislodging ice that had formed on Luke's jacket. "Brother."

Devon's expression turned serious. "We need to get you warmed up. Fast."

That felt like a good idea.

There was a gasp from the people who'd gathered around, pressing blankets on him. Luke looked over his shoulder to see what was happening.

The bank, a formidable brick-and-wood structure, seemed to be twisting. One corner sank lower. Then the whole thing seemed as though it was suspended in air before it shifted and dissolved like a computer-generated image in a movie. Pieces ripped and fell away before the building itself succumbed to the force of gravity. Within moments the bank was entirely gone, the water swallowing the real estate as if it had never existed.

Safety deposit boxes included.

———

"Luke!" Emma could see a silhouette that looked like her husband in the headlights of a vehicle. His movements were sluggish, and several men were helping him walk.

He'd been hurt, as Olivia had feared!

"Luke!"

He turned as though hearing his name on the wind before trudging along again, a man who looked like Devon propping him up. Emma cupped her hands around her mouth and called again. Someone hooked an arm through hers, leading her toward Luke. Her leg ached, and she hobbled, trying to keep up.

"Come on," the man said, "he needs to be warmed up." It was Scott Malone. He was tall, broad, and his strides so long that Emma had to struggle to keep up, her feet splashing in water that was so cold it hurt.

He threaded his way between vehicles, sweeping her along with him, and she jumped as she heard a cracking sound. In the shadows across the raging river, a large tree crashed into the water, disappearing within seconds.

Scott led her to a car where Luke was being pushed into the backseat. The police truck was parked beside it, its colored lights rotating and lighting up the night.

Red. Blue. Red. Blue. Nothing good ever came with those flashing colors.

"The hospital is likely overwhelmed," Scott told Devon, who was helping Luke into the car. "Try and warm him up at home. If you don't see improvement within fifteen minutes, bring him in."

On a cross street Emma saw an ambulance flash by, and tears pricked her eyes as she realized it could be going to help someone she knew. Scott pushed her onto the seat beside Luke.

"The bridge to the cabin is closed," she said.

"I've got this," Devon stated, starting the rusty old car she recognized as his. For the mayor he sure didn't put much effort into looking the part. She could see how her sister, who had often been frustrated by the expectations they'd grown up with, likely found him refreshing. Exactly how Emma found the entire town.

"B-b-brave," Luke said to Emma, his teeth chattering.

Scott closed the door and patted the trunk once. The car pulled away, Devon honking to get a cluster of men to move aside, the heater cranked to maximum.

"I'm sure you were very brave." Emma rubbed a hand across Luke's shoulders, making the silver plastic wrap designed to reflect his body heat back at him crinkle. She had a feeling it was merely reflecting the frigidness of the icy water that soaked his clothes.

"He's hypothermic. Don't rub. Just press heat into his core," Devon commanded from the front seat.

Emma wrapped her arms around Luke, the wet cold seeping through her clothes everywhere the blanket didn't cover him.

"No," Luke said. "Y-you w-were."

"Me?"

"Videos." His shaking was uncontrollable as he met her gaze.

So much sincerity, respect and honesty. And there was something else there, too.

Maybe regret. Maybe humility.

He let out a giant shudder and hunched farther into the seat to preserve what little body heat he had left.

"You okay back there?" Devon asked. He looked over his shoulder to check on them as he pulled onto Main Street.

"I don't know," Emma replied. Luke's lips were blue, his face so pale.

She worried he wasn't going to make it.

"I'm sorry, Luke. I should have listened to you instead of going off on a whim. I probably ruined everything."

He shook his head adamantly as they pulled up in front of a cute house. Devon's house. The home Olivia had chosen over Luke's luxury quarters that overlooked the ocean.

Emma flashed a glance at Luke, worried he might refuse to go inside. "We have to get you warmed up," she said gently.

She scooted out of the car, her calf muscle aching, her shoes squishing on the car's wet flooring.

"Are you sure we shouldn't take him to the hospital?" she asked, noticing how uncoordinated Luke was as she helped him climb out.

Devon shook his head. "We need to move fast," he muttered, clasping Luke's arm again.

Olivia came to the door, her expression frantic. "Devon?" Her voice was high with fear.

"Luke was in the river," Emma said.

"Saving my dad's car and all the family photos," Devon said, his voice thick.

Emma looked at Luke for confirmation, but he was solely focused on putting one foot in front of the other.

"We have to warm him up," Emma said.

Olivia was still standing in the doorway, blocking the way, her eyes wide. "My water broke."

Devon, who had nudged his shoulder under Luke's arm to help propel him up the steps, turned white, then swore under his breath. "Are you sure? You're not due for another three weeks."

"I'm sure," she said in a trembling voice.

"How far apart are contractions?"

"It's time to go."

"Olivia, you're going to be fine," Emma said. She addressed

Devon as she tried to take Luke's weight. "I've got this." She really didn't.

Devon began barking out commands, hustling Luke into a room just off the kitchen that looked like a home office slash guest bedroom. He vanished midsentence, talking about putting on water for tea, then reappeared moments later, his wet boots leaving dark spots on the carpet. He plugged in a space heater, aiming it at the futon couch, which he yanked out into a flat bed, scraping paint off the wall in the process.

"Get him out of everything wet and under the covers." He pulled a stack of blankets out of a small closet, dumping them on the bed.

"Devon?" called Olivia, her voice high, breathless.

Emma felt the need to run to her, but Luke, who was always so capable and strong, didn't look like he could stand on his own.

In the kitchen the kettle whistled and Devon disappeared again, returning in a few seconds with a cup of steaming water, a tea bag floating in it.

"Take off your clothes as well as his and hold him tight. Warm him up. A bath is risky. The extremities hold enough cold to freeze the heart. Heat the core, then hands and feet. Keep extremities out of the bath and down from the heart."

Emma tried to breathe through the fear. If she messed this up, it could kill him.

"P-p-photos okay?" Luke stuttered.

Devon gave a quick, "Don't know," as Olivia called him again. "I have to go. I'll leave my car in case you need to bring him in."

Devon closed the bedroom door, and not too long after Emma heard the front door slam.

Skin to skin. Body to body.

Luke had slumped onto the bed, the reflective blanket dropping to the floor as he struggled to get out of his jacket, his arms barely functional.

Emma yanked off his boots, then went for the coat. Then his

shirt, which was stuck to his skin. He was so cold the chill was radiating off him.

"Pants." Luke tried for a smile.

"I know," she said softly. "Sexy, isn't it?" She undid the button at his waistband, the fly. She pressed him backward onto the bed, carelessly piling blankets on him before she tried to shuck the wet jeans from his legs.

The denim finally came free, the sudden lack of resistance sending them whipping against the wall behind her and a shadow box crashing to the floor.

Luke had the blankets clutched against his chest, looking helpless.

Emma pulled off his underwear, then tucked the blankets around him. He gave a small smile.

"Don't get any ideas about make-up sex," she scolded.

She aimed the heater at him. The tea was still too hot to drink. There was nothing left for her to do but climb into bed with him.

She'd done it before. Why was she hesitating?

She dropped her coat on the floor, kicking Luke's wet clothes into the corner.

She hoped Olivia was okay.

Luke, as if reading her mind, said, "Go. She might need you."

"*You* need me," Emma said uncertainly.

"I'm f-f-fine." Another shudder went through him.

"No, you're not," she said with a sigh. She dropped her pants. Then her shirt.

"S-sexy," Luke said.

She put her hands on her hips. "Did you wade into that river on purpose? What if Scott was the one who'd had to warm you up? Hmm? Or Mary Alice? She uses her bra as a purse. Imagine how comfortable it would be cozied up to that. Then where would you be?"

"W-w-warm me," he said.

"I'm still mad at you," she replied as she dived under the covers, giving a squeal as her flesh hit Luke's freezing body. "And I wouldn't do this if there was a chance that you'd survive without me."

His grin looked more like a grimace.

"And you can just cut that smile, because if you *do* survive this we're going to have a very long talk, as well as sign some divorce papers."

LUKE CLUNG to Emma and her heat. "Are you warm enough?" he asked her as she let out a shiver. His jaw was no longer chattering uncontrollably.

"Warmer than you," she said softly.

"Not saying much." His entire body felt clenched from the cold and as though it would never be warm again. But Luke could feel his feet again—they hurt.

Just like his heart.

...as well as sign some divorce papers.

"The truth is, Emma…"

She tipped her head up so she could see his face.

"The truth is…I wanted to give you the rest of my money so you could finish your project. Step out of the way so you could launch it in the way it deserves."

"And?"

"The money was in the bank."

"And what? You can't remember your password?" She looked amused.

"The bank washed away tonight." It had felt right helping Devon's dad, even though it had cost Luke a few million. And yet he knew he would make the same choice if faced with it again. He still would wade into that river, and not just because it had him curled against the woman he'd thought would never speak to him again.

"Banks are insured, but Luke, you don't have to put more money into this product. It's *ours*. Even if we don't continue to work together on it."

"It was in my safety deposit box. Not insured, and quite likely never to be retrieved."

"Oh. Wow. I'm sorry."

"And the truth is I'm no longer wealthy." He waited for her to withdraw, pull away. Instead she tightened her grip, infusing him with even more warmth and making his throat thick with emotion. "I have nothing to my name beyond my apartment, our agreement and anything that comes from the line."

A sharp feeling of failure cut him deep.

"You still have Cohen's."

He still had his resort in the Caribbean, too. But in his mind it always had been, and always would be off-limits due to the way its proceeds helped those in need.

"Everything I want is here in Blueberry Springs, but my wife is planning to leave me," he whispered.

She didn't reply, simply rested her head against his chest. It was all he could do to hold back the emotion that threatened to overtake him.

EMMA LIFTED her cheek from the warm spot she'd created on Luke's cool flesh. He had stopped shivering and was going to survive.

He'd been a definite jerk earlier in the day, but then had gone and chosen to save someone else's photos over money. He'd helped Devon's family.

But he'd also tried to pay someone to hide the photos she was proud of. And yes, having them released right now wasn't awesome. At all.

"Why didn't you save your money?" she asked.

He shifted and looked away. "I thought about it." He drew a shaky breath. "Stupid, I know, but what I did felt right. Cory was willing to wade out for those photos and I just…" He shook his head. "He could have been swept down the river. He's going to become a grandpa tonight."

"*You* could have been swept away."

"I know. I asked Devon to cut me free at one point."

Emma felt that wrenching in her chest again. As if the weight of the pickup pressed on her as she fought the tears, imagining what it might be like if Luke had been lost tonight.

She would be a widow.

She didn't want to be one. Or a divorcée, either.

But she also wanted a man she could trust. One with the same game plan as she had and no secrets.

He seemed to gain new resolve as he said firmly, "People are happy without money."

"What will you do about the blackmailers?" She hated to ask it, but had to know.

Luke shook his head. "A woman once told me to stop hiding behind my money and be a man. Own up to my past mistakes. She showed me how to take the power out of their moves by beating them to the punch. Revealing your own secrets takes away their power to hurt and destroy you."

Emma felt a prickle of worry. Her earlier wig reveal may have taken down the company. "I'm not so sure that's true."

Luke tipped up her chin so she'd meet his eyes. "I am. I've made a lot of mistakes, Emma. I've put money ahead of everything, thinking it was the security I was seeking. And I was wrong.

"If you'll have me, I'd like to keep working with you. Although I understand if you choose not to. But either way, it's been an honor to work for you." He gently touched her bottom lip, letting a draft of cool air under the covers.

When Emma met his eyes she knew it was the Luke she loved who was talking, who was asking to stay.

She said yes.

1 2

*L*uke wiped away Emma's happy tears.

They would remain business partners, but he wanted more. He wanted all of her. All of her trust and love.

He brushed the hair from her face. She was wearing her wig, still not quite believing in her strength or beauty despite her words in today's video.

"Will you show me the real you?" he asked quietly.

"What?"

He kissed her slowly, unsure whether she'd reject him. He tenderly stroked her cheek, kissing her as light as a butterfly, showing her with his body what she couldn't seem to accept with his words.

She was his everything.

He hesitated, then reached for her hairline. "I want to see the real you. The one you keep hidden. I discovered her here in Blueberry Springs and she's the best woman I've ever met. I fell in love with her, EmmaLu." He found a hairpin that kept the wig in place, then hesitated. "Will you trust me?"

Her eyes darkened and she eased away.

"Please?"

240

He knew she felt exposed. He was asking a model, a woman who'd always been rewarded for her beauty, to show him what she thought was ugly.

"For your husband." He gave a slow smile and he watched her try to bite back her own, her wet lashes creating the most beautiful star shapes framing her eyes.

She slowly pushed herself into a sitting position, her body bare before him like a pinup model. The air from the heater was warm, but he tenderly tucked the blankets around her as she hesitantly lifted her hands to her hair. She removed a pin, then another. Her blue eyes would dart to his, and he was careful not to spook her even though her trust was breaking his heart. She was so vulnerable, so…breakable. And yet so strong.

He sat up beside her, helping her peel back the wig. There was a cap underneath and she unpinned it as well, then tossed it to the floor, giving him a shy look from under her lashes.

She was the most beautifully real thing he'd ever seen.

"Your new hair is so much darker."

She raised her hand, self-consciously tugging on it as though that could change its color, its length.

"May I?" he asked, reaching out. He slipped his fingers through her short locks, slowly, tenderly. She looked petite, vulnerable and her eyes drifted closed, her chin wrinkling as she struggled with emotion.

"It's soft." He placed a kiss on her cheek, just under her lashes.

Her blue eyes opened, piercing him with how bared she felt. It was like a current and he treaded carefully, afraid to break what they were building between them.

This was real.

"I love you, Emma Carrington. All of you. If I have you—" he swallowed a lump of emotion "—I have everything this man needs."

Tears rolled down her cheeks, fat and quick.

She opened her mouth to speak, but had no words. He pulled

her close, caressing her, loving her. And before long they were united, sighing with the satisfaction and freedom of being utterly in love.

———

LUKE WAS FINALLY FEELING human again, and not just because of the way he and Emma had come together, unclasping the last pieces of their armor and letting them fall. The room was warm, as was he, even though the heat hadn't fully penetrated his bones. Emma, however, had a sheen of sweat over her skin. That perfect, kissable skin, which became exposed as she slipped from the covers, grabbing her clothes.

He wanted to pull her back into bed.

It was predawn and he didn't think Emma had slept much. Neither had he, for that matter. All he could think about was the fact that she hadn't returned the three words he found himself longing to hear.

It made him think of what Olivia had told him—that Emma had passed him up all those years ago so her sister could have him. A woman who'd never truly loved him. Was Emma a repeat?

"Let's go get our vehicles, and see how Olivia is doing," she said.

A few hours ago she had placed his clothes in the dryer, and she went to retrieve them now, limping in the process. Where the SUV had hit her there was an angry, multicolored welt. It made him hate himself, the bruise a visual reminder that he'd failed her by not doing the right thing. It brought with it a near-crippling fear that it could have been so much worse, and that the nightmare wasn't yet over.

They slipped into their clothes, his still warm from the dryer and the best feeling in the world. He wasn't sure what the river had done after they'd left, where his truck and the rented Jeep would be and what condition they'd be in.

"Emma?" he began. He wanted to ask if the two of them were okay, but found himself at a loss, unsure how to navigate the foreign emotional waters. Instead, he simply said, "Thank you."

She nodded, not quite looking him in the eye. She didn't seem to know what to do with herself now that they weren't in bed. He could tell she was already doubting how she'd let him in, exposed her rawness, and that she was doubting the power of their moment, trying to withdraw, trying to find a way to call it a mistake.

He opened the front door for her, checking to make sure it was safe, and was assaulted by the sounds of birds chirping like nothing was wrong in the world. A woman he now recognized as Devon's good friend Nicola was pushing a double stroller down the sidewalk, and she called out to them, "It's a baby girl!" She pointed to Luke's truck parked at the curb. "Keys are on the visor." She smiled and carried on.

Blueberry Springs. If he had kids he'd pull up the last of his stakes in South Carolina and move into the first available home for sale here, even if it was the small cabin, which had grown on him in an unpredictable way.

"I missed being there?" Emma said softly.

Luke's heart dropped, knowing Emma had counted on being there for her sister. "I'm sorry."

They silently climbed into his truck, and found the keys right where Nicola had said they'd be, driving to the river.

Emma had left the Jeep near the edge of the rising water, but today, the only sign the river had been that high was the swath of debris left where it had raged over its banks.

It was going to take a lot of work to clean it up and repair all the damage.

Emma got out of the truck, pausing to look at him. "I'm going to go see the baby and Olivia."

"I'll follow you."

She gave him an intrigued glance, but said nothing.

He followed the green Jeep to the hospital, then parked beside Emma. He wanted to pull her into his arms, kiss her, love her. Instead, he stood beside his truck, the door still open. He'd invited himself along, and wasn't sure where the pressing-his-luck line was currently located.

Emma limped toward him slowly, as though uncertain herself. As she drew near, Luke hoped for a kiss, but knew he would easily settle for her not sending him away. Despite how they'd bared themselves to each other, they still hadn't had that big long talk she'd promised.

She paused in front of him, her expression unguarded, but unsure.

"Luke Cohen, you owe us a lot of money."

At the sound of the gruff voice, Luke instinctively stepped in front of Emma, pressing her toward his truck's open door. He turned to find three men closing in.

The streetlights brightening the hospital grounds had winked off; the parking lot practically empty as daybreak stretched into early morning. He wished Emma would leap into his truck, start the engine and hightail it out of there. But she kept holding on to his elbow as if he was her life raft in a stormy sea.

One of the men cracked his knuckles.

"We released the photos when you didn't pay up," another snarled.

"We're not giving you a dime," Emma said, leaning against Luke's shoulder as if he was holding her back from taking a swing. "You did us a *favor* releasing those photos."

The men shared an uncertain glance before shifting their weight and stepping closer.

"You had your warning shot. Now it's time to pay up." One of the gang produced a metal pipe and swung it jovially, eyeing Emma's leg.

Rage built inside Luke like a primal being rising from the

dark, ready to lay the world flat. His words came out like pellet shots. "You hit my wife?"

"You can't scare us," Emma said.

These guys weren't looking to cause some negative publicity, they were looking to hurt her. The woman he loved.

"I'm calling the police," Emma said loudly.

The men had a hearty laugh, and Luke felt Emma shrink against him. He tried to subtly wave her into the truck.

"If you don't pay, we'll take our debt in pain." The leader began counting things off on his meaty fingers. "You owe us for the government bribes. I bet you won't think revealing that one is a favor. The media payoffs to keep things hush-hush about Carrington…"

"What payoffs?" Emma asked quietly.

"Ho-ho! This makes it all so much better." The first man bent over laughing and Luke wondered what his head would look like smashed in, thanks to his truck door.

Luke shrugged, letting go of the pride that had caused him to hold on to his secrets and shame for much too long. "Em, I paid the press with some high-priced ads, in exchange for them not running anything negative about you, your family or either of our companies last summer. I also spent time living in a homeless shelter."

She quirked her head. There was no judgment, no pity in her expression, simply curiosity and maybe a little confusion.

"I lived in one for almost a week." He turned to face her more fully, ensuring he didn't leave his back to the men, who seemed to be reassessing their game plan. "When I was nine my mom left my dad, but her cousin wouldn't take her in. My mom went back to my father. She's always felt controlled by him. He doesn't give her…"

Financial freedom.

They'd left with money, but in Arizona…the casino. She'd lost it all. Who did that when they had a kid waiting outside?

An addict. That's who.

Luke thought of the big shopping sprees. His father's constant need for money.

He'd been covering for Charlotte for years, hadn't he? Taking the brunt of Luke's anger and disapproval.

His mom had said she'd doubled the money she'd taken out for her condo's down payment. How long until she lost everything Luke had given her?

"Yeah?" One of the men piped up, a hint of desperation in his voice. "How would that look? The mighty Cohens living in a homeless shelter."

"You know what? Tell the world. I don't care. Good came of it. I help tons of communities with social assistance programs both here and in the Caribbean. And spread those photos of Emma some more. Really milk it. They'll be good publicity for the new business line she plans on starting."

He had no idea if she planned to, but with her business sense, he hoped so. It was time for her to stop holding back.

To Luke's surprise, Haddie stepped from the shadows. "Don't worry, if they release something negative—I'll write a counter article about all the good you've done, not only in this town, but overseas and in the various states, as well."

"It won't matter," another man said. They were starting to cluster, looking slightly panicked. The one smacking the pipe against his palm was no longer looking quite so brave.

"The past can't hurt me any longer," Luke stated. "Sure, I've done some stuff to protect my family that you could twist around in hopes of making me look bad, but the people who know me best won't be swayed, and I've come to realize that making money isn't everything." He wrapped an arm around Emma's shoulders, drawing her against him. "Some things are more important than that."

Haddie waved someone over. It was Scott Malone, with Logan and Zach close behind.

"These men confessed to the hit-and-run?" Scott confirmed.

Haddie nodded. "They took credit for it."

"Who *are* you?" Luke asked her suspiciously.

"FBI." She gave a sheepish smile before flashing her badge. "I've been investigating your father for almost a year, although you suddenly became much more interesting with this whole mess."

"Will you still write that article?"

She merely raised her brows in reply and Luke shook his head at himself. "Right. Sorry." Stupid question. She wasn't a reporter. He turned to Logan and Zach and asked, "Do you two work for her?" By the sound of things, he'd hired the men around the time Haddie started investigating his family. Had he been paying them to snoop on him and his family?

Logan stood at ease. "When agent Goodchild approached us we shared what we knew in order to help protect you, sir."

"Protect him! Who's going to protect us?" called one of the men. "Cohen's is corrupt! They hid stuff! We were bringing it to light."

Scott began reading the thugs their rights. One of them tried to hoof it out of there but Logan reached out a beefy arm, knocking him to the ground.

Maybe he was worth the money, after all.

"Don't worry about these guys," Logan said. "Haddie's going to sort things out. You two are free to go."

Luke took Emma's hand, placing a gentle kiss against the back of it. "Come on. We have a niece to meet."

EMMA WAS STILL PONDERING over the past day and all that had happened.

Luke, her husband, loved her. Truly, genuinely loved her. The real her and not some image, but the person she was even if it changed from day to day. The person who'd grown and evolved in Blueberry Springs.

She'd felt so exposed after making love without her wig, as if she'd revealed everything down to the raw bits that hurt. It wasn't until Luke confronted his own pain and his past out in the hospital parking lot that she felt he'd finally let go and allowed himself to be exposed to that same raw level.

She'd thought he would break, every shifting emotion etched on his face. The fear, the anguish. The enlightenment, before he finally stood up for himself.

That was the moment when she'd realized they were going to make it.

Then, when the kerfuffle was over, they'd gone into the hospital to see the new parents and meet their new niece.

Luke had smiled, clapping Devon on the back and congratulating him, saying, "Way to go, brother-in-law. Take good care of them."

Brother-in-law. Emma had never dared think beyond the piece of paper that had created a union neither of them had ever planned to advertise.

She'd had a difficult time holding back the tears, and had instead turned her attention to gushing over her perfectly healthy, not-quite-term niece, Abigail Joan, and her sister, finally a mom.

But Olivia's focus hadn't just been on her new six-pound child, it had been on Emma, too. She'd squeezed her hand and told her to hang on to Luke. To not let him go no matter what.

It had been an emotional twenty-four hours, and by the time they'd made it back to the cabin, the bridge having been reopened as the flood waters retreated, Emma had fallen into bed beside Luke, and slept nearly until noon.

She left the bedroom, slowly working the stiffness out of her injured leg, to find Luke fixing brunch in the kitchen.

She loved him and he loved her. That made her smile, her whole body warming.

He moved around the room as if he owned it, as if he could command the pans to turn out perfect French toast, scrambled eggs and more just with his assertiveness.

"Hungry?"

She smiled again. "Insatiable."

"Ready for that long talk?" he asked, setting her breakfast in front of her.

She stared at the plate. She didn't know where to start their discussion, so blurted out what felt like the most important part. "I'm not going to divorce you, but you can't give your mom the inheritance."

They were both quiet for a moment. "Okay."

"Unless it's in a trust or something."

"Agreed." Luke paused, a brief look of sadness washing over his expression. It vanished as he added, "I have something to show you." He turned a tablet to face her, the screen for their preorders open.

She was no mathematician, but she'd guess the number she was staring at was at least a few hundred, if not thousand, times more than it had been the last time she'd checked. Which would have been yesterday morning. Before the videos, the flood, the baby. It already felt like a week ago.

She met Luke's gaze.

"It's not a glitch," he stated.

"It's got to be. Or a prank." She took the tablet and began tapping various boxes and buttons, diving deeper, trying to make sense of the incredible increase in orders for the new product line. These were the kind of numbers they were hoping for a month after launch, once they had a little word-of-mouth going, once they'd proved themselves.

"No prank." He woke up his laptop and tapped on his keyboard before turning that screen to face her, too. It was for her Real Beauty video. Her hand automatically went to her short hair. The comments numbered in the tens of thousands.

Emma grabbed her phone, which she'd left facedown on the table beside her purse when she'd arrived home hours ago, completely exhausted. She turned it over, checking its screen. There were hundreds of missed calls, email notifications and more.

She thought she might faint. There was no way she could keep up with all this. She needed an assistant. And maybe an assistant for her assistant, if things continued like this for more than a day or two.

Her blood went cold. What if they were all nasty phone calls? Hateful emails?

"They love you," Luke said, as though reading her thoughts. He'd always seemed to have a way of doing that.

"Are you sure?"

He took the tablet, placed it on the table so he could grasp her shaking hands. She was like he'd been after his dip in the raging river last night—trembling uncontrollably.

"EmmaLu." He tipped her chin up. "This is it. This is what you were hoping for."

She nodded mutely.

"I love you, and I'll be right here at your side through it all."

Emma met his eyes and knew that was true, and that she couldn't have chosen a better partner.

"I love you, too, Luke. I have since I was a kid."

He gave her a crooked smile. "Remind me to tell you a story of how I had this inappropriate crush on you when we were younger."

"You didn't."

"You made me laugh," he said simply. "Still do, EmmaLu."

IT WAS launch day and Luke was feeling nervous. Things had been insane since the flood. Totally, unpredictably insane. They'd had to hire eighteen new staff just to handle the preorders that had swamped their system after Emma's beauty video turned the world on end.

After they'd made love like two souls joining, and had agreed to stay together, he'd naively thought everything was going to be simple and easy. He'd thought wrong. All You had exploded and they hadn't stopped running since. Running toward today. Launch day.

They hadn't even had time to consider a sprawling four-bedroom home when it came onto the market, choosing instead to stay in the small cabin where everything was already set up and at their fingertips. However, last month they had taken a few hours out of their crammed schedule to claim his inheritance, setting up a trust for his mother after taking a small portion to help with the additional explosion of All You startup costs. More greenhouses, more staff, more everything.

And his mom? She'd moved back in with Franklin. Go figure, but Luke understood that love made a person do things that seemed strange from the outside.

Despite the lack of time Luke had had to spend with his wife, he knew she loved him. He could see it in the way her smile turned shy, the way she no longer fussed with her short hair when he was with her.

They'd hired just about everyone in town to help fill the half million orders, and the community had come together in the most amazing way. He was proud to be able to cohost a launch party for everyone who had wanted to come, and it was strangely satisfying being able to feed everyone under a series of large tents. It was nearly bankrupting him, but then again, without Blueberry Springs, they wouldn't be where they were.

And they were in a good place. A very good place.

And Emma… She was a shining light, a powerfully intelligent woman.

Man, did he ever love her.

He smiled at his wife from across the tent. She looked up, as though sensing he was thinking about her.

"Something's wrong with the microphone," the man beside Luke said. He was tracing the wires that radiated from the sound table set up at one end of the expansive white tent, across the mountain grasses that served as the tent's floor, and toward the stage and various speakers.

"I'll help." Luke leaped onstage and started fiddling with the microphone, planning to tap it until the issue was resolved and sound was restored. He waved to his protégé, Jay, who happened to be the younger brother of Trey, the kid he'd promised to cover the costs of college for. After the flood, Luke had requested he mentor Jay who had an interest in all things business and often tagged along to minor meetings.

The guy at the soundboard moved his hand like a puppet, indicating Luke should talk.

"Want to go for it?" Luke asked Jay.

He nodded and quietly spoke into the microphone. "Testing. Testing. One, two, three."

The technician gave him the signal to keep going.

The crowd was watching and Jay backed away from the microphone.

Everyone was waiting for their host to say something. Seeing as the event was about him and Emma, Luke figured he might as well get things moving and welcome everyone. He indicated that Jay could go back to his seat where Trey had been fixing a wobbly table leg, and adjusted the microphone stand, raising it to his height.

"Hi. I'm Luke Cohen, and I'd like to welcome everyone to the launch of All You, a product that couldn't have happened without Blueberry Springs, these beautiful mountain meadows, and you.

Thank you all." He paused to wait for the applause to die down. "How are you tonight? Hungry? If so, do check out the spread Lily Harper, our local caterer, put out for us. Amazing meatballs, Lily. And I heard Jill Armstrong's door prize is spectacular. Great soaps and other products. Make sure you grab her business card on your way by the prize table."

He and Jill had had a long sit-down before concluding that Cohen's and her products weren't quite a match. She'd met with Burke Carver of the Sustain This, Honey online store, but he'd turned her down, and she'd decided momentarily to continue to refine her products before striking out again in a few months. But in the meantime, Luke would do all he could to help her.

The master of ceremonies was still moving around at the back of the tent, not quite ready to take over. Now what? Luke had started the ball rolling. He couldn't just let everyone sit and wait.

"So, I heard this joke from Beth Wilkinson's kid." The crowd groaned, and he saw Emma roll her eyes from the back of the tent, where she was bouncing Olivia's baby girl, trying to burp her. Emma gave him a look as if to say, *"Really, Luke? A joke in public?"*

He smiled, shifting his attention back to the crowd. "You know Beth?" he asked, before laughing. "Of course you do! This is Blueberry Springs. I'll bet most of you are related to her or went to school with her. Do we have a relative in the audience?"

A few people raised their hands, and an elderly lady raised a glass of what looked like sherry.

"I raised her!"

"You must be Gran," he said.

"Sure am! Have you seen my boyfriend, Reggie Max? He was at the open bar and I think he must have gotten drunk and fallen off the side of the mountain."

A few people laughed, as someone led an older gentleman her way.

"I think it's pretty cool how everyone in town helps each

other out," Luke said, before realizing he was speaking out loud. "I really do. It's different from the city—a good different—and I've learned a lot." He paused and lowered his voice ever so slightly. "Like never tell Mary Alice a secret."

"Hey!" the woman clucked from her spot in the middle of the tent. People were laughing, turning to check out her reaction.

"I know, I know, Mary Alice. But it's true, right?"

"Shush, you!"

He grinned, knowing she didn't take offense. "Anyone need a mint? Mary Alice is keeping some warm between her girls."

More laughter. The loudest from Mary Alice, who yanked a tin of mints from her bra and waved it in the air.

"Seriously, though," Luke continued. "This is a great town, full of wonderful people, and I'm happy you're all here tonight, and that you didn't get lost due to our instructions. You know, turn right where Olm's homestead used to be. Then right at the old mine." More laughter sounded. "Anyone know where Benny's restaurant used to be? I heard Emma convinced Lily to rebuild."

There were whoops and hollers of approval.

"Oh, and the joke. Right. I almost forgot. What did the firefly's mom say when he aced his flying exam?"

He paused, caught sight of Emma watching, a smile lighting her entire being.

"Way to glow."

He got moans and a few laughs.

"You thought I was going to buy you all a round again, didn't you?" Luke noted that the MC was waiting at the side of the stage, enjoying the show. "Well, don't worry. Emma and I are doing that tonight, too. The bar is open. Thank you, Blueberry Springs. For everything."

"To the man of the hour!" The MC had stepped to the microphone, and started clapping for him, but Luke waved him back.

"Nope. To Emma! It was all her."

She had given her niece back to Olivia and was standing

beside the MC in a white sundress, her short hair in a cute pixie. Luke smiled. She was gorgeous, real and the love of his life.

How many parties had Emma thrown in her life? But this one was different. It was special.

And there was one man who'd made it so. Without him believing in her she wouldn't have made it this far. And she knew that without her, he wouldn't have, either. They were a good pair, strengthening each other and working together in the spirit his grandparents had intended.

In some ways, she wished this was their wedding reception.

She hadn't told him that, though. Despite agreeing to not divorce, they'd barely had time to breathe lately, let alone work on their relationship.

It had taken all her courage last night to tell him she didn't want to return to the lovely shores of her South Carolina hometown. She was a mountain girl now. Once you'd had the satisfaction of pulling your truck from a ditch with your proverbial bare hands, why would you ever leave that?

He'd smiled knowingly, but not said a thing. She wasn't sure if that meant he planned on returning to Cohen's next week, as their agreement stated, or what.

She glanced down at her hands. For the past month she'd been working without nail polish, since it always chipped as she'd rushed to do whatever was needed to keep them on their tight launch schedule. She'd painted her nails a pale blue today and they didn't seem as honest.

She smiled at the thought of showing up at a party without nail polish. She could almost hear the whispers behind her back. And yet here in Blueberry Springs she knew that would never happen.

Last night she'd had a new ending to her driving dream. The

brakes had worked and she'd stopped the truck when she'd wanted to. Then she'd put the vehicle in gear and steered it forward, down the road to where Luke was waving to her, looking handsome in a tuxedo, his face lit with a smile. She'd discovered what her precious cargo was, too. It was her niece, Abigail. Sitting all innocent in her car seat, wearing a cute headband sporting a giant flower, with a big gummy smile for her auntie for pulling it off. For saving her. A new generation of Carringtons.

Emma glanced up. Luke had taken to the stage again. Since the flood, he'd been helping out with the other volunteers around town, fixing the parks, yards, streets and businesses that had been ripped apart by the river in March. Now he was onstage, looking so handsome and real that she felt her heart flutter. He was hers.

He had his arms slung around two of the guys on the volunteer crew as if he was one of them, and she realized that he was. The head of the crew was speaking. "Luke, we'd like to name a park after you."

"What?" He jerked in surprise, his cheeks pinking. He dropped his arms.

"You helped us out at great risk and peril to yourself."

"Everyone did."

"We want to show our appreciation. Not just for that night where you saved a large chunk of our local history in the way of the photos in Cory's car, but for the little things, like restocking our sandbags after the flood." Luke tried to protest but the man laughed. "We know it was you. You also donated your backhoe to the town."

"Nah, I just wanted cheap storage. I can still borrow it whenever I need it."

Everyone laughed, filling the tent with the sound, before the leader continued, "You chipped in for benches, loads of gravel. You even bought us all lunch and drinks at Brew Babies. You're one of a kind and your generosity of spirit has not gone unnoticed."

"I was just doing my part for my hometown," he said quietly.

He met Emma's gaze and her heart sang. *Hometown.*

"Why don't we name the park after the town's founder, or for our future generations?" Luke suggested.

The audience whooped.

The men shifted offstage, the presentation over, leaving Luke to stand there with the microphone. He looked at Emma. "I love you, Emma Carrington. And I want to marry you. For real. Forever and ever real. Will you marry me, EmmaLu?"

Her feet began propelling her forward as she nodded, trying not to sob with joy. He was off the stage within moments, his arms around her, his lips upon hers. When he came up for air he said, "From now until the end of time."

She laughed, reaching up for another kiss.

"Oh, and by the way, my mom has this great place in Indigo Bay reserved for a wedding reception. Are you free August 28?"

"I am." Emma looked out at the townspeople surrounding them. She couldn't imagine getting married without them present.

Luke seemed to think the same as he said, "What do you say we hire a private jet and bring these yahoos out for a nice Southern wedding?"

She nodded and laughed in delight.

He raised his voice to the crowd. "Wedding date August 28. I think that makes Mary Alice a winner of the town bet. We'll send a jet for you all. Invitations will be in the mail. Or we'll just have Mary Alice take care of it all."

"My dears, it would be my pleasure," she called out.

Luke pulled Emma into his arms again, kissing her long and slow, and in that moment she felt like the luckiest, most beautiful woman in the world.

EPILOGUE

Emma stood in the white, floor-length wedding down designed by her sister. She felt every bit the princess she'd imagined being on her wedding day, and she couldn't wait to see Luke's expression even though they'd been married for almost a year and were practically an 'old married couple' according to some of her friends. Her short hair looked cute and fun. Pretty jeweled clips held it back, and her veil from Ginger's store hung down her back.

Olivia was fussing over her, and it was almost time to walk down the decorated aisle in the Portia House ballroom in Indigo Bay. Emma and Luke had had to push their wedding reception from August to December—right before Christmas—due to time conflicts with their work, but now, at long last, they were finally renewing their vows like they were having a real wedding in front of their friends and family.

Olivia dabbed at her eyes. "I'm so glad you two found each other. I'm sorry I stood in your way for so long." She dabbed at more tears.

"You didn't. Everything worked out like it was meant to," Emma said, her own voice choked with tears. She gave her a tight hug before changing the subject. "Is our little flower girl ready?"

Her sister lifted Abigail Joan from her car seat. Olivia was going to walk down the aisle ahead of Emma, with the precious Abigail Joan in her arms.

Someone had found Luke's safety deposit box miles downriver, and had brought it on the chartered plane from Blueberry Springs to South Carolina. It had been presented to him at the rehearsal dinner last night, and Luke had laughed in delight. He'd opened the box, discovering more moldy money than anyone had ever seen. Wini, the Blueberry Springs bank manager, had assured him that despite the ruined state of the bills, they were still considered valid currency and that she would personally ensure he was properly credited for the money if he brought it into her branch. Once it was rebuilt next year, of course.

Luke had laughed and thanked her, closing the box and setting it aside.

Emma knew the find had been unexpected, and that he would likely tuck the money away, replenishing his emergency fund.

They'd spent a lot of time talking together over the past few months as they continued with their product launch. It had been insane and Luke was planning to pass the CEO reins of Cohen's over to his cousin Cash. Just as long as he didn't do something rash like blow things by taking Luke's former assistant—who'd put her blood, sweat, and tears into organizing today's celebration—to bed, he'd do just fine with the task of taking over the company. But if he sent Alexa running like one of her former bosses had, Cash would be lost. A man swiftly heading downstream without a paddle. It was that simple.

Luke and Emma had also hired Jill to help run the All You line despite Jill still wanting to launch her own products someday. Apparently things hadn't worked out with Burke Carver at the Metro Conference—at least not in a business sense. From what Emma had heard, the two had enjoyed some more personal moments together and she suspected that Jill was hoping to see Burke again.

But really, all the woman needed to succeed was the right partner.

Just like Emma had found.

She smiled and moved toward the door, saying to her sister, "It's time."

Emma walked down the aisle, her hundreds of guests a blur as she headed toward Luke, throwing herself into his arms. He kissed her slow and deep, their love stronger than ever.

"It's a good thing we told him you wanted to kiss the bride this time," Emma said softly, pausing to kiss Luke again as Zach read through the vows like he had at their original wedding.

"I haven't gotten to that part yet," Zach grumbled.

"It's the most important part," Emma said, arms hooked around Luke's neck so she could keep him close for another kiss.

"The one mistake we need to keep repeating," Luke said.

"Only it wasn't a mistake."

"Fine," Zach said with a sigh. "You two are already married so..." He raised his voice. "Without further ado...you may kiss the bride. Or, Emma, kiss the groom. Whoever wants to go first can dive on in and make this official. Again."

Emma giggled as Luke dipped her backward, kissing her.

———

ABOUT THE AUTHOR

Jean Oram is a *New York Times* and *USA Today* bestselling romance author. Inspiration for her small town series came from her own upbringing on the Canadian prairies. Although, so far, none of her characters have grown up in an old schoolhouse or worked on a bee farm. Jean still lives on the prairie with her husband, two kids, and big shaggy dog where she can be found out playing in the snow or hiking.

Become an Official Fan:
www.facebook.com/groups/jeanoramfans
Newsletter: www.jeanoram.com/FREEBOOK
Twitter: www.twitter.com/jeanoram
Instagram: www.instagram.com/author_jeanoram
Facebook: www.facebook.com/JeanOramAuthor
Website & blog: www.jeanoram.com